Right
After
the
Weather

Carol Anshaw

FIG TREE
an imprint of
PENGUIN BOOKS

FIG TREE

UK | USA | Canada | Ireland | Australia
India | New Zealand | South Africa

Fig Tree is part of the Penguin Random House group of companies
whose addresses can be found at global.penguinrandomhouse.com.

First published in the United States of America by Atria Books,
an imprint of Simon & Schuster, Inc. 2019
First published in Great Britain by Fig Tree 2020
001

Printed and bound in Great Britain by Clays Ltd, Elcograf S.p.A.

A CIP catalogue record for this book is available from the British Library

ISBN: 978-0-241-39280-5

www.greenpenguin.co.uk

Penguin Random House is committed to a
sustainable future for our business, our readers
and our planet. This book is made from Forest
Stewardship Council® certified paper.

For Joy Harris

and

in memory of Shirley Hazzard

For my next trick, I'll need a volunteer.

—Warren Zevon

Right
After
the
Weather

desk

On the fourth floor of a warehouse under the long stretch of the Green Line as it heads west out of the Loop, Cate prowls across a vast plain of old office desks. A walk through the decades of the previous century. She travels from linoleum to fake wood to real wood to scarred metal. She is looking for a particular desk. The play—*At Ease*—for which she is designing the sets, takes place in the late 1950s, on a military base in Georgia. She needs a metal desk, olive drab if possible. She has found two possibilities, but one is too small and one is tan. This will be the desk of the closeted drill sergeant. She decides to go with the larger one and spray-paint it at her shop. She snaps a couple of pictures, measures it with her tape, then pencils these dimensions into sketches of the play's two sets. In the second set, the desk will be covered with a mattress and used as a bed.

Her cell makes the sound of a coin dropping into an old pay phone, a notification sound Maureen put on Cate's phone so she'd know it was Maureen calling. Maureen's photo appears on the screen, to the side of a text dialog box. The picture was taken on one of their early dates, a couple of months back now. Maureen is in a theater seat, leaning sideways to fit in the frame. Looking terrific in an effervescent way.

what's up?

Cate never knows how to reply to this vague sort of question.

looking for a desk

can I see you tonight?

going to neale's yoga class

ok. so, tomorrow then. already excited.

Advances in communication technology have made Cate's life so much smoother. She is bad at phone calls, especially bad at making them, possibly interrupting someone in the middle of something more important. She hates hearing that small adjustment in someone's voice. Now she almost never has to hear it. Probably the best phone calls of her life were the vintage ones, the hours she and Neale spent on the phone late at night as teenagers, luxurious conversations, artifacts of an earlier civilization. Also artifacts of who she and Neale used to be when they were trying to assemble the universe.

Now her phone is mostly a tool for semaphoring whereabouts

and plans, for taking pictures of stage sets and furniture, interesting colors, appliances of the past.

Maureen's phone, on the other hand, is her best friend. Everything in her life is filtered through it—information received, confirmed, replied to, shared. Not to mention recorded with the phone's camera. One night when the two of them were hanging out on Maureen's giant sectional sofa, Maureen startled herself.

"Wow. I almost forgot. It's Jill's birthday." Which prompted her to send a small burst of texted good wishes punctuated with a selfie of her waving. "I know they're stupid," she said, but kept on tapping in emojis of firecrackers and a cake. Jill is not a person, she's a decrepit barn cat who belongs to one of Maureen's stable of once lovers/now friends.

The dinner Maureen is already excited about is her treat at a ridiculously expensive restaurant. Cate hopes her pair of dressy pants is clean and pressed. As soon as she slips the phone back into her pocket, it starts ringing, an actual call. She looks at the screen. It's Raymond. The guy doing the lights; she has to answer.

"What I'm thinking," she tells him, "is big lights for the drill scene, big Georgia daylight. Then a creepy sort of pale, late-afternoon darkness for the sex scene in the barracks."

"I can definitely do creepy," Raymond says. "Make it double creepy if you like."

Cate lies down, stretching out across three desks. "We need to pump up the visuals on account—"

"On account of the play sucks?"

"We can help, though." No one wants to write or direct or act in a bad play, but bad plays do happen. And when they do, everyone concerned, Cate believes, needs to do their best to save the play from itself. When it was written, *At Ease* was a story with a gay subtext in a time when queerness was too naked to present directly; it needed to be discreetly dressed. It needed underwear and an overcoat. The drill sergeant's murder of a corporal in the second act is ostensibly military discipline gone too far, but beneath it bubbles jealousy and self-loathing. The drill sergeant seethes at a crummy affair the corporal is having with an unhappily married nurse at the base hospital. Sometime in the 1950s this was put up on Broadway or near Broadway with not Ava Gardner, but someone sort of famous— like Carroll Baker or Shirley Knight—playing the nurse. And so the company is putting this relic up to honor its place in gay history rather than for its watchability.

She slides the phone back into her pocket and lies very still. The damp autumn day outside gets filtered in here through groaning radiators, the light sifted by grimy, wire-meshed windows, then carried down on the dust that occupies the air in this sealed-away space. An el train hurtles past, sucking every other piece of noise out of the air, leaving behind a brief wake of silence.

From here, she enters a mental space she gets to by way of a deep tunnel. Once inside, she can realize a set to its smallest detail. She can see the actors bring the set to life. Sometimes she casts the play with perfect actors. Oliviers and Branaghs and Redgraves. Inside her imagination no flubbed lines trip up the dialog, no tape mark is overshot, no doorbell rings randomly, off-cue. Even a play as bad as the one she's working on now can at least get bathed in a glow of respectability.

She rolls over and idly tugs open the drawers of the very old wooden desk on which she's lying. One contains a short stack of yellow dog, the cheap, porous paper reporters used for typing copy back in the day. Somebody else's day, before her day, but she knows what it is. She has become a historian of small visual details. These pages are still yellow at the center, faded to gray at their edges. In the top drawer she hits pay dirt—two ornate fountain pens, Esterbrooks, their casings marbleized Bakelite, one deep red, the other brown— the sort of small detail that subtly lends a period play authenticity. She slips them into a jacket pocket. She will ask downstairs if she can have them. She'll give them the number of the desk. They'll get it out somehow. She's never asked how they perform the extraction. The desks are impossibly cheap.

warrior two

"Your right knee should be directly over your ankle." Neale walks among the students, tracing a winding path between their mats. They are in warrior two, an easy lunge with one arm stretched out in front, the other behind. Neale puts her hands on Cate's shoulders and gently presses them down, a little longer than necessary. An adjustment, but also a tiny piece of connection in their long friendship.

Taking classes at the studio, Cate can observe Neale in her floral movements, folding this way, then that, bending in a nonexistent breeze. Neale doesn't look like anybody else. She doesn't even look like her parents, who are short and nondescript and careworn. She appears to be composed entirely of recessive genes. Movie-star threads in her DNA. This doesn't make her vain, but she definitely operates out of a keen awareness of her body. This is where her confidence lies. She walks into a room and can calibrate how much of it she occupies.

She's careless with her beauty. She often gives herself (terrible) haircuts. Wears a couple of pairs of jeans she's had from when they were called flared, through a long period when they were so out of style they weren't called anything, to the current moment, in which they are called modern boot-cut. She broke her nose twice playing volleyball in college, and never bothered to get it reset. Now it just (beautifully, of course) detours a little at the bridge. She carried herself with assurance even when the two of them were teenagers. Neale never went through an awkward phase. She's always been physically arrogant. Riding her bike through storms, dodging falling tree branches, exploring construction sites. Cate, her hand already damaged, was hesitant about making wrong moves.

Cate is not a natural yogi. She goes to classes because it's a way to hang out with Neale.

"If you find your attention drifting," Neale is saying now in her tranquil yoga voice, "return your focus to your breath."

Cate tries to follow this suggestion, but it's not easy. Although she is glad she has breath, keeping track of it is never interesting enough, and so, almost immediately, her focus loosens and she drifts off into a thicket of random thoughts. Paint she has to buy for the desk. A nearly due credit card statement on which she at least has to pay the box. Otherwise they will tack on their 270 percent or whatever interest fee.

"Bring your right foot onto your left leg." First Cate wonders how this will be possible, since she is in a lunge. Then she sees that Neale and the class, in her absence, have moved on to tree pose, standing balanced on one foot. She repositions herself awkwardly and is able to pull her attention way over to her breath for maybe a second, before it once again gets yanked off, this time into replaying something really stupid she said to Hugh Prendergast, the director of *At Ease*. From there, Mick Jagger and Jack White jump in front of a microphone, their mouths as close as lovers', singing *Gimme little drink. From your loving cup.*

When the class is over, Neale asks if Cate can come home with her to fix a blocked drain.

"This is why I hang out with you. For the social life."

Then she loiters in the lobby while Neale hugs prodigal students newly returned to the fold, offers workarounds to young women with shin splints or ankle sprains. A lot of the reason people come to yoga, Neale says, is to get a pastel sort of attention from the instructor, encouragement and understanding that's not about the rest of their complicated lives.

When the two of them are finally in the car, Cate says, "Do you think Joe is trolling social media, asking girls at school to send him nude selfies?"

"Oh God, no!"

"I read this article—"

"You know what? I'm just going to stop this speculation in its tracks. NO. Joe is a complicated kid navigating a difficult landscape. And he is just hitting puberty. But he is also one of the most decent humans on the planet. He is not asking girls for nude photos of themselves."

"You're right, of course you're right."

"I'm sorry I clipped you. I just so totally believe in him. Even if I wind up being interviewed. I mean, when he turns out to be the Fox River Killer. And I'll be saying he was such a good, quiet boy."

———

"Joe!?" Neale goes in the back door first and shouts up the staircase.

"In my room." A muffled shout. "Kiera's here."

"Are they doing homework?" Cate lies next to Neale on the kitchen floor, at the ready with a wrench, a plumber's snake, a plastic tub, a rag that was recently a T-shirt.

"They don't really give homework anymore. The kids are too busy with their after-school activities. Joe has band practice until five, three times a week. And then they're too exhausted. Their parents are exhausted, too. Everyone goes around in a stupor." Neale's voice is deadened by resignation, also by coming from inside a small cabinet. She comes out with a fairly large smear of troublingly colorful plumbing gunk across her forehead, in her hair.

Cate says, "Maybe you should be doing something to give yourself a little quality time. I'm thinking crystal meth."

"Can you hand me the rag?"

"I saw this documentary and there was this toothless mother in front of a farmhouse and she was saying, 'I get the kids off on the school bus and then I put the baby down for her nap and then it's my me time, when I do my meth.'"

Joe moves into the kitchen stealthily, startling them both when he says, "Good thing I was upstairs when you needed help with that. Hey, Cate." He says this without making eye contact. He and Cate both hate eye contact. Also hugging. They stick with fist bumps. They are close in their own way. She was there when he was born. Not having gotten it together to have a kid of her own, she mooches a little of him off Neale. She's tried to occupy a place somewhere between parent and friend and aunt. Nondisciplinary like a friend.

Older, with good advice at the ready, but not the aunt whose crepey, powdered cheek he's required to kiss. And after Neale's marriage was over and Joe's father was off to India, Cate tried to be around even more. But as he heads into adolescence he has started building in a little distance.

"What's up?" Neale asks him.

"Just listening to some, you know, music or whatever." Which, of course, means noise music. He and Kiera and their friend Theo listen to this deconstructed sound on their headphones. To Cate it sounds nihilistic: well, of course—that's the point of it. The kids go to noise concerts together. They follow a local duo, Japanese sisters called the Mexican Porno Nuns. When it's Neale's turn to take them to this or that venue, she wears earplugs and covers her head with a hoodie and stands in the back so she's not an embarrassment to them. Joe would like to make noise music himself, but does not have an acoustically insulated studio where he could practice. He is second percussion chair in the school band. His noise music demonstration for the band director—opening pre-shaken pop bottles to a tape of a woodpecker—got him a respectful hearing, but he is still confined to triangle, tambourine, and maracas. To be played in sync with the rest of the band. "But really, do you need help down there?"

Cate watches him scrabble around in the cupboards like a raccoon.

Neale has her head back inside the cabinet. "No, I've got this little situation under control. You do your share. You catch bugs and take them outside without killing them. You handle the recycling. You keep your room not a total mess."

He nods at the justice of this assessment, then takes a carton of milk and a box of doughnuts and heads back upstairs. Watching Joe come into himself makes Cate envy Neale. But Cate has never had the money or a partner willing to shoulder the burdens of parenthood. Her one husband, so far back now, was not interested. And now, at forty-two, she'd probably have to get fertility treatments or in vitro and wind up still single and fairly broke, but now with triplets. Or she could adopt, which would have the element of good deed to it, taking on someone who might need a break. But this would have the downside of responsibility for a complete unknown. The nature part would already be in place; her input would only be the nurture. Which seems more than she might be able to handle on her own; a solid partner in place would help, and she doesn't have one of those. None of this keeps her from wishing now and then that she was having the experience of raising someone, the million small moments of guiding and being surprised by a child.

And she sees it as an inequity between her and Neale, a badge of maturity and wholehearted engagement with life that Cate lacks. She does have Joe in a peripheral way. She gets to enjoy the issues and problems and solutions around him, second-guessing Neale. Now she says, "Doughnuts? I thought you were going to stop buying those."

"I know, but he loves them. They probably won't do much damage now. I mean you never hear about teenagers having clogged arteries, or being on statins. I have to pick my battles."

"If he and Kiera are up there listening to music on their headphones, isn't that sort of lonely?"

"No, they're probably texting each other."

"Oh."

"I know. It's weird, isn't it? How talking isn't so big anymore. But in the new way, they're super-close. Some of what they're about is making themselves look bigger together than they would be alone. I hate how scary school is now. Maybe the scariest place outside of those warlord areas in Africa. You have to have a buddy. Being alone attracts trouble." A longish pause, then Neale says, "Euwww. Very bad under here. Can you hand me that tuppery thing? I've got a real mess going."

Cate shoves the plastic container into Neale's fluttering, gunk-covered hand. She knows she will likely receive this same container, rinsed out and filled with cookies, at Christmas. Neale's housekeeping tempts the fates, all of them. From the outside, which is even worse than the inside, the house looks like the house in *Psycho*. It's an artifact of Neale's marriage. She and Claude were going to be urban pioneers in their dicey neighborhood. They were going to rehab this crumbling monstrosity. And then the marriage was over and Claude was off to India, leaving Neale in a perpetual state of disillusionment. Also only a block over from a sketchy patch of halfway houses and vacant lots with their own furniture, home to a vibrant drug marketplace staffed by serious guys in enormous jackets. But she's staying. Partly a political statement, partly out of stubbornness. She's the guy who makes them build the new freeway around his shack.

She emerges with the leftover container, now half-filled with what looks like shoe tongues boiled in sludge. "Where does this even come from? It's like someone is running a workshop down here while we're asleep."

She's the soul of do-it-yourself, a continuing student at YouTube

University. She has taught herself to rewire lamps, fix the toilet when it runs on, glaze windows. She does her own oil changes. This is a stare-down of small challenges. Of course, it's also about the financial pit, staying a ways shy of it. She has small savings and a going business with her yoga studio. And now with the new healthcare, she and Joe have decent insurance. The policy she had before only covered catastrophes, and even those had catches and loopholes. Because she'd had fibroids in her twenties, they'd only insure her from the waist up.

"Maureen's taking me to some foodie restaurant tomorrow night. It's trending, apparently, whatever that means. I haven't even heard of the place. She had to get the reservation a month ago."

"She's plighting her troth." Neale dumps the sludge into the trash, washes her hands in the sink.

"Maybe."

"Doesn't it feel like she's on a mission? Isn't that a little scary?"

"No, no. I'm grateful she's after me. I think she's my best shot at making something more than another pile of tinder. Something to live in, not set fire to. All that wastable time I had? I used that up. I have to get down to business now. It's not old age I worry about—I haven't even gotten to that worry yet—it's middle age. I don't want to be in my fifties and in some lesbian sinkhole. Alone, obsessed with gluten. Accumulating cats. Old cats with health issues that keep me housebound with their medication schedules. Maureen is part of my new plan to keep that from happening."

To herself, she calls this new plan Plan C. She didn't really have a Plan A. Plan B was using her MFA to get a tenure-track teaching job. But by then she was doing sets for Adam Pryor and thought settling into academe would pull her off the artistic path. Now Adam is gone and Cate is broke. Drifting, but now into the reeds.

For a long time, her circumstances didn't seem reduced in comparison to anyone else's. Cate had a cohort of theater friends who were staying alive on a week-to-week basis. Everyone had fifty dollars in the bank. They made ten-dollar withdrawals from the ATM. At first she didn't notice that their ranks were thinning. Somebody got married, then had twins. Somebody moved to L.A. for a movie and is now in a lot of movies. Her friend Brooke now heads up the theater department at a private school in Oak Park. Two guys who did excellent sets struck out on their own to become decorators, filling houses for wealthy clients on the North Shore—a more lucrative end of their trade. The friends came and went all along, but as time went on, more of them went than came. And many of the replacements were from a further subgeneration assembling their own cohort. By then Cate had spent the postdivorce remnant of her twenties pushing furniture around darkened stages, sleeping with the girls in backstage black, smoking dope, reading Victorian novels. Now even her thirties are behind her, a third of them spent on Dana in an underside life—freezer burn on her elbows, sleepless from 4 a.m. phone calls that might only last a few minutes but kept her awake through the rest of the night. All of which has landed her exactly here, in her early forties, standing on a hard patch of bare ground and clear horizons, trying to set off in some better direction.

Plan C attempts to find this direction via four main points:

+ Firm up employment (steady job at design house, maybe full-time gig at some school).

- Unlatch from Dana and get a real girlfriend.
- Don't take money from parents.
- Brush teeth two minutes two times a day (get timer).

Neale pulls a bag of taco chips out of a cabinet. "Your problem is how hard it's going to be to find someone to follow Dana. To match that ferocity."

"Yes. That's the bitch of it, right?"

palate cleanser

She's mortified by her appetizer. On the menu it sounded fanciful. Now it just seems decadent, and decadent is always embarrassing. Like Roman orgies in movies where servants are peeling grapes for the reclining emperor, where the guests are eating off human tables—naked women on all fours.

"I feel a little weird eating, you know—I guess I didn't think it was going to really be gold. What's it doing? Being a little metallic glaze on whatever this tiny egg is? Whatever bird it came from. I hope not a parakeet from some Thai forced-hatching factory." She pokes through the thin skin of gold leaf and they watch the yolk seep up. Neither of them says anything when Cate lifts off the gold film and sets it on the rim of the plate. They sit across from each other at a table much larger than necessary for two people eating dinner. It's a size more appropriate to spreading out maps, plotting a voyage or a war.

"I know, I know. It does seem like what they were probably eating in the dining room of the *Titanic*. I didn't know it would be this fancy, hardly anything *is* anymore. Except this place, I guess." Maureen's sympathy has a hollow ring to it. She actually seems quite comfortable spearing a forkful of foie gras (for Christ's sake), nestled in a pillow of salted cotton candy. Cate has brought up issues of animal cruelty before, and Maureen always seems sensitive in the moment, deeply nodding her support, saying annoying stuff like, "Poor things, they can't speak for themselves so we have to help them." But then she will turn around and tuck into something like this.

Cate scans her from across the table. As a costume designer, Maureen of course costumes herself. Her clothes make tiny statements without calling attention to themselves. Odd collars, the occasional hat. She has an extremely articulated tattoo on one shoulder—a Japanese fan. She wears a lot of pale green, also navy, to set off her hair, which is dark red, Botticelli crinkles, both bunched up and falling down.

Tonight would probably be a good time for Cate to reveal her discomfort about over-the-top restaurants like this one. But she can't find her way to that conversation. Maureen loves expensive dining, and can afford it. She has spent the past decade dressing actors, for plays, musicals, sometimes operas. Operas, Maureen says, are the costume designer's diamond mine.

In the end, Maureen might be too different from Cate, but they are only at their beginning, and Cate is not ready to give in to that notion just yet. The thing is, Maureen fits perfectly into the future Cate hopes to have. She's totally adult. She has investments. There's a financial advisor in the wings. She is funny and large-hearted, ardent in bed, and beautiful in a recovered way that stirs Cate. As though she has sprung back from something difficult, but is made of denser material because of it. Cate still thinks there's a chance that with her she might make a respectable partnership. Important in a real-life way, as opposed to the elaborately fantastic scenario she spooled out with Dana, who nonetheless remained firmly attached to her partner. Remains still.

"Sometimes I think you might be too good-looking for me." Maureen reaches across the table to pluck a hair from the cuff of Cate's jacket. This is a kind of thing she says. Romantic prompts. What would be a good response to this? Cate, by her own standards, isn't all that attractive. She's awkward, gangly with her height, as though she's still adjusting to it. Maybe she has something small going for her, a serious expression, like that of a reporter in a war zone, or a doctor about to give bad news. A face that is flat planes and abrupt angles. She also got her father's ice-blue eyes, which adds another element to the chill. She does know this severity holds value in particular situations, incipient romance being one.

But now she has to get serious instead of just looking serious. Living casually in the moment seemed so vibrant, but has left her looking over her shoulder at a pile of used-up hours and days, hearing the scratchy sound of frittering. If Graham hadn't bought the condo for her, she'd still be living in her rental apartment with seventy-two coats of paint, cabinet doors that stuck even when they weren't shut. Silver-painted radiators that lay dormant for hours, then banged to life in a mechanical riot that would blast heat through the place in such an overwhelming way that she could leave the windows wide-open for those cool February breezes. She has come to understand that room temperature in the demographic she aspires to is a more personally controlled business.

Maureen inhabits this thermostatted demographic. She owns a co-op on Marine Drive, has an Infiniti that still smells new. She's on the board of something that puts disadvantaged kids into musicals on nights when the theaters are otherwise dark. She has won three Jeff Awards to Cate's one—Maureen's for equity productions, Cate's for one of the sets she did for Adam Pryor. Like all his work, this was a small play with large ideas.

For a long stretch, her career strategy was simply attaching herself to Adam Pryor. They had interlocking artistic views. The plays he directed got serious attention, which brought her sets the same sort of respect. And then he was walking on Wabash one day a year ago, at three in the afternoon, when an elderly woman mistakenly wearing her reading instead of her distance glasses, jumped the curb and killed him instantly. This was devastating to Cate personally; they had an intricate friendship, a matched sense of what was important, what was ridiculous. More prosaically, in terms of work, she was suddenly unemployed. Doing the sets for a play as dismal as *At Ease* is the kind of thing she thought she was beyond. And yet here she is.

Maureen is saying, "My sister is coming for a visit. I'd like you to meet her."

"Sure, great. I always envy people who have sisters. Especially when they're close."

Maureen hesitates, then says, "Yes. We are close." She suddenly looks uncomfortable. Probably from the goose liver. She pushes her fingers into her big hair, not in a coy way, more maniacal. Like Mr. Hyde rousing himself from sleep in Dr. Jekyll's laboratory. "What I'm trying to say is, there was a time when we were even closer."

"When you were kids."

"No. After we were both out of school and on our own. For a while then we were, you know, involved."

"Oh." Something slippery and cold flushes through Cate, the eel-like sensation that accompanies unwelcome information. As she searches for a response, she focuses on the remains of her egg as it is taken away by a silent waitperson, replaced by a teaspoon's worth of pale green shavings of something frozen and glistening. The server explains the palate cleanser. Cate can't listen.

Once the server has walked away, Maureen says, "I just don't want there to be any secrets between us." At exactly this instant Cate is thinking everyone should really hold on to their secrets, edit the worst lines from their personal résumés. This piece about Maureen and her sister, for example, would have been an excellent edit. Now, though, the cat's out of the bag. Now the cat is hopping all over the place, demanding attention.

"How did that happen anyway?" Cate tries for a neutral tone, as though she's asking about a tour of the French countryside on which Maureen and her sister took the optional side trip to see the cave paintings.

"Oh, she was coming off a divorce and she was needy. And of course, this was California. Also the nineties. You know."

Clinginess or historical period or seaside locale don't really seem extenuating enough circumstances.

"Were you in love? Was it that sort of thing?" She doesn't even know why she's asking. Would it be better or worse if they were or weren't?

"It was more a way we had of being together. You'll see when you meet her, Frances is just an intensely charismatic person."

Cate looks around, suddenly awkward at having this conversation in a public place, but then she notices the hanging glass panels, some elaborate baffling system. The other customers exist somewhere else on the dining matrix, all of them in parallel, convivial but hushed universes.

"This is kind of—well, you know—unusual."

"I didn't mean to shock you. By now I see it as something small and far behind me. A tiny part of someone I was for a little while."

In some precisely measured time frame, the vessel (something between a bowl and a plate) that held the sorbet or granita or whatever is taken away, replaced by a nubbly deck-of-cards rectangle. Sesame-crusted tofu striped with two sauces, pale pink and yellow. The server extends white-gloved hands toward Cate. The hands, palms up, hold a napkin, which in turn surrounds a heavy silver eating utensil with which Cate is completely unfamiliar. As Cate takes this narrow, flat, shovel-like implement, she sees the waitress look for a couple of nearly invisible but definitely extra clicks of time at Cate's hand, her left. By now, she has a full repertoire of deft moves to replicate the functionality of a complete hand. But having only the first two fingers and a thumb to work with makes this particular gesture look like the claw in a game machine, picking out a toy. This doesn't bother her. One thing Cate is not self-conscious about is her hand.

The esoteric sauce shovel makes a surprise second appearance after dinner when they're in the car and Maureen pulls it from her coat pocket. Cate can't help looking appalled at it; she can feel her eyes bulging.

"What—?" she says.

"Shh shh," Maureen says, placing it in Cate's lap. "Just a little souvenir. Now, should I turn left or right? Say you'll come home with me. I don't think we can go back to your place."

"I think I need to go back, though. Graham's been so down. Sometimes he forgets to walk Sailor." Graham is living with her in a temporary way after getting tossed out by his latest wife. Cate was his first wife, a million years ago.

"Is that situation starting to bug you?"

"He's so depressed. I can't just show him the door. And he's really no trouble. He mostly stays in his room. He hired a cleaning person. He orders in for us from Dean and DeLuca. I eat more Italian artisanal cheese than anyone outside Umbria."

"It just seems like a peculiar arrangement is all."

Like the arrangement where your head was between your sister's legs? Cate thinks, but doesn't say.

"Then maybe we could just drive downtown, then back up to my place. It's a beautiful night." Maureen rests her hand on Cate's thigh in a proprietary way. In the close, leather-upholstered, Bose-speakered interior of the Infiniti, things heat up a little. Cate notices how great Maureen smells. The car heat ramps up some spring-forest cologne she's wearing. Vetiver and woody smoke and desire cloud the air, obscuring the giant chunk of unfortunate information now bumping around in the too-little space between them. Maybe it's not so important, this thing with her sister. Maybe Cate's being prudish, old-fashioned. Maybe it's really less important than the silverware thievery. She needs time to think about all of this.

base camp

It's a little before 2 a.m. Tonight they blocked *At Ease*. Her first chance to watch the actors negotiating her sets. A gloomy evening. Her sets are fine, but everyone knows the play stinks. Still, tickets have already been sold, ads placed. The show must go on. Cate took the job to pay respect to gay history, but she has an argument going with herself about whether even the better plays from earlier, benighted eras—plays like *The Children's Hour* and *Suddenly Last Summer*—are too worn-out and anachronistic to put on for twenty-first-century audiences except as history lessons.

As she comes into the alley behind her apartment, Cate looks up and sees a wavy blue-green light in the room Graham is using. As soon as she is through the door, she's in the new sort of quiet she has grown accustomed to: refrigerator hum overlaid with an intermittent narration coming off the internet as it bleeds out of her spare bedroom. Cate enjoys Graham's company and is kind of crazy in love with his dog, Sailor. She has never had a dog, didn't know how great it would be. Now she wonders how she got along without one. Graham and Sailor moving in with her was supposed to be a temporary situation, just until he got back on his feet after his most recent marital breakup (he is now two wives farther along from Cate), but man and dog have been here three months now and Graham is still off his feet. All that seems to have happened is that he has become increasingly nocturnal, interactive with the web. Watching someone from somewhere talking into his—in fewer instances, her—webcam. Different voices come in on different nights, but all with the same dark, knowing tone, a tone that has a sideways delivery, a hand in front of it.

When he sees her in the doorway to his room, Graham puts up a Metallica playlist on Spotify. For masking purposes.

"How's it going?" She looks in. The desktop computer's screen-saver is luminous with the pale aquarium colors of the Zapruder film clip. JFK's motorcade coming through Dealey Plaza in a repeated gif, a mood enhancer, the way lava lamps used to smooth out the vibe for seductions, only in Graham's room the mood is paranoia.

Her arrival stirs Sailor. He must've been totally sacked out; usually his nose is at the door when she comes home. He unfolds and frees himself from the nest of cords and cables under Graham's worktable. Standing on his hind legs, his front paws on her shoulders, giving off a dry, delicious warm-dog aroma, he's tall enough to be a dancing partner. She acknowledges this by doing a quick mambo step, then gets him down on the floor and sits next to him; then she flips him over like a pancake and scratches his stomach. He appears to be a mix of something red—Irish setter maybe?—and Lab. And whatever else. He's a glorious mutt.

Cate doesn't pay as close attention as Graham does to the machinery of government. She reads the *Times* online every morning, political pieces in *The New Yorker*. She does get-out-the-vote work for Democratic candidates around elections, and is grateful to have had, at least for the last eight years, someone smart and well-intentioned in the White House. Maybe she's been on cruise control because of that. But she understands Graham's suspicions, and knows what he believes—about lobby-purchased legislators, gerrymandered congressional districts, suppressed votes, backroom deals, enforced inequities, suppressed science, dark money shuffled and laundered endlessly, the planet poisoned, vats of chemical sludge dumped into rivers at night—is true. Where there used to be a few things to seriously worry about, now there are way too many. He is fixated on the death of privacy, the amount of personal information available to whomever is interested in obtaining it, and the really bad uses it might be put to. And how unaware of this exposure most people are. He believes the world is in the golden age of internet naiveté. Philosophically, he's a disciple of Edward Snowden.

A smaller invasion of Cate's individual privacy is Graham's open-ended presence in her apartment. Her spare room has been taken over with command-post electronics and a giant bed he had delivered soon after he arrived. It goes up and down, can be hard or soft, hot or cold. Plus, it vibrates. Other than this anomalous room, her apartment is of a piece, a set of sorts. Well, of course it would be. The play would be titled *1944*. She's fascinated by this period, which she knows mostly from a love of its movies. She loves the furnishings, the reliance on hats, the cavalier smoking, the enormous cars. She has combed junk shops for old furniture from these days gone by, reupholstered several pieces herself in dark mohair. Maroon and moss green. She painted the walls the color of a paper bag. Possibly too much bamboo. A heavy, standing ashtray is surrounded by a population of emphysemic ghosts. She enjoys standing in one room or another, surveying the total effect, also the small pieces that make it up. Her bedroom furniture is of a heavy, dark wood with lighter panels of inlay. She has an indigo chaise by the window, lampshades with fringe. Framed and hung rotogravure portraits of movie stars from the studio days.

Graham is spoiling this "curated" (she only ever uses this word to herself) environment. But he's a good friend, not to mention he bought the apartment for her.

When she gets out of the shower, she can hear him chatting with Lucille Rae. On the screen of one laptop, Lucille Rae is peering seriously at the camera. Behind her head and shoulders are shelves crammed full of teddy bears. She appears to be sitting on the teddy bear subway at rush hour.

Graham holds up the laptop and Cate waves at it. "Hey, Lucille Rae." Lucille Rae lives in the Black Hills in South Dakota, which she's certain lie on top of huge hidden bunkers filled with recorded phone calls.

Having come farther into the room, Cate catches a whiff of mustiness off Graham, mustiness and herbal supplements. When did he start looking and smelling like a nut? He's developing tics. Rotating his head to get a crick out of his neck. Picking at his fingers, tearing up the cuticles until they bleed. He doesn't wash his hair, wears it pulled back in a greasy ponytail. When did he start sleeping in his clothes, or maybe it's that he's working in his pajamas? Hard to tell with the garments—there's really no other way to describe them—he wears. Hemp and unbleached cotton, drawstring closures. He looks like someone who has an entourage of naive followers.

Fate dealt Graham a joker. He only intended his big, cheerful play to be a temporary financial solution. He wanted to make a play to which you could bring your nephew, your lover, and your great aunt. He didn't allow himself any artistic intentions, just stuck to the template of combining surefire elements of Broadway blockbusters. These included:

+ cuddly animals;
+ amateur detectives;
+ inspirational songs about possibilities, potential, romantic happiness, durable friendship, and beating the odds; and finally,
+ audience interaction (children pulled onstage from their seats to dance with Petey Panda and his friends; an audience-chosen ending).

He put all this into a jumberator and what came out was *Pand-a-Rama!*, which by now has had two Broadway runs and has four touring companies roaming the world, a movie version, a novel-ization, a video game, and a line of detective panda action figures. He will never have to work again in his life. He will always be famous for this unsinkable piece of junk.

What the indignity bought him is endless time to write and pro-duce plays that are brilliant but so obscure and opaque hardly any-one comes to them. The shows are elaborate puzzles the audience must solve. People don't want to work this hard for their entertain-ment, or take notes in the dark (he provides lighted pens). Or come three nights in a row to see all the acts necessary to complete the "geopolitical acrostic."

His obsession with surveillance has taken over his writing. The play he's working on now takes place in a single room, underground. There are only two characters. They are not friends; they've just been assigned together to the room. They wear identical gray jumpsuits. They are both listening in on phone calls. Their only interaction with each other is when they take off their headsets for a coffee break. They only talk about the coffee, although *coffee* may be a code word, also *stale cookie*. It is never clear who they work for, who is benefiting from their machinations. They might or might not be facilitating something that might or might not be a zero-sum endgame, and the winners are not going to be regular people, or even, necessarily, humans.

The audience, he's told Cate, hears every phone call. What he's trying to capture, he has told her, is a very slight amount of change. Picture a vacant field on a cloudy day at five-eighteen in the afternoon, then at five-twenty.

The whole apartment smells of chemical lemon. Which means Pledge. Which means Jennifer was here today. Jennifer is a small, amazingly industrious woman Graham pays to come in every week to clean. When she leaves, the entire apartment is immaculate. She has three cell phones (also four passports under different names; Cate went through her purse once), which she sets out on the kitchen counter while she's cleaning; she is vigilantly poised for incoming information. Her driver's license identifies her as Raluca. She comes to work in a fur coat. She told Cate she made it.

She comes from terrible poverty in a beautiful setting in the Carpathian Mountains, a rural area, grindingly poor. Cate stands a little in awe of Jennifer. She has lived through extreme cold, hunger, and fear. She had three root canals done without novocaine, just gripping the arms of the dentist's chair. She has triumphed over circumstances of poverty and ignorance and is now negotiating her way through a culture that does not value her. Still, it's better to admire her from a little distance. To enter into a conversation is a step into quicksand. Her main topic is her various ailments. (She has so many that, if you added up all of them, Cate once figured, every single part of her body has hurt, blown up, been infested with ringworm, or suddenly prolapsed. Or itched like crazy, or, according to her, really needed to be sawed off.) She has a boyfriend, who is hiding somewhere. From Interpol. Cate didn't know Interpol still existed. Whatever he did was not his fault. Legal maneuvers are being arranged. Things may or may not work out. Once she gets going, there's no stopping her. She doesn't break for breath or paragraphing. Interaction for her is you nodding at her rhetorical "Do you know what it is that I am saying?" tagged onto whatever run-on sentence. There's no polite way to extricate yourself. If they are both at home, Cate and Graham work a system where, after ten minutes, one goes into a closet and calls the other, pretending to be someone important with something crucial to be attended to. Immediately.

It's easier to just be out on Wednesdays. Even Graham finds somewhere to go.

"Hungry?" he says now. He and Sailor have followed Cate into the kitchen. "New supplies for base camp." He nods toward the table. Ripped-open Dean & DeLuca FedEx cartons with their arctic blocks of Styrofoam padding, their steaming packets of dry ice, clutter the surface. Large chunks of cheese, three bottles (one already open) of Pouilly-Fuissé, a package of shrink-wrapped blinis next to a jar of caviar, a crock of vegetable pâté.

"Not really. Mostly I'm exhausted."

Sailor has positioned himself close by her side, which, not co-incidentally, puts him near the cheese. She takes a few of the crackers billed on the package as "handmade in Abruzzo." She imagines old women in a small factory bent over as they shape cracker dough into deliberately asymmetrical squares. "I'm just going to give him a little snack." She unwraps a chunk of Humboldt Fog, breaks off a piece, and tucks it between two crackers. Sailor is sitting up on his haunches, his head cocked to one side. Even mooching, he looks majestic. He was less majestic when he arrived. After a few months living in the midst of Graham's disintegrating marriage, Sailor looked middle-aged. Heavy, slow, fur clotted, one eye crusty with what turned out to be a minor infection. Since he has been here, Cate has taken him to the vet, put him on a feeding schedule, and added green beans to his dinner. She takes him on a couple of walks every day to supplement whatever Graham doesn't do. They are still participating in the fiction that Sailor is his dog.

"Do you ever feel, deep in your heart, that Lucille Rae might be a crackpot?" Cate has just poured herself a glass of a dramatically expensive wine.

"No, she's not a crackpot. The crackpots are all focused on stuff that's already gone down. Falling towers and missing planes. They're nostalgists. Whatever bad thing that's already happened isn't going to happen again. At least not in the same way. It's much harder to look ahead and beyond. To use events predictively. To form the near future, give it a shape."

"Okay. Then what is she digging up in hillbilly holler?"

"Don't call her a hillbilly."

"Well, she *does* lives in a hilly part of the country."

"It's not the hill, and you know it; it's the billy. You wouldn't like it if someone referred to you as a Chicagobilly. Just because she wears terrycloth and her hair is fluffy, you don't take her seriously. Did your set work tonight?" He is always happy to steer the conversation toward *At Ease.* Eleanor Quinn, his most recent ex-wife, the one who threw him out, plays one of the main characters. He loves hearing anything unfortunate about Eleanor.

She's an impressive actress; she's only attached to this stupid production as a favor to the director. That she and Cate are involved in the same play isn't that much of a coincidence; the world of Chicago theater is like a tangle of double-sided sticky tape.

"My set isn't up to the task of saving this play. Some things shouldn't be revived. *Revived* implies something that was once alive. Here's a line." She pulls the script from her messenger bag, flips through it, then reads aloud.

"'You hate me because I remind you of your mother.' I mean, you can't use that line. Maybe Sophocles could have, but—I mean, really. How's yours going?"

"Still tinkering with act six."

By 3 a.m. they have polished off one bottle of wine and half of a second, and are now walking Sailor together. Sailor loves this. He pushes his chest out in pride at showing off his family, although at this hour no one except barflies is out and about. This is a real fall night: skittering leaves along the pavement have replaced the summer's cicada din. A Peapod truck wanders by once, then again.

"Something is definitely off about that," Graham says. "Do they even offer three a.m. deliveries?" But this doesn't throw him into a spiral of worry that the van is a secret CIA surveillance vehicle. He is too distracted, teasing apart the threads of Eleanor's complex personality. Cate doesn't see any complexity to her at all. While she can subtly delineate any role she plays, in real life Eleanor is just a blunt instrument of ambition, also deeply unpleasant. It's a mystery to Cate why Graham is hung up on her. In spite of the fact that, at the end of their marriage, she put a live rat in the glove compartment of his car. Cate is at a loss in advising on the more terrifying variants of love.

the scary hand

Down on Blackhawk at her workshop, Cate spray-paints the desk for the sergeant's office in *At Ease*. The shop is a small brick building on an industrial block south of the North and Clybourn junction. The rent is ridiculously low. Her landlord appears to have forgotten her. He hasn't raised the rent in five years. If he does, she probably won't be able to afford it anymore.

Warm air is coming in gusts, and she is dancing around outside the back door in a mask and goggles, dodging the paint as it plays in the wind. Her workshop is in a neighborhood of factories, but also dance clubs, and she notices that a small pack of large women who all seem to be costumed as Adele are running with peals of hilarity across the street. Warming up for some later, main event. They wave at her, possibly thinking her mask and goggles are a postapocalyptic costume.

Shit, she thinks. Halloween. She's late. Trick-or-treating has already begun.

She finishes up, then tents a tarp loosely over the desk. She needs it to dry by tomorrow morning, when Stig will come by to help load it into her SUV and get it to the theater.

Halloween in the city has been escalating the past few years. Now the parties start the weekend before, and trick-or-treaters are a mix of kids and adults. It's five when Cate gets to Neale's house; the winds have died down and evening is coming in—mild, with a thin glaze of winter approaching. The crowd is already swelling. Trick-or-treaters flood the sidewalks and parkways, a renegade traffic jam, stumbling over their elaborate costumes, blinded by their masks, urged by their parents toward the candy.

Lawns set up as small graveyards also feature zombies emerging from holes in the grass. Feet stick out of a glowing Weber. Fog billows from doorways. A couple of guys lie in their front yard moaning, knives stuck in their bloody chests. Behind one front window obscured by a translucent shower curtain liner, stooped ghouls creep back and forth, then press their palms wildly at the window as though trying to escape. Someone has hung a giant plush-toy tarantula from a tree branch over the sidewalk. It's on an elastic string and a pulley, and drops down on one unsuspecting kid after another, so there's about a scream a minute.

BLOOD—5 CENTS

with a pitcher and cups is offered at an unattended card-table stand.

Almost as many adults as children are in costume. Pennywise

the evil clown is popular this year, along with a strong perennial contingent of SpongeBobs. A significant part of the population has made its own costumes, some so idiosyncratic you have to ask, "What are you?"

"I went out for a look earlier. We've got some stiff competition this year," Neale says as she hangs a cardboard sign in the front window, drawn to approximate neon tubing:

BATES MOTEL

VACANCY

"What do you think?" Joe says about his costume. He has just come out onto the front porch. Kiera is right next to him. She's wearing a lime-green jacket and dark green tights. Joe has on a white dress shirt he asked Neale to get him at Value Village. This now has the initials NV markered in monogrammy letters on the front pocket. He's also wearing a Richard Nixon mask he must have found at one of the pop-up costume shops along Clark.

"We're *together*, that's what you have to think about," Kiera says.

"You're green with envy!" Neale says, and both kids start laughing so hard they have to hold each other up. Sailor jumps up on both of them, to join in the fun.

"Do you think everyone will guess right away?" Joe says, his voice boxed in by the mask.

"No," Cate reassures them. "It definitely takes some putting together. I didn't get it until your mother did. What's the Richard Nixon part, though?"

"Just I don't like my face so much tonight. The mask is good." Cate wonders what this is about, this self-consciousness. He is a beautiful boy.

They're itching to go. Sailor thinks he's going with them, which he is not.

Cate thinks Joe is a boy out of his time. He lives in a culture he has created to the side of his peers. The good thing about this is Neale doesn't have the standard-issue parental concerns. She doesn't have to worry about him spending too much time on video games, since he doesn't play them. She doesn't have to worry about him getting a concussion on some playing field, since he is not interested in team sports of any kind.

His interests are obscure. The noise music. According to Neale, he listens a lot—maybe too much?—to William Basinski's *Disintegration Loops*, essentially the sounds of a tape wearing out as it plays over and over for hours. And of course, there are the Mexican Porno Nuns. He's also into film history. None of the other kids are, and so he watches old movies, sometimes with Neale, but more often by himself. He can stream almost anything he wants from the twentieth century. They go downtown to the Siskel Center or over to the Music Box for what he calls the "theatrical experience." Neale is grateful for Kiera's presence, Theo's too, to dilute Joe's solitude.

"I can drive you over," Neale says.

"Actually, it's like two blocks away," Joe says. "At Michael's house."

"Don't cut through the vacant lot," Neale says.

"I know. We won't. I mean *of course* we won't."

Once they're gone, Neale says, "What's up with 'actually'? Suddenly it's all over the place. Isn't 'actually' supposed to imply a mistake being corrected? I don't believe I said anything that would require a correction."

"I think it's a little snippiness entering the larger conversation. I get it all the time. Like I call someone's office and an assistant answers and I ask if I can speak with Mr. Boomba and she says, 'Well *actually*, he isn't here.'"

"I've noticed that, too. It's probably part of something bigger. It's probably hooked up somehow with that voice sales clerks use at Banana Republic, high-pitched and so insanely cheerful you're supposed to understand it's ironic. That it means they hate their job and think you look fat in the sweater and are an idiot to pay as much for it as you are."

They set up their candy distribution point on Neale's front steps. They offer fun-size Snickers from an orange plastic bowl with a creepy gray-green rubber hand coming out of its center. A motion detector sets off the hand whenever someone reaches for the candy. At the moment, it's responding to five grabby little Spider-Men.

THANK you!!!! the creepy hand screeches in a loud, witchy voice while it squirms around a little. Other times the hand cackles **HAP-py Halloween!!!!**

Sailor is unflapped by these spasms; if he has to go past the hand to get the candy, he will. Cate gets him to move around to her other side and puts the bowl between herself and Neale and he simmers down. Being part Lab, he's in general a laid-back guy. He leans against Cate, watches the action, plots how to get back around to the Snickers.

When the spider-kids have squealed at the scary bowl, taken

candy bars, and begun their retreat toward the sidewalk, Cate, holding the bowl, says, "Just think. This was someone's *job*. She got home
from the casting call and told her husband, 'Honey, I got a gig today.'
And he said, 'Oh baby, that's great. What's the play?' And she said,
'Well, I won't be on a stage, it's more of a dramatic-narration thing.'"

"'But with a big impact on the audience,'" Neale says.

Neale goes inside, then brings out a couple of Coronas. They each
eat a fun-size Snickers. Sailor gets a Milk-Bone, then Neale says, as
she does quite often, "I'm a terrible parent." This time it's about Joe's
lunch. He's been getting the one they sell at school. "He insisted. It's
apparently social death if you bring a sandwich in a bag from home. I
never thought to ask what the school served. I guess I was thinking of
the old cafeteria with ladies in hairnets ladling out vegetable soup, but
now it's premade meals, and I asked if they offered vegetarian options
and he gave me the look of welcoming me to the planet, and so I gave
in and now I just pay for the lunches at the beginning of the week.
Then he started getting zits and I asked if the lunches had any fried
foods in them. He said a better question would be if they had any
unfried foods. Like yesterday it was fried chicken tenders. What *are*
those even? Chicken rectums? The vegetable was fries and the dessert
was fried apple pies. I've got to figure out some other way. Maybe I
fix him a lumberjack breakfast and he just brings an apple for lunch,
then I fix something intensely nutritious for dinner. Something with
kale. Why didn't I twig onto this sooner? I know why. Because just
handing over the lunch money was the path of ease and ignorance."

"Don't beat yourself up," Cate says, and brushes her two knuck-
les across Neale's cheek.

There was a time when this contact would have been way too loaded with subtext. Cate and Neale have been friends since ninth grade, through Cate's straight years, then her fake straight years, then her coming out after holding on to the secret a little too long. She was already sleeping with women by the time she told Neale she thought she might be interested in sleeping with women. Their friendship for a time became tentative, folded around confusion, hovering over its former version. They had to not talk about whether Cate had been in love with Neale, which of course she had. And whether Neale aided and abetted that, which she probably did. Now all that is far behind them. While she can remember particular events, Cate can't call up the emotional content anymore, even though there was so much of it. This, she supposes, is the drape that closes off pain so everyone can get on with the rest of life.

"Do you think this is the worst house on the block?" Neale says.

"No. The green house is the worst."

"Because they keep chickens in the back."

Neale's neighborhood is changing, bettering itself, but slowly. Tonight they get a few upmarket kids, like Frida Kahlo in a body cast with a chubby Diego Rivera. But there's still a steady traffic of dispiriting visitors. Earlier, a homeless sort of couple showed up—a large, lumbering guy with a childlike face and a cartoon—Cate couldn't make out the character—tattooed on the side of his neck. With him was a small, wiry woman, eerily tan and smelling of washable parts that hadn't been exposed to daylight or water in a while. "Trick or treat," they said, in tandem, with absolutely no human inflection. Candy-seeking cyborgs. Sailor growled. Cate distracted him. It's embarrassing when your dog growls at people because they are poor. Or in wheelchairs. Or fat, which sometimes happens, and who knows what that's about.

And there are still more to come—whole families, children and adults, none of them in costume. One has just arrived, each member holding out a thin plastic grocery bag.

Trick or treat, hahahahaha!!!! the witch's hand screams at them.

None of them squeals or laughs or smiles or even seems to take notice of the writhing hand or its crazy talk. They appear beleaguered. All of them have combed but extremely dirty hair. They are wearing super-cheap sneakers that appear to be made from cheesecloth and Styrofoam. Maybe this family has just arrived from someplace where they have already been seriously scared, not just by a crappy rubber hand. Each of them, including the mother and father, takes two Snickers, and then they all turn around to trudge off to the next house.

"Hey!" Neale shouts after them. "Hold on for just a sec." She raises her index finger, then gets up and goes inside and is back with her wallet. She pulls out a couple of twenties and pats them onto the father's palm. Both parents look at the money and nod, then leave. Cate knows how improvident this is, given the financial situation of someone who owns a yoga studio and cannot count on as much as she'd like for support from an ex-husband who lives in Pondicherry, where he has put aside material concerns. But it's no good scolding someone for her generosity.

Neale looks in the bowl. "They've cleaned us out of candy. I'll go get more." She ducks just inside the front door and grabs what's left in the bag of Snickers, dumps it all into the bowl, setting the hand off on its entire litany of proclamations.

THANK you!!!! Trick or treat, hahahahaha!!!!
Come here, take some candeee!!!!

The flow of trick-or-treaters starts to wind down. The hand screeches on. It seems to be on a roll—maybe there's a short in the circuitry. The two of them stare at the hand as though it's a hysterical friend, and then Neale reaches underneath and switches off the bowl. Now seems like a good time for Cate to bring up the matter of Maureen and Maureen's sister.

"So, you know—Maureen?"

"Well *actually*, I don't. And I think I'm going to need to sometime soon. Give her the gimlet eye."

"Right. We need to set up something."

"What? What were you going to say about her?"

"Nothing. It's nothing, really." Nonetheless, after a little more holding off, she winds up spilling the beans. She's using Neale as a litmus test. She's the most principled person Cate knows. So it's surprising when Neale says, "Oh, that's nothing. That taboo was put in so people didn't have babies with pinheads. I think when it's between sisters, it's not really a problem."

"Really?" Cate says, so grateful.

"No, not 'really'! What are you even saying? She had sex with her *sister*? For *years*?!"

"Well, only a couple, I think. Years."

"The sister who's a weaver?"

"Quilter."

"Oh well then, okay."

"It probably took care of that boring lull after holiday dinners," Cate says.

"She never should have told you."

"Well, I'm meeting her tomorrow, the sister. She's in town. We're all going out for tea."

"Nice. Very Jane Austen." Neale stands to look at a house down the block, which still has creepy fog rolling out its front windows and door. "I know this goes against reason, but I felt better about you when you were with Dana."

"You were totally against it! Remember? 'Afflicting someone's relationship.' 'The sleazy nature of an affair.'"

"I know, I know, but I was impressed at the amount of connection you had with her. It's what everybody wants."

There are levels, a lot of people don't see that. You can live around here and still have self-respect, work a job. Have a good lawsuit going. But there are also people out here existing on a lower level. They no longer make any food. They eat tamales cold from the can. Or dinner can be Hershey's Kisses. When the gas company shuts off their heat they burn wood in the old fireplace. The flue doesn't work right anymore, so the living room is usually filled with smoke. And then on top of that they themselves smoke, cigarettes and weed and hash and crack and meth. Whatever's around. I'm talking about Irene, of course.

You have to think of her as someone who's going to be moving on; think of her heading for the West Coast, or Alaska. The leaving she's actually doing is dying, but in a beautiful kind of slow motion. There's a little less of her every day.

Where I see myself is a level or two up from her. I have regular work, nights at the Citgo. I can make a spaghetti dinner, with a salad. Plus, I am just stronger for being a man, and younger, and into drugs only recreationally, not as a total lifestyle. This is how I am able to help Irene, to push a soft pillow between her and the hard ground when she falls.

We are in bed in the back room of her place eating Halloween candy. Snickers from those good-looking babes in the run-down house. By now the mattress has gray, shiny marks where our bodies lie through the day. We fall again and again onto these reserved places. When it gets too gross, we'll just bring in another mattress—the alleys are filled with them. If it's full of bugs, we toss it and find another. This afternoon we are bug-free and happy under a pile of old quilts someone left behind. Things turn up at Irene's, and also disappear. The quilts might be gone tomorrow, but there could be a new sofa (new to us anyway) in the living room. I have no idea about the flow of all this stuff. It's like there's a hole under her rug and a steady cargo comes in through it and then goes out again. We use a lot of what are scraps to most people. We haven't gotten any help like education or rich relatives. We have to make our own help.

"Are you still with me?" she asks. She has just shot up. This has moved her to a space not really here. Near here. I watch her and eat a packet of candy corn.

"I'm staying under the covers until I can make myself get out and dressed. That might be about Tuesday." We are on the near edge of November. Although we live in a city, we are also on the Great Plains. The fierce weather doesn't care much about our little human constructions. And now there's no rhyme or reason to the jumble of hot and cold, or the extreme ways they show up.

"I'll check in with the Administrators. See if they can crank up the heat a little." We have gas again, but Irene is stingy with it. She is joking about the Administrators controlling the heat, but she also fears and worships these personal gods. The Administrators are all women. Irene believes in them along with dark magic of all kinds. She thinks cards can tell your future and crystals can heal you, and that everything interesting is happening inside electric air that hovers around us. She thinks the dead have things to say to us, especially those who are dead by our hands. I have killed one man, and it was to make an important point. Irene has killed three people, at least that she has told me about. These were freelance jobs she did for money when she was younger and had her act more together, her hands steady. She's long past that sort of thing now. She's old and weak and lazy. Still, her past does make me keep an eye on her. Sometimes she will pull her gun from under the mattress and stick it in my shorts, and if it were someone else, I'd know it was just part of a game, but with Irene, I stop whatever we're doing and say, "Baby. Put it away."

femininitea

Rain from a sudden storm hammers against the huge windows of the classroom. Cate walks among the bent heads of twenty students. None of them has hair that is completely an actual hair color, as opposed to green, or blue. A few years ago, every one of them would have been wearing a hat. And none of them—she doesn't know why not—ever turns the lights on. They work by the light of their desk lamps, like old accountants. "Can someone flip on the ceiling lights? Raven?" Fluorescents flicker to life and Cate turns her attention back to a student's computer layout of today's assignment—the office set for *Glengarry Glen Ross*.

"You have to keep checking against your drawings for scale. This would be a desk for Paul Bunyan. *And* his blue ox."

The student, Dequan Chang, looks up, blinks a couple of times, then asks, "Who's Paul Bunyan?"

Cate is grateful to have this adjunct job. She only has two courses a year—one grad and one undergrad section of set design. The school is prestigious. Georgia O'Keeffe went here. Claes Oldenburg. Elizabeth Murray. The architecture department has interesting faculty and attracts talented students. It plugs her into the design community. She could not live on the salary, but it does come with health insurance. It provides her with the closest thing to a financial floor she has ever had. A full-time, tenure-track position would make her totally solvent, but then she would have too little time to design sets, a chronic dilemma.

From class she rushes north, surfing a water-lashed Lake Shore Drive, happy she let her father talk her into all-wheel drive, nice and grippy. With cars, she takes his advice along with his family discount.

At a red light, she checks in the rearview to make sure her face doesn't have any glue smears or patches of sawdust from the classroom. She circles around Andersonville, looking for a parking spot in the baritone thunder, branch-cracking lightning. She texts Maureen.

parking nightmare. b there soon.

Maureen looked so good in terms of early impressions. She came with so many features, like one of those knives that are also bottle openers and screwdrivers. She's financially solvent. A little older than Cate. Hot in a restrained way, which is to say, hotter than unrestrained. The play they worked on together was about the last days of Marie Curie, as she pressed on with her science even as she weakened from radiation sickness. Cate loved that Maureen spent an entire day hunting down a particular shade of green rubber for Madame Curie's lab apron. A professional perfectionist. Everything happened so quietly, a small collegial friendship that opened into an attraction. A lucky break for Cate. She's not much good at making the first move. She's a lot better at standing still and waiting for whomever to show up and make her desire half of a coincidence.

In addition to their work, she and Maureen have a few ready-made, overlapping interests. They both love the same TV show, about a married couple of undercover KGB agents. They've started talking about a trip—Maureen's treat—a small-ship cruise to the Inner Hebrides. Now, though, there is the sister to factor in. Maureen has arranged for the three of them to meet up this afternoon at Kopi; she loves the hippie atmosphere of the place.

Because of the storm, the place is underpopulated. She sees Maureen with a woman quite a bit blowsier, but definitely bearing a family resemblance. They are sitting at a back table, by the travel store that occupies the rear third of the place—racks of hemp clothing, shelves of Lonely Planet guidebooks, a stand of jaunty felt hats. As Cate approaches, Maureen's sister stands and opens her arms. Frances is from Oregon; Cate has noticed a north-coastal (both coasts) phenomenon of unwarranted hugging. She tries to duck the incoming embrace.

"I'm afraid I'm a little wet for hugging."

"Nonsense," Frances says, a little too loud for how close she is to Cate's ear. "Where I come from, this is a sprinkle."

Maureen says, "We've been on the couch last night and today." Cate can see she doesn't mean for this remark to be alarming.

"We watched two seasons of *Mad Men*, which I never saw before," Frances says.

Frances is in Chicago on her way south and east. She sells quilts as well as restores them. This expedition is a search for hidden troves, mint-condition quilts tucked away in hope chests for a hundred years, saved for "good," a day that never arrived. Arkansas and Pennsylvania have been high-yield states for her on earlier scouting missions.

Frances is what Cate would describe as recently pretty. Her long hair, brown as opposed to Maureen's red, is pinned up with clips of silver and feathers, then falls in other places onto the shoulders of a wraparound sweater. Everything about her clothing is complicated, swaddling. It's hard to see where one garment leaves off and another begins. Vaguely spiritual jewelry is also involved, a shimmery shell on a leather string around her neck. Deep purple shoes with turquoise laces, and the ends of the laces have charms dangling from them. She appears to do most of her shopping at Renaissance fairs. Cate was expecting someone else entirely, someone sullen with something about her that could, with the right lighting, be irresistible. Patti Smith maybe.

Frances is very different from Patti Smith, also very different from Maureen. Cate thought maybe Kopi would be a little too corny. But it turns out to be perfect for Frances; she even orders one of the teas Cate and Maureen make fun of. Femininitea. She laughs at herself for ordering it. She's a good egg. It's hard not to like her.

Cate imagines Frances's house, which Maureen refers to as a cottage. Woodland tones throughout, that goes without saying. An already overstuffed sofa further cushioned with large pillows, a couple of heavy throws. A rough-hewn table, its top a repurposed barn door. Set out on this would be an arrangement of rocks with words etched into them.

harmony. acceptance. purpose.

Two plump cats and a carpeted kitty condo. Cate doesn't particularly like herself when she sums up strangers like this, by their decor—especially when it's decor she's imagining for them—but this doesn't stop her from doing it.

"So, if you don't mind me asking," Frances says, taking Cate's bad hand, turning it over, rubbing it between her own thumb and middle finger. "What happened here?"

This almost never happens. People are usually too polite, or squeamish. Or they don't want to risk hearing something gruesome. But Frances inhabits a sharing culture; she has probably offered up a lot of her own private stuff in group therapy sessions and sweat lodges and the tents of tarot readers. By now, she probably expects returns on her investments.

"Workshop accident. When I was a kid," Cate says.

"Oh, honey. That must've been the worst day of your life."

"Really the worst day was when the fingers came out of the dressings, and the grafts hadn't taken."

"Oh. I'm so sorry," Frances says, covering at once the accident, its aftermath, and herself for bringing it up.

"It's an old story by now. And I can do almost everything with what I still have." She picks up her teacup, sets it down as a little demonstration. "My two big pieces of luck were not losing the thumb and that it happened to my left hand."

Maureen comes back from the counter with two enormous

pieces of carrot cake. "I thought we could share," she says to Cate, who's wondering how three people are supposed to share two pieces of cake. Then she says to her sister, "What did you think of that yellow quilt on the back wall?"

Cate is distracted by the carrot cake, one piece of which she is already tearing away at. She worries that she eats like someone in a federal prison. Table manners are just one of a list of small social concerns she should probably have sorted out by now, but hasn't. Interrupting is another. As soon as a conversation is behind her and she's alone, she goes over it like she's casting runes. She worries that she was finishing everyone else's sentences, or lurching wildly off-topic. Also she often, after the fact, takes herself to task for the darkness of her humor, for not gauging if it will be welcome in the circumstances. Maybe this or that ironic remark was taken seriously. Or, worst of all, maybe she has bad breath. She never forgets this about someone; it always haunts her memory; she doesn't want her breath haunting anyone's impression of her. So she checks along the way of a day, breathing into her cupped hands to see if anything's amiss, asking Neale, if she's nearby, to take a whiff. She pops mints. No one is going to run into ambient garlic while in conversation with her. Or worse, that steel-mill aroma she sometimes picks up off others; she assumes this comes with heavy vitamin regimens.

While Cate is mired in these shallows of self-loathing, Frances freewheels into a long, extremely dull story about the difficulties of restoring an 1840s cross-stitch baby quilt. The problem is getting yarns to exactly match the historical colors. From the sound of things, Frances either gives away a lot of her work or trades it for firewood or honey or massages. Her house has only a woodstove for heat. In a way, hers seems a life full of small adventure; looked at from another angle, Frances seems to be about one step shy of slipping off the grid entirely.

If Cate met her with no backstory, she would only find Frances a sunny, placid woman hanging on to a '70s lifestyle that was mostly over before she was born. She tries to catch a glimpse of some spark between the sisters, but can't see anything. She tries to fit their affair inside a box labeled "stuff that happened years ago," but that doesn't neutralize it. The sisters are kind to each other; there doesn't appear to be any rivalry. Which is nice to be around, but now, of course, tainted.

By how, and how often, they refer to their childhood, it's clear this was a happy place for both of them. Their parents were in the movie business in L.A. Their mother was a seamstress at Disney. At home, she made clothes for her girls, often matching outfits, as though they were twins. Frances threatens Cate with home movies of them riding in their own Mad Hatter teacups, spinning around and around in a scaled-down carnival ride their father—a metalworker, a fabricator of special effects—set up for the kids in the acre of desert that was their backyard.

"Whee!" Maureen trills.

Cate can't tell if they are being ironic about the teacup ride, or not. "Do the teacups still exist?" Cate asks.

Frances says, "Exist?! We still *ride* them when we go home. Round and round we go." Cate assembles a mental picture of this, but she can't make it a good picture.

"Danny refuses," Maureen says. "He thinks it's infantilizing." Danny is the brother with a silly-seeming but fierce addiction to aerosols. He huffs. Maureen has barely mentioned him. Cate suspects there's a fair amount not to mention.

So here's a new piece, Cate thinks. She envisions Maureen and Frances, now too big, stuffed into their teacups, their brother high, spinning in his own way, in a lawn chair. She needs more anecdotes, more evidence on Maureen. She's looking for extenuating circumstances. She's not sure if the teacups are redeeming or damning.

Frances gets a call on her cell. The picture that pops up is of a guy in a camouflage balaclava. "My old man," she says. "I'll take it outside."

"White Water Jack," Maureen says, once Frances is outside. "He's a guide. In a town as small as Maupin, he counts as a celebrity."

Cate pictures Frances and Jack together in a yellow blow-up raft, shouting happily as they roar down the middle of a river.

"Can you come over tonight?" Maureen asks this shyly.

"Oh boy," Cate says. "I'd feel a little uncomfortable, I guess."

"Don't. You don't have to. Frances won't mind."

"Well, *yeah*? That's the bad part, that you have to say that. That there's a reason she *might*."

"Oh, I think the teacups are worse than that thing. I honestly thought I was using good judgment not telling you about the ride." She is speaking softly, close to Cate's ear, and the smell of her breath—clove and smoke—is arousing. Cate has noticed this aroma during other intimate moments with Maureen, but only just now does she realize what it means. Maureen is a secret smoker. Or tobacco chewer, although that definitely seems less likely. She employs some clovey cover-up. She stands in the alley behind the Lyric exhaling plumes of smoke, in the company of her cohort, her shrinking demographic. Cate can see her so clearly, having a conversation in the alley with the theater janitor and a nerved-up soprano who's one of the townspeople in the second act.

Something about her breath and the soft brush of her mouth against Cate's cheek and the emptiness of the café and Frances being outside in the snow prompts Cate to turn to kiss Maureen, and then kiss her again. Maureen is a world-class kisser. Put that in the plus column.

Cate tells her, "I could probably kiss you all afternoon. Make a little spectacle in here. But instead I'm going home. I need to reflect."

"Oh, don't do that."

As they stand on the sidewalk outside Kopi, Cate looks down and notices the purple of Frances's shoes bleeding into the turquoise of the laces. Chicago is tough on whimsy. A small van speeds by, splashing them as it goes. The van is from Toaster, a diner quite a ways down on Lincoln (*way* out of this neighborhood) owned and operated by Dana, who is supposed to not be contacting Cate. This little bit of stalking is interesting, and should be annoying. Discouragingly, Cate is more flattered than annoyed, but then she doesn't have time to be either, as the van keeps heading north up Clark and her phone starts ringing in her parka pocket. A 212 area code. Cate assumes it's Love Salvage, a Manhattan prop house. They have the real 1950s venetian blinds Cate is scouting for the drill sergeant's office, and they're cheap. Of course the fat kind are being made again, but they look historically phony. The old ones are yellowed from all the smoking done in the offices where they once hung, their tapes nice and grimy. It's a look that's hard to create retroactively.

"Work call," she tells Maureen and Frances as she gives them fist bumps, as a jokey good-bye to avoid hugging. "I'm going to have to take it."

"Hey, Cate." Not the salvage place. It's Ty Boyd, artistic director of Ropes and Pulleys, a very good off-Broadway company. She's met him a couple of times in her previous life as Graham's wife. He tells her they're putting up a play about Vita Sackville-West. "Do you know who she is?"

"Virginia Woolf's girlfriend, yes? Lived in a castle? There. I've run out of knowing about her."

"Woolf was just one in a long string of willing victims. Vita was a serial cad. It's a good story. Lauren Mott wrote the play and so Molly Cracciolo is directing. They both liked what you did for Marie Curie. They wonder if you could come out and talk with them about doing the sets." This is one of the eerie aspects of theater. You never know who's blowing through town, dropping in on your play.

"Well, Jesus. I'm flattered to be called. They're my idols," Cate says. "Ever since *Gauntlet*." Cate stands in awe of art that can work people into a lather of love and hate. That would be every one of Lauren Mott's plays.

"Well here's your shot at working with them. I'll send you the script. We'll need ideas for four sets. Just as a way of starting the conversation. They'll be talking with a couple of other designers, so it's a tryout of sorts, but a friendly one."

She thinks, this is how the wind shifts. "Sure. I can push some other stuff out of the way." This other stuff is pure invention. She has no further commitments, no employment for the foreseeable future.

She was just about to hit up her father for a "loan." She knows he will never turn her down. Because he loves her, but also because of her hand. She hates using this, even though it's only ever tacit. But she does do it. If she actually gets this job, and the play goes big and that gets her more work with these two icons—

She's way ahead of herself.

————

"Hey Nathan."

I don't know who this guy is. He's just somebody coming out of the john, one of the too-many people living here. Irene likes company. She also likes her dope delivered. People know to not show up empty-handed.

Inside I lock the door, take a leak, then sit on the toilet with the lid down. The tub has a dry, ancient atmosphere. No one has actually taken a bath in this room for some time. The bar of soap in the little soap dish in the wall looks like a piece of bleached bone. The scum that rings the inside of the tub has also aged into something hard and permanent. This room is a sort of religious sanctuary, a tabernacle of what is worshipped here. On the lip of the sink, I lay out a line from a private stash of brown. I don't have enough to share with anyone in the living room.

I can hear Irene from all the way down the hall, through the door. She's holding forth, wandering down memory lane. "During my heyday . . ." Her voice has the sound of maracas, as though little beads are rattling inside her throat. I tune out the rest of what she's about to say, which will just be one or another story about her musical career, singing torch songs in what she calls cocktail lounges, but the truth is they were really just dives. The Bad Alibi.

Whiskey Heaven. Places that didn't even have a piano. Irene brought a boom box. Basically she was doing karaoke and passing the hat. Irene holds on to this image of herself that is not really long gone, more like it never really existed in the first place.

She has an audience for these stories, though. Tonight it's the guy from the john, plus the Mexican father and son, and Betty, who has been in that chair for a couple of weeks now. She must get up to go to the bathroom, but every time I come into the living room, she is still in that chair. Betty's aspiration is to become a cocaine addict. This is a financial matter; at the moment, she can only afford to be a tweaker. She is one of the few people I've known who enjoys both uppers and downers. She's happy either way. Her mind is pretty well gone by now, along with her teeth.

I have to leave for work. I help out financially. I'm Irene's helper. Before me, she had another guy. Dusty. Before him she had Lois. Both of them are dead now, Lois OD'd and Dusty fell asleep behind a truck that backed up and rolled over him, then rolled over him again going forward. She enjoys the tide of people who come in, then seep out of her life, the life around her. It's her house; it belonged to her parents. She pays taxes out of stuff we steal, then sell. Because she's the owner here, she calls the shots.

—Get me some nuts, she'll tell me and I'll come back with something nice, mixed nuts in a can. Not just a bag of peanuts. I know not to get her crappy nuts.

—You're a sweet man, she'll say. I like her to boss me around.

She says she doesn't know why she is still alive. She hasn't had a sober day since high school. She has taken some kind of drug most of those days. Even as a teenager, she and her mother took speed as a way of dieting and feeling like superheroes. The two of them vacuuming at midnight, or coloring each other's hair or painting each other's nails, each nail a different color.

After her parents died, Irene had the house to herself. She caught a lucky break. Some of us have never caught a lucky break. A lucky break could have made a big difference for me. I've had to make it with no luck at all. It's okay. I'm not complaining. Most of the people here haven't had any luck either. The drugs even the playing field; when we're high, we have huge futures and big plans to fill them. The stealing is just to get the money to buy the drugs. Plus I try to only steal from the sort of people who do have luck.

When I get to work, a few of the fluorescent bulbs are flickering over the pumps, but fuck, it's like ten degrees out with the wind. Those suckers are going to have to get changed another night. I'm busy anyway, thinking amazing, important thoughts. I haven't had a customer in maybe an hour when I hear the thumps of a huge sound system. I don't like the looks of the guy getting out of the pimped Camaro. Too skinny, weird beard. Also, I don't like the neon piping beneath his door. I set my face into something like a big stone as the guy pushes a twenty into the pass-through. He wants fifteen dollars of premium and two Kit Kats. I keep my eyes locked on his as I push the candy through and punch in the amount on pump five.

I've never been held up at the station. This is my value to Sabir. He can leave me in the booth, go home, and get a good night's sleep knowing no one will ever try to rob me. I weigh probably three hundred pounds. I'm six foot two. I have no muscle or strength, but you can't see that from outside the booth. From outside the booth I am someone you would not want to mess with. I enjoy this about the job, my power. Also, I love the smell of gasoline.

a very bad day

"Tragic buffet table. Those hot dogs were in that slow cooker for at least a couple of days before we got there." This is Arthur, Neale's father, sitting in the front passenger seat, critiquing the food at the campaign office. Cate sits beside Neale, both of them slouched across the back seat of Arthur and Rose's menacing Dodge Challenger. They are politically progressive and concerned about the environment, but they are also from Detroit, and have always driven union-made American muscle cars like it's part of their belief system.

Cate sits behind Rose, noticing her long, salt-and-pepper hair tied in an elaborate knot at the back of her neck. She has worn it this way since Cate has known her. At one time she was pretty in a hippie way, like those small women folk singers who wielded big, acoustic guitars. Over time, particularly time spent trying to mend a broken world, her features have loosened. Her eyebrows, which used to be dramatic, are now caterpillars. The lid over her right eye now sags. When she was younger, Cate wished Rose could have been her mother. She was so not-Ricky. She was the first woman Cate knew who had tattoos. From where she sits, Cate can see the fading peace symbol on the side of her neck.

When she met Neale, Cate loved to go to her house after school. Rose would be there, ready with her stripped-down version of the mothering shown in TV commercials. She wouldn't bake cookies, but she stocked rolls of Pillsbury dough in the fridge so the girls could bake their own. While they waited, she'd get out a globe so old several countries had to be redrawn or renamed with a marker. They went through the *New York Times* until they found a story. Indira Gandhi, assassinated. Why? It was Rose who gave Cate the idea of a larger world, and that even if she was only a teenager in a smug suburb, she was part of that world. Because of Rose, Cate has volunteered around elections since she was in high school.

They are heading back to Chicago after getting out the vote in a town in western Michigan. The town is really poor. A lot of the voters on the Democratic rolls there live in rural versions of projects—town houses with dirt front yards, nobody outside, not so much as a potted plant in any window. Cate isn't sure if they are really going to make it to their polling place today. It's hard to counter their apathy.

"Good cake, though," Arthur says. "The poppy seed."

Rose is driving in her usual limit-pushing gear. She has spent her entire adulthood fighting for civil rights, opportunities for women, justice for the wrongfully imprisoned, open arms for refugees. But once these humans are behind the wheels of other cars, they become, if not the enemy, at least the competition. They need to be tailgated out of the fast lane, encouraged with a quick, prompting honk just before the light changes, flipped the bird when they try to cut into the front of a line she feels they belong at the back of.

Cate settles into her portion of the back seat, which is to say a burrow she has made in a high drift of lawn signs and door-hanger cards whose usefulness has just expired. On the other side of this (now) litter, Neale is eating half a tuna sandwich she grabbed off the food table at the headquarters. Cate is playing *Toon Blast*, a game on her phone that has already sucked away months of her life when you add up all the bits of hours she has played, lured in by big rewards like a smashing-hammer icon, or a power-drill icon to destroy color cubes.

But although they are tired, none of them is worried. The outcome is in the bag, isn't it? Other Democrats in less dispirited places will carry the day. Still, Cate is nagged by the subdued atmosphere in the campaign office.

They go to the apartment of Rose and Arthur's friend Maury, where there's to be a gathering of the faithful. Maury orders Thai, opens a bottle of wine. Five of their union-organizing friends arrive. Everyone settles in.

The returns are disturbing from the start.

"Red states," Rose says, dismissing them.

"I think I'll head out," Cate says an hour later, when she has begun to get queasy. "I'm going to the pool. That trick worked for me the night the Cubs won the Series. Things weren't looking good, but by the time I swam, then got back, they were on their way to the win."

No one is listening to her. Everyone in the room is magnetized by the bad news flooding out of the TV. It's as though the television is in meltdown, but of course it is actually the country.

The pool trick doesn't work this time. She's the only one in the water, sequestered for an hour, but driving home, the radio is a torrent of gloom. Sailor meets her at the door. Graham is in front of the TV in the living room, which is running but with the sound off. He's on the floor, rolling and covering his head. He's not saying anything, just rolling back and forth.

She crouches down beside him. She rubs her hand over his hair. She scratches Sailor's chest. "Guys, I think I'm going to take an Ambien and go to sleep. I just can't think about this anymore tonight."

Maureen calls. She was at what was supposed to be a victory party, but everyone is just going home now. "Nobody even said good night. They were like miners going into their own private tunnels."

"Let's talk in the morning. I know waking up will be slamming into an abutment, but eight hours of whatever's just happened will have passed."

One of the happiest moments of Cate's life was in front of another TV, eight years ago, waiting through another set of returns, when Barack took Ohio, and so the presidency. Now all that is about to be pulled inside out.

Even medicated, she can't sleep. In the kitchen, Graham is still up.

"How will the world survive this?" he asks. It's 4:30 a.m. He's sitting at the island, hunched over, drinking coffee. His ponytail has come undone; his hair hangs Christlike to his shoulders; he's in his own private Gethsemane. "The people who voted for him. I feel like I should have gone and talked with each of them. Brought charts, scientific articles, photos of melting glaciers, dying polar bears, shown the value of immigrants, how much better it is to consider races and genders equal. I should have told them coal mining isn't making a comeback."

"This is very bad, but a lot of it was mechanical malfunction. Too many things are wrong with the machinery. All the gerrymandering. The voter suppression, the low turnout. The obsolescence of the electoral college. Many more people voted for Hillary, but we're going to have him for president. We need to sit with this for a while," Cate says. "Then get to work turning it around. Get inside the wheelhouse and start pushing against the heavy wheel."

"The surveillance is going to get much worse."

"Let's take a break. Let's walk this dog." Sailor concurs by swiping at the back of her shin. "When things get bad, he always worries it's about him."

duck egg

She stands in the ankle-deep water that slides across the sandbar, kicked up into spray by the dogs running its length, then back again. The water is a cold that eventually becomes bearable. The sky holds the vibrant blue of renewal, a postcard of spring. All well and good, except this is the second week of November. (The first week, it was raining, then freezing.) Through the morning, the temperature has drifted up to seventy. Of course this can't be right, and is surely a harbinger of floods and fires to come, dust storms, mud sliding into living rooms, deadly whirling winds plucking off roofs. Still, it's impossible, just for today, not to be viscerally thrilled.

Sailor leads a pack of dogs he has whipped into a lather. Most are not as fast as he is, and drop away after one sweeping circuit out of the lake, onto the beach then back into the water. By then he is left with only another big dog—a loose-limbed Ridgeback. They fool around a little, chest-bump, then go down to the lake for a drink. Sizing up the possibility of friendship, finding a match in size and weight, energy level, good smell. The two of them slam against each other as they run in sync, taking the turns wide, angled low. From the side, they look like a single dog in motion, and then they are out of the water, up on the beach, then back in again. Cate has noticed that these sorts of temporary attachments, once formed, are exclusive. For their short duration, they are powerful. If a third dog tries to edge in, he gets barked away.

Watching Sailor run is a furious pleasure. He's an Olympian in his prime. Cate is a forty-two-year-old woman with crappy knees from too much running on concrete through her twenties and thirties. She will never know what it feels like to be young and light on four legs. Tuning in to Sailor is the closest she will get. He watches her peripherally. Then, as he passes, spraying Cate lightly with the water flying off his fur, he looks back at her and grins. The dog beach is about him, but it is also about the two of them together. It is where she is learning about dogs. She's a beginner. Graham never comes along with them; he is plageophobic, also anxious about melanoma.

A significant number of the surprised have shown up. The beach resembles its summer version—bustling with dogs and humans. People are dressed in variations on a new climate-change style— autumn resort casual. A lot of parkas with shorts. T-shirts and wool watch caps. November is the new August.

Sailor and his friend are now standing side by side, stock-still, biting hard on opposite ends of a short branch. Their serious jaws are clamped tight in a silent, stationary battle of wills. And then the stick loses all value and they are boxing in the shallow water. She doesn't sense the presence of another human until a hand wraps around her arm just above the elbow, thumb pressing hard into her tricep, a gesture so familiar, so stupidly arousing.

Everything about Dana is trip-wired. Distance is Cate's strongest line of defense and when Cate insisted—this was about a year ago—Dana reluctantly agreed to stay away, but now she appears to have gone rogue. Even not counting her stalking Cate on Clark Street by Kopi, this is the second time in the past few weeks she has turned up. The first was maybe accidental—maybe—at the Jewel, in front of the fish case. Cate was looking at the different kinds of salmon. She was just about to say "Coho" to the fish guy when she noticed Dana over at the meat counter and so did a one-eighty into the cereal aisle in a determined way, as though her cart was pulling her along like an old lawn mower. So that was the Jewel. Dana doesn't go to the supermarket to buy meat. She owns a restaurant and gets her groceries wholesale. Today is one step farther over the line. Since Dana doesn't have a dog, a chance meeting at the dog beach has zero element of chance to it.

Cate turns and runs into a bit of trouble getting to "hi." She can't even look straight at Dana. Even now, she isn't up to that. Even now, she is only up to looking at Dana's feet, blocky, with an errant hammertoe on the right. She has taken off her shoes and socks and is now, like Cate, up to her ankles in zippy-cold water. The starter switch of hope flips inside Cate, followed by discouragement that she still feels this much. And that's what it is—all feeling. Electric impulses light up in tear ducts and pulse points, private parts (which suddenly feel much less private).

Breaking free from Dana was one of the original pieces of Plan C—her taking-charge plan, authoring her own narrative, blah, blah, blah. Moments like this, though, make having a plan seem ridiculous. But maybe Dana coming here means something's up. Something big. Like breaking up with her girlfriend. But all she has to say for herself is "I'm sorry. For bothering you. I just miss you too much."

"Oh man, I hope so. But this is exactly what you are supposed to *not* be doing. This is still the part where you stay away and I get over you. And anyway, shouldn't you be asleep now? Why am I seeing you in daylight?"

"Scouting out provisions. I'm just back from Indiana. There's a woman in Michigan City who raises ducks for eggs. Have you ever tasted a duck egg? They're fabulous. Deep-orange yolks." She pulls one out of her jacket pocket, hands it to Cate.

"I just had gold leaf on a coddled egg the other night," Cate says.

"I know that place. A lot of, you know, *sophistication* going around these days."

Dana's place, Toaster, is a retro-hip twenty-four-hour coffee shop on Lincoln. She works on a higher plane than gilded eggs. Scrambled duck eggs fit the narrative of her menu. Parisian baguettes she bakes herself. Nothing arch, just better in terms of ingredients and preparation. Working on a play a block away—this goes back to the beginning, years ago—Cate and Adam Pryor and Lonnie McKeen, the lighting designer, would get together there for tech meetings. The attraction Cate felt toward Dana was so dense it had its own place in the booth. One night as they were leaving, Dana slipped Cate her cell number on a pack of matches, like they were in a 1940s detective movie.

At first it was just about sex, a secret affair. The secret part was so Dana's girlfriend, Jody, wouldn't get hurt. Jody is embedded in Dana's life because of something Dana at first didn't want to elaborate on. Initially Cate took this to mean Jody was fragile and needed to be taken care of. But it turned out the obligation was rather Jody having saved Dana. The specifics of the rescue were cards Dana kept chested for a time, but eventually laid down as troubles with addiction. Until then Cate had thought cocaine was an occupational hazard mainly for rock musicians and stock traders. But apparently apprenticing in high-wattage kitchens was, for Dana anyway, more manageable with coke. And then the coke was the problem. And then with some incredible amount of patience, a draining of their accounts for high-end rehabs, Jody pulled her out of all that. Dana thinks she owes her life to Jody. How can Cate get in the way of that? How can she even want to?

But when she tried to pull back, she found her principles had been shredded by desire. Principles lay in ribbons around her feet. She had allowed herself to fall into a ridiculous sort of heart-throbbing love based on small, colorful explosions of urgent sex and careless revelation. Huge amounts of self-exposure made possible by containment in a cloister. Over time, these revelations accumulated into a potent sort of knowing obtained by confession. Eventually, she and Dana found themselves in a place where they knew each other better than they knew anyone in their real lives.

Cate's life was a cycle of concentrated time with Dana followed by delicious aftermath. Cologne trapped in a scarf. The chorus of a song, maybe "Stolen Dance" played on Dana's cell as it rested on a box of four hundred eggs, then later turning up on the radio while Cate was driving. Then the thuddy drop into the gray scale of actual life. Then the longing, then the return to the scene of the crime for another crime or two.

The GPS and time stamp of the affair were the hour between Dana arriving at Toaster for the night shift—relieving the day cook and waitress—and the arrival of Felipé, who worked the front of the restaurant at night while Dana cooked and also did the baking for the day to come. Or on the other end, the nights when Cate, sleepless anyway, would drive over to Toaster at six in the morning to grab a cup of coffee, then a bit of making out in the freezer before Dana was expected home. Once in a while Dana engineered a situation where she could get away to meet Cate at her apartment or workshop.

From the first, Cate wanted more of Dana than she was ever able to get. It wasn't a good position, always wanting more. This never brings out the best in anyone. It went on until Cate stopped liking herself. At that point she thought: *Enough*. Stopping was harder than she'd imagined it would be, but she did it, and she has stuck to it.

But even right now, having successfully come through over a year's withdrawal, and with her good reasons still marshaled, Cate's resolve has drifted into a small fantasy in which Dana suggests a cup of coffee. Then the small but peppy sex mouse in Cate's brain starts scrambling around to think what coffee shop nearby might have a single-occupant bathroom. She feels sensible for confining the fantasy in this way. Running with it would allow visualizing just a stall, in any restroom, even one in a scary park bathroom with sheet-metal mirrors and broken locks and puddled floors. Worst, she can tell that Dana, standing inside Cate's silence, has sensed the existence, if not the particulars, of the fantasy.

Sailor comes whipping by. Cate doesn't bother telling Dana that he's her dog. Dana doesn't need to know her dog. Dana no longer has any sort of purchase on her. Cate turns back to look hard at the horizon where the lake is steaming up a little, the last of the recent rain lifting off. She hates how much she feels exactly now, when she would have hoped to feel nothing.

Sailor loops around, then jumps up to put his front paws on Dana's shoulders and bounce off. *Of course* he'd like her.

"Could we get together tonight, late? You know, to talk. I'm so flipped about everything, our country. My mind folds in on itself when I try to make sense of what just happened. And my own life without you. I need to talk. Jody's out of town. Her sister's having a lump removed from the back of her neck."

"Cancer?"

"No, it's some better kind of lump. A cyst maybe? But her sister wants Jody's support anyway. Their family is basically one group hug."

This is a rare piece of domestic revelation, that Dana's house would be vacant enough tonight for Cate to pay a visit. Cate waits a beat for that invitation, which doesn't come. Cate has never been inside Dana's house. She knows where it is and what it looks like only from Google Street View.

"You can't come by my place. Graham's split up with Eleanor. He's staying with me for a while. He would definitely notice your arrival. Then he'd put together an intervention. The kind where guys in black burst in and put a bag over my head and take me by my arms and haul me away. Until I come to my senses." She pauses, then, a little too late, remembers Maureen. "Plus I'm seeing someone."

"Yeah," Dana says, dismissing this as an irrelevant detail, getting back to logistics. "Then what about Blackhawk?" Cate's workshop.

"The problem isn't locational, it's that I don't want to wreck any more of my life being in stupid, tormented love with you." Cate enjoys hearing how confident she sounds. Also how she can finally look straight into Dana's eyes (unfortunately fascinating chasms, they're the green of the flesh of a lime) as she says this. But they both know that, caught in a weak moment, maybe even the next time Dana shows up wherever, Cate's better judgment could crumble and wind her up

on the movers' blanket thrown onto the big table at the workshop—
fucking. Then, worse—crying. Mercifully, Cate's phone hisses in her
pocket. She pulls it out and puts the duck egg in. A text from Maureen.

can u c me?

followed by a string of question marks and emojis of puckered
lips. Maureen is deft, sometimes even ironic, with emojis. They
may be the language in which she was born to write. At first Cate
takes this message to mean Maureen is asking if she is free to
meet up, then understands it means she is here, at the beach. Cate
left her a voice mail earlier saying she was so depressed about the
election. She thought Maureen would just call back, but apparently she has instead shown up. Cate looks around until she spots
her, standing atop the rocks above the beach, waving, smiling.
Impressive timing.

"That's her?" Dana says, peering in Maureen's direction. "Okay.
Right."

Cate doesn't know what Dana can be dismissing from a hundred
feet off, but it's a conversation she hasn't time for. She pulls up her
hood, clears her throat, and starts walking. She half-turns once, to
hold a hand up to Dana. A waveless good-bye. As though they are
just a couple of regulars at the dog beach. Sailor follows Cate. When
they get up to the patch of grass that overlooks the beach, he ambles
off a little way.

"Hey," Cate says.

"One of your beach buddies?" Maureen says.

"Someone I used to know. You run into everyone here sooner or
later."

She hard-shifts into the election, what it's going to bring. They guess around a little.

"Big cuts in funding for the arts," Maureen says. "But let's be happy while we can. About your good fortune. This play is going to be a big break for you. Molly Cracciolo and Lauren Mott. You're moving into the stratosphere." Maureen is so happy for her it makes Cate a little high all over again. She goes on. "Off-Broadway, for one thing. Bloomsbury, for another. The 1920s. The 1920s in England. Those will be sets you can really sink your teeth into. Those rickety wicker lawn chairs. Interiors—those mullioned windows and velvet drapes. That *really* heavy upholstery."

"But they want ideas in three weeks. Three weeks minus the four days since they told me. They FedExed the script."

"You can do it. You don't have anything left to do on the army thing, right?"

"Previews start Thursday. I'll be so glad to have this behind me. I'm not even putting it on my résumé."

"Look how fast he is," Maureen says, meaning Sailor, who has left them to take a final loop around the beach, leading a fresh pack of small, yapping dogs around a curve. Cate has to keep an eye on him. He enjoys rolling puppies and certain small dogs, which is fun for him, but sometimes not as much fun for them. When she looks across the beach, Dana is no longer there.

"He learns a lot here," Cate says, turning back. "Like, he's learned to take the inside and lean low going around the bend. He learned how to swim when I started bringing him here in September. Another dog taught him. Sailor just followed him in. They learn from each other. It's cool to watch."

Maureen grabs Cate's hand and pulls it around to the small of her own back. "I haven't been this crazy about anyone in a long time. I thought maybe that wasn't going to happen for me, that I'd become too alone, too critical, too particular. But now this. I didn't tell you about me and Frances to freak you out. I wanted to walk across the bridge between us. How can two people be close if they cling to their unknowability?"

Although a lot of Maureen's relationship analysis sounds like it came out of the same factory as the inspirational rocks Cate imagined for Frances's living room, she can hear the sincerity within what she is saying. She can also hear the shell of the duck egg cracking in her pocket. She tries to cover by speaking a little louder. She hopes it's not leaking through.

"I'm not judging you on any kind of moral basis. But it just— it seems like you and your sister were in an actual *relationship*. I've never had the issue come up before. Or even heard of anyone else having it. I guess that's a little troubling."

"It wasn't exactly a relationship. We saw other people."

Everything Maureen adds to this story only further tightens Cate's cringe.

Maureen is ready to brush away the subject. "You're going to have to get more information on me. So this thing doesn't stand out so much. We need more space filled with more details."

Cate nods, then looks over at Sailor, who is sitting at attention, begging a treat off someone way down at the end of the beach. He sees her, though, and by the time she and Maureen reach the parking lot, he's caught up with them. She doesn't need to look back; she can hear the clink of his tags behind her.

excursion

She loves to swim, but some winter days are not for diving into even indoor water, and she just heads for the gym.

The guy on the treadmill next to Cate today isn't watching ESPN or CNBC, but rather the closed-circuit camera in the gym's daycare room. Two toddlers are rolling a giant ball back and forth, rolling and laughing. The guy is in his fifties; she hopes the girls are his granddaughters.

Unlike him, most of the people who work out at this gym are inconspicuous, interchangeable; they don't show up on her radar. She probably doesn't show up on theirs. Over time, though, a core group has sifted out. The really sweaty guy, the corpulent priest, the scary anorexic. The lady cop with the terrific body and year-round tan from the beds in the gym's basement, but so tough it's hard to imagine working up the nerve to have sex with her, although Cate does imagine.

This noninteractive companionship is comfortable for Cate.

She used to swim or go on the mill two or three times a week, but since the election she works out almost every day. She needs to burn off a morning film of despair. She avoids the news stations on the monitors hung from the gym's ceiling. To make forty minutes pass beneath her notice today, she watches a show about women buying wedding dresses. Two brides are being featured on this episode, both much older than women Cate would put in the virgin bracket, older with a bit of wear and tear. In photos, their fiancés look like bar bouncers. These weddings are not their firsts, but both of them say they want to feel like a princess on their big day. The bridal party of friends and/or relatives tears up as their bride emerges from the fitting room in a sequence of strapless gowns. One is fixed on the idea of "bling," and they find her something with a cascade of rhinestones down the front. The other wants "a full mermaid," which is apparently beyond her budget. The wedding party shares a moment of sorrow.

Maybe, Cate thinks, this show seems insane to her because she is queer. Maybe if she were straight, she'd be thinking about a full mermaid and should she get a second dress for the reception (a chronic consideration on the show). Maybe queer weddings will eventually get pumped up like this. She tries to remember her wedding to Graham. She was twenty. He was so different from anyone else she'd met—playful, original. They'd have sex, then talk through the night about art and life. They floated big ideas. This was before *Pand-a-Rama!*, before all the money. They had the ceremony in a friend's apartment. She wore a sundress from the Gap. He wore jeans and a thrift-shop dinner jacket. Someone took pictures, but she doesn't know where they have drifted off to. Pictures weren't so important then; they weren't so much a validation of experience. Back then, you had experience, later on memories, then you came across a small pile of old snapshots in the back of a drawer and thought how skinny everyone was back then.

The belt slows to a stop. The guy on the next treadmill is gone; so are the little girls on the closed-circuit TV. The daycare room is empty.

When she gets home, the little lobby of her three-flat is stacked hip-high with Amazon envelopes, squishy mailers, and boxes. She brings up as many as she can. She drops them to the floor to unlock the front door. Sailor's nose is in the space created by her opening the door an inch or two. He licks her hand—more specifically, he licks her phantom fingers. He gives her this exact same lick at one point or another in any given day. He is probably the most empathic creature she will ever know.

Beyond him, a distinct shut-in smell greets her. A fusion aroma of Kleenex and orange juice. Sheets that could use some freshening.

Graham looks way too startled when she puts her head into his doorway and says, "Hey. *Beaucoup* d'Amazon for you. Some in the hall, some downstairs. I couldn't get all of them up at once. What's up in here?" *Here* meaning his room, also the internet, also his mind. He plays Nine Inch Nails's "The Hand That Feeds," to cover their conversation. He points to the walls, then to his ears. When his phone buzzes and skitters around on the desk to announce a text coming in, he takes a look at the message, which appears to be a map.

"Lucille Rae. She's found a likely data storage hub out in the desert in Nevada. She spends a lot of time on Google Earth. It's beginning to pay off. We need to get a jump on things before January. Before move-in day at the White House."

"Do you think he's going to bring all that gold dictator furniture with him? And why aren't you Skyping with her?"

"We have to be more careful now. We use something else now. It's encrypted. And it disappears. What I'd like is for you to use it, too."

"Why do I need to message you? We live together. You're here all the time."

"Just do this. Please. It may come in handy. I want to be able to reach you in case the shit hits the fan. Give me your phone. I'll set you up."

She wishes he was in here looking at porn like a normal recently separated guy. He's in his fifties now; the thing of being a decade older than Cate seemed hip when she started up with him. She was in her early twenties, wandering around in an inchoate sexual half-sleep where she only knew she didn't want any of the guys who were interested in her. She wanted something different, but what? So then it was a younger guy, then a couple of black guys. Then when she did sets for one of his plays, it was Graham. He was so compelling, she thought older must be what she'd been looking for.

They were together almost five years. And then she met a woman—a terrible woman, as it turned out, but with a lot of power and ramped-up pheromones—and Cate couldn't fit her own response into a small box. What happened was nothing like a crush.

She came out to him almost as soon as she did to herself. She didn't want to be a jerk to someone who'd been so kind to her. And his kindness has continued. Here it is, a decade and a half later, and she is so queer, and he has two more marriages behind him, is vastly wealthy, and now maybe a little crazy. And yet, life is long, and here they are, living together with a shelter dog, subsisting on a diet of curated cheese and buttery chardonnays.

"Why don't you take Sailor out for a spin? You know." She sniffs the air and nods her head at their gorgeous dog lying like a cutout on the carpet. "Where there's smoke, there's fire."

"Sure. I can do that. I haven't really been out all that much today."

"In all this national uproar I forgot to tell you, I got a call from Ty Boyd." She tells him about the play and her chance to do the sets.

"Oh, Catie, that's so excellent. Really, really. I feel the big time rushing at you. And you'll love working with Ty. I should call him. It's been a while." Meaning he will never call.

In the shower, Cate thinks how Graham's belief system with its complex architecture that used to seem a little too complex—now, in this new normal—is beginning to look almost reasonable. In an increasingly crazy world, Graham doesn't stand out so much. But he's still crazy. Most of his money is now in gold coins in two banks in Singapore. He had to fly there to set up the accounts, and he hates flying. Actually, what he hates is leaving the apartment. Her apartment. Amazon is a big help in this respect. When she's showered and dressed, he's back from walking Sailor. Now he's ripping open one of the larger boxes. Inside is about five feet of crushed paper stuffing and a small box.

"Toothpicks," he says sheepishly.

"Couldn't they find a smaller package?"

"Sometimes this happens. I always assume some sort of nervous breakdown at the warehouse. I ordered these yesterday after I ate one of those Greek spinach pies."

While it's okay for Cate to think he's troubled, she doesn't want other people to. Much better he stay a little mythic. She has quit gossiping about him with Neale, and has avoided the matter entirely with Maureen, who knows everyone in the realm of Chicago theater. All she knows is that he's staying with Cate while coming out of his marriage to Eleanor. By sequestering him, Cate is trying to buy him time to get his act together. Still, she probably shouldn't be the only friend he talks to in person.

She asks if he wants to come to Mariano's with her. "We're out of everything."

He astonishes her by saying okay.

"Look at this." They're in the produce department. "You can get salad in a *bag*."

"Well, *yeah?* How long has it been since you've been grocery shopping?"

"Hey!" He turns to show her a small tray of tuna maki. "Right in the grocery store."

"They have sushi everywhere now. I saw some in Walgreens the other day. Pretty soon it'll be in vending machines. Convenience marts in the desert. It's kind of frightening. I mean, it *is* fish. It came out of water somewhere, sometime, and it's still raw."

She's slightly embarrassed to be out with him. When she first knew him, he was a sharp dresser. An excellent hunter-gatherer in thrift shops. When the money started pouring in, he switched without a beat to shopping on Oak Street. Now, though, he hardly ever wears anything but shapeless garments. If she didn't know him and just saw him for the first time right now in putty yoga pants and a sand-colored tunic, she'd guess: alternative-medicine practitioner. Specialist in cranial-sacral therapy.

At the checkout he's fascinated by the small bottles of energy boosters. "What do you think happens after the five hours? I guess you'd want to make sure you weren't still on the icy highway in your big rig. You'd want to make sure you were already tucked in at the roadside motel."

"Maybe a glass of wine?" She nods at the pretentious in-store piano bar, but she can see he's done.

"Probably better to head back now," he says, looking a little sweaty.

———————

Basically, security is a state of mind. People are afraid to get on planes but there's a way bigger chance they'll get killed in their own car. They put all sorts of locks on the front of their house, but leave the backyard gate unlatched, or the garage open, or put in a fence that's low enough to jump.

In the afternoons, when many people are at work or out shopping, Irene and I take walks in the neighborhood. First we jiggle doorknobs and look for windows left open. Today she has to break a basement window with a little duct tape and a quick hammer tap. Irene is a small person and can slip through. She's elastic, like a rubber band. Like a mouse. She pulls away the glass and drops through, then listens for the possibility of anyone else in the house. If it's all good, she lets me in. If she hears voices or footsteps or the tapping nails of a dog, she slips out the back door and we're done there. We have to leave empty-handed, which we hate to do after having gone to the trouble. But if somebody comes in while we're already there, we're forced to deal with them. This involves physical connection and ups the ante. We never bring her gun. A gun carries the possibility of worse consequences.

This house is dark and empty. This is totally the house of rich homos. It's not that I'm all that perceptive. I'm not thinking this because of their fruity furniture or going through their CDs. Right in the first bedroom we go into, on the dresser there's a framed photo of two guys with hairy chests, holding each other in their faggotty arms. Both are middle-aged and balding, one heavyset like me.

We don't discriminate. We don't make judgments on anyone. We are only there on business. We are after certain things. Jewelry, iStuff, smartphones. We have buyers for these. Irene goes through dresser drawers, nightstands, boxes high on closet shelves. She pulls books out of bookcases and throws them to the floor. You'd be surprised how many people think that inside a book is a sneaky place to store cash. Or that the sock drawer is a genius place to hide jewelry. In the bedroom dresser here, I find a gold chain brace- let under the socks. Then I take a look through the bedside drawers and come up with a few poppers. In the medicine cabinet there are several bottles of Xanax. Someone here must be very nervous. I pocket the bottles. Irene comes in with a Bose radio, drops it in her shopping tote. I show her the bracelet.

Before we leave we usually do a little crazy shit. Like here she finds shoe polish and writes

FAGS MUST DIE

on the bathroom mirror, then I squirt some dish liquid on one of the pillows on the bed. This is just to scare them out of calling the police. It's good if they think we are freaks who might come back.

We go out the back way, through the kitchen. Outside, in the alley, it's nearly dusk. I put my arm around Irene's shoulder. We go to the Mexican chicken place for a little dinner.

at ease

Cate knows most people are attracted to working in the theater because of the hubbub—the accumulating and quickening pace of getting something ready, the fluid (sometimes romantic) camaraderie of cast and crew, the excitement of having pulled together and done something as a team. The last-minute crises (lead actor comes down with flu, uncle's mustache goes missing between acts) and their rushed resolutions (understudy steps in, passable mustache is cut out of an old fake beard). The thrilling sounds in the darkness beyond the stage—the satin shiver of coats being shed, the light flapping of programs being opened. The quiet that descends on the room as the stage lights come up. The hoped-for perfection of performance.

For her, it's different. She's not a particularly social person. Out of necessity she has developed into a team player, but for her the best part happens when she is alone, reading the play and imagining it at work on the set she will create. Filling in the negative space between the actors, giving them what they will require for whatever moves they make. She starts with inspiration drawings, then uses Vectr to make 3-D renderings of sets. She also makes models. Old-fashioned, but they still give the most reliable idea of what the finished set is going to look like.

For local shows in small venues, she roams around prop rental houses, or more often junk stores where the used this or rented that can be obtained. What she's bought, she modifies with paint, hammer, glue. She's a little skittish around saws, still.

What happens during the performance will then be snug inside its setting. Once the curtain goes up, Cate's job, for the most part, is over.

Tonight, the opening night of *At Ease*, she lies up in the fly gallery with her assistant, Stig. From this perch, if she drops her head, she can see Neale and Joe in their seats. They come to opening night of anything Cate works on. If the subject matter is too adult (a revival of *Bent* when Joe was only nine), Neale comes alone. Tonight, Cate is embarrassed that they are going to witness this loser, but she couldn't put them off. She tried. It's hard enough just to lie above this play and see it herself. The company could have had a million-dollar budget and the play would still sink with the weight of its awfulness. Below, Eleanor Quinn is giving everything she's got to one of the terrible lines she's been dealt.

"I lahk a uniform on a man. Even bettah, I lahk the uniform on the floor next to my bed."

Eleanor is playing Layla, the voluptuous nurse on the bleak army base. Layla makes the best of her situation by bedding enlisted men. The one she's speaking to now as they pass an afterglow cigarette back and forth lazily in the midafternoon, in an empty barracks, is Corporal Mason, who will be murdered in the second act.

When Eleanor gets to this terrible, Mae West line, Cate and Stig cut their throats with invisible knives, hang themselves with imaginary nooses. The line is the cue for the closeted, jealous Sergeant Tragg—Corporal Mason is a hunk he'd like to bed himself—to come briskly through the door and discover them. Howard Foster, the mildly famous, occasionally Steppenwolf actor they've borrowed to add name recognition to the cast, is at the ready, behind the door, positioned to come abruptly in. He has a stomachache tonight and Cate is worried this will prevent him from bursting through with gusto. As often happens, it turns out she's worrying about the wrong thing. What she should be worrying about is the crummy door, which is made of some pulpy wood that bloats in ambient humidity. They've planed it twice, but it appears to have swollen again and is now keeping Howard from doing any bursting at all.

"Fuck," Cate says. Although they are so very close, only a few feet away, the distance they need to cover is, regrettably, vertical. They can't drop straight down to help; they'd wind up in a pile of their own broken ankles. They have to run a gauntlet of steps and ladders to the stage.

Meanwhile, as Howard continues to give the door hearty thumps with his shoulder, Eleanor and Denny Cochran, who plays the corporal, at first pretend not to hear the thudding, and, with no further lines, start making out, then add some sexy moaning. A thin ripple of laughter lifts off the audience. After what seems like an hour but is probably no more than a minute, Cate and Stig reach the door. Stig nudges Howard aside while he hits the door with a brick wrapped in a sweatshirt. The scene lumbers on from there, a cart with a broken wheel.

———

Later, Cate is too dispirited to chew out the stage manager, who was smoking a joint out back when his door stuck.

"It was a dumb play anyway," Joe says once he and Neale are backstage. "The door just made it a funny play."

"Just put it behind you, honey," Neale says, bracketing a hand around the back of Cate's neck. "Come by in the morning. We'll cheer you up."

"We can make pancakes," Joe says, which causes tears to loosen in Cate's eyes.

Behind Neale, Cate notices Graham go by, toward the dressing room. What's *he* doing here? But before this thought gets to its question mark, she knows it's Eleanor.

"Nothing you did made that play any worse than it already was." This is Maureen, who has found her way into the small huddle. Cate introduces everyone, then puts a stop to the general consolation. "I know the sticky door wasn't my responsibility, but it was part of my set and that makes me look bad. If I keep working on plays this terrible, plus doing such a terrible job on them, I'll probably eventually be banished. Lightly. Casually. I'll have to do dinner theater in the Wisconsin Dells. Or dinner theater in the round. Where the stage revolves. Do they still have those?"

"In Florida," Maureen says. "I think they still have them in Florida. But you won't have to go there. This is just a small reversal, a small erasure on your résumé. You're lucky it didn't happen anywhere important."

Cate thinks it's good that Neale's first impression of Maureen is seeing how kind she is, but almost immediately the moment evaporates and Neale is steering Joe outside, home to bed, waving over her shoulder as they go.

"I'm going to draw you a bath," Maureen says once they're at her apartment. Maureen has taken a particular direction with her apartment decor—Midwest by midcentury. Furniture blond as Doris Day. Breakfast nook in the kitchen. Rooster-print wallpaper. Cate flatters herself that there's a subtle but distinct difference in the ways the two of them have taken up themes from the recent past—that she, Cate, is paying homage to the '40s as a significant period in design while Maureen is just fooling around, being lightly ironic, stylistically winking. Cate knows she can be a terrible snob along these lines.

"You've started getting the *Times* delivered?" Cate notices a copy on the kitchen table, still folded in its blue plastic wrapper.

"Not really. Just I like that Thursday Styles section, so on Thursdays, I pick one up. You know, from someone's doorstep."

"Someone was doing that to me once in a while, so I got up really early one day and brought my paper in. I slipped it out of the wrapper, unfolded it, sprinkled a nice layer of cake flour onto the surface, then carefully folded it back up and slid it back into the wrapper. Then put it back on my doorstep. If the culprit picked it up I figured he wouldn't open it until he was nice and settled in his bus seat." Cate is trying to head off Maureen's celebration of her shabbiness by gently implying that someone suffers in a small way from having their paper taken. This has no effect at all. Her reply is, "Oh, you sly devil, you." And from there she quickly gets back to coddling Cate.

"A proper bath is just the thing when you're upset. I'll put in some soaking crystals I got the other day from Merz. Blueberry Blossom."

"I don't think blueberries even *have* blossoms, do they? And I never really take baths. I'm kind of a quick-shower person." The prospect of getting undressed and into water is not, right now, particularly appealing.

"Come on. Give it a whirl."

When Cate is finally obediently in the tub, Maureen sits on the toilet lid and de-pills an old sweater. She has a little shaver for this purpose. Maureen is encyclopedic in matters of fixing things. Her phone holds a compendium of go-to people for every possible small problem. She is also encyclopedic regarding do-it-yourself tricks, household hints. Many of these are from old books she has lifted from libraries and the kitchens of her friends' mothers. So many of the fixes are for problems that no longer exist. No one really needs their hat blocked anymore (whatever that was), or their clothesline strengthened for extended use. No one has time to flameproof Halloween costumes by dipping them in a bucket of water and boric acid. On occasion, though, you might be interested in getting chewing gum off the back of your pants (soften with egg white, then put in the washer), and Maureen's there for you.

When she's done with the sweater, she brings out her stash of weed. Scrawled in marker across the top of the baggie is

WHITE WIDOW

She sits on the edge of the tub and sifts a teaspoonful of finely ground weed into her vape. When it's ready, she takes a long, slow pull, then tilts the mouthpiece toward Cate.

"Thank you for all this," Cate says, then takes a hit.

"I'm trying to do right by you." She scrubs Cate's shoulders with a puffy net thing. "I've misspent too much time on my way to you. You are a delightful person. Kind and thoughtful and, most important, you are not mentally ill. So I'm making a big play for you. I am squandering my blueberries."

"What happened tonight just seems part of the everything going wrong in a larger sense. Maybe this new America won't be as bad as I'm worried it will—"

"No, I'm pretty sure it's going to be worse. But we'll work at getting in the way." In Maureen's worldview, everything is fixable.

Cate lifts the comforter to get into Maureen's expensive Swedish bed, and a sultry aroma escapes. Maybe she sprays her sheets with a signature perfume. Sexually, Maureen is more advanced than Cate, or maybe more jaded. Certainly more artful. Because she handles fabric all the time, the pads of her fingertips are rough as a dog's paw. This is a nice feature she comes with. She also has a nightstand with a drawerful of lubricants, sex toys in lurid colors, with tricky protuberances. In their abundance, the toys embarrass Cate. They make her think of oppressed Asian women pouring hot-pink silicone into penis-shaped molds. Some of the toys are also a little scary. They look like they'd take you to a different place than a regular orgasm. Tonight Cate prevails and they have sex with just their bodies. Cate is too worried about her faltering career to get into it, although she pretends. She never wants anyone to feel bad in bed if she can help it.

Maureen's affair with her sister is fading and blurring. There were, of course, mitigating circumstances, although maybe it's just that circumstances usually mitigate. Frances is five years older than Maureen; she was off to college while Maureen was finishing up middle school. They almost didn't grow up in the same family. Then, when Maureen was just out of CalArts, she got a job doing costumes for a summer theater production of *South Pacific* in Eugene, Oregon. She stayed on with Frances after the play opened. They went to a sweat lodge, also a massage workshop. That's when the monkey business started.

And at that time Frances, from photos Maureen has shown Cate, was not seductive exactly, but had a definite ragged blondness to her. And the whole thing seems to have had very little carryover into the years since. It's not like Maureen was molested by an archbishop, and ever since has had to get her sexual partners to wear vestments. What Maureen and Frances did was a now-and-then thing, a way of hanging out together like other sisters share jewelry or bleach each other's hair. Except that it was having sex. That Cate is working so hard to find Maureen's dark secret diluted by these additional facts probably means they are going forward.

She gets a text from Graham, who for no given reason—meaning he has hooked up with Eleanor—says he just took Sailor for a walk, but will be out for the rest of the night, can she get back soon?

"Can't you stay over anyway?" Maureen says, reading the message over Cate's shoulder. "It's too cold out to go back to your place."

"I can't."

"What would happen if you didn't? Just this once?" The question is accompanied by Maureen placing her hand on the left cheek of

Cate's butt and gently pulling her closer. Cate sees she's being sub-jected to a little test of her affections.

"Well, he'd probably hold it as long as he could, then he'd pee on the floor, which would shame him. And then he'd totally panic because I still hadn't come home. But that's not going to happen."

It's little stuff like this about Maureen, more than the sister busi-ness, that makes Cate slow down and take a harder look at her.

When Graham comes home two days later, all Cate can say is, "Oh, please."

"I can explain."

"How can you be doing this? After the rat? After telling me that what you really wanted was to hack her to pieces, then spread the pieces over a parking lot on a hot sunny day, then shovel lye over the whole mess?"

"It turns out we weren't as far apart on things as we thought. Mostly it was a small cluster of misunderstandings. And it's not like we're getting back together. We're just exploring the territory."

Cate can't see any point in bringing the discomforts of reality into this smoothed, burled vision. It would only mean a few tiring, reason-able conversations where he'd act as though he was listening and then go back to Eleanor anyway. Cate can smell a reunion a mile off, but there's nothing to be done about it. It does say a lot about her opinion of Eleanor that she thinks Graham going back to her would be worse than him continuing to hole up in her spare room Skyping with Lucille Rae. Worse than him peering through the night at downloads in that tiny white type on a black background, what lives behind the smooth interface of the regular web. A marginless scroll of speculation.

pleasant travel

"Scary." Neale notices a new beauty shop/reflexology place called Bionic Hair. This particular stretch of Broadway has businesses that seem to have slid in from a parallel universe, or a lost time. Pleasant Travel. The Double Bubble bar. The Loving Hut vegan restaurant. Neale is riding shotgun in Cate's car, twisted into a position that would only be comfortable for a yoga teacher. She's swiping photos right and left on her phone. She's on several dating apps. So far, none of this activity goes beyond her thumb. Although she'd like to be having sex with someone, she's leery of bringing home random guys from the internet, especially with Joe there and all the complications around that. Who she'd like to be with is Claude, her ex, Joe's father. She is still hung up on him; this puts a definite crimp in her forward momentum.

"What do you think of him?" She holds the phone out toward Cate at the next red light.

"He looks like Conan O'Brien. I mean, the exact hair thing."

"Which would be okay, unless he's deliberately trying to look like Conan O'Brien. That would be a problem."

They're running errands. They enjoy driving around together, which they've been doing since they got their driver's licenses in high school. Today they start out at Cermak, a global supermarket with extremely cheap vegetables.

"If we knew what these were, we could save a lot of money by eating them." Neale takes a picture with her phone of a hairy, dark brown root that's on special. Cate gets bok choy and head lettuce, cherries, then lingers in the Indian aisle picking out a frightening jar of mango pickle for Graham, who's a hot-pepper addict. They drop off a pair of Neale's boots for new heels at the shoemaker on Damen, then head down to Costco for paper towels and laundry soap. Dog food. Small vats of yogurt. By midafternoon they are smug with thrift.

Neale doesn't exactly know how much more crucial the penny-pinching is for Cate, doesn't know that Cate routinely takes cash advances from her viable credit card, while another carrying scarily high interest is maxed out. Financial management that's barely a step up from going through the couch cushions for loose change. If Cate didn't have the adjunct position, with its benefits, she wouldn't even be able to dangle where she is, off the edge of the middle class. If she weren't subsidized by her parents, she would only be living in one of the higher echelons of poor.

For her pride's sake, it's especially important that her parents not realize how crucial their support is, how cheese-paring her personal economy is. So today at Costco Cate splurged on a shrimp cocktail platter as her contribution to her mother's Thanksgiving dinner tomorrow. As soon as they've left the store, she regrets the purchase.

Instead of retro-glamorous, Ricky will see it as outdated, a sad attempt at irony.

Neale says, "Thanksgiving seems antithetical to everything about your mother. I mean first of all, Ricky doesn't really eat. And I've never seen her particularly thankful for anything. Whatever she has, she got it herself, with her bare hands. Hands and claws. And I have to say, she has never seemed particularly sympathetic to Native Americans. Or Pilgrims, for that matter. Holidays are just shit, aren't they? But look. All you have to do is make an appearance. You've got your shrimp, your expectations are low. You're good to go."

"No. I can already hear the force field of her disappointment, waiting up there. Buzzing."

"Yes. Of course. I can see her pulling her expression into place. That little twitchy thing she does around her mouth. The way she folds her expression into something that subtly implies diminished expectation. Slightly disappointed is her neutral, resting state."

"I think most of her disappointment is around my being queer."

"Oh no, it goes way beyond that. She'd also like you to have some sort of regular job. She'd like you to be working on Broadway shows. But if you were, she wouldn't like the particular show. And she doesn't care for your hair. She told me you look like a boy from an English boarding school. She'd like for you to go long and ombré."

"The hair thing." Cate runs a hand through it. "At least I won't have to have another depressing conversation about the election. It's only been a couple of weeks. There's a possibility my mother hasn't heard yet that there *was* an election. Why do *you* get to have warm, friendly holidays?"

"Well, friendly, yes, but you know parties at my parents' aren't exactly warm. More like spirited. All those old lefties in a small, enclosed space. All those saggy sweaters, all that corduroy. This year it'll probably be a wake, a funeral for democracy. My parents have worked their whole lives for equality and diversity, the good of the common man. What's coming is going to be a total teardown of all that. That guy's going to come in thrashing at everything decent and good. Thrashing with a machete."

"I know."

"There's going to be a women's march. Around the inauguration. My mother's working on it. It's going to be big." Then she puts a light, restraining hand on Cate's arm. "I need to talk with you about something. It's Joe. I need you to tell me what to do."

"What is it? God, I hate to ask."

"I went through the browser history on his laptop."

"Porn."

"Well, of course. I mean, he's twelve. And I wouldn't worry about busty babes, or even blow jobs. But what I found was *Czech Fantasy 8—Part 3*."

"Oh, I really don't want to hear this, do I?"

"I'll be vague. It's a glory hole sort of situation. Wandering guys with their dicks poking out of their jeans. Naked women are behind the walls. The guys wander around trying out one hole, then another. Like they're shopping. Then the camera switches behind the holes to where the women are lying on their platforms. They are deeply bored. Like they're thinking they don't get paid enough to do this. Like they wish they'd brought their phones so they could play *Toon Blast* while they're getting banged. They're not attractive or aroused. Neither are the guys. Everyone has skin problems. They all look like they've already given up hope for anything good. Doesn't this seem like too sad an idea of sex to have at twelve?"

"He probably just tripped over it cruising through regular videos."

"But maybe not. Maybe *all* his fantasies are Czech. Maybe he's already seen numbers one through seven. Maybe because he doesn't have two happy parents to model healthy sexuality for him. And I don't know what I can do about that. I'm in a business that's like ninety percent women. I'm never going to find anybody new. Anybody good. I'm worn out. And too alone. I hate going down in the basement to replace fuses at night. Not to mention living in a house that's so old and unrenovated that it still *has* fuses."

"Don't they have internet locks so kids can't get to that stuff?"

Neale pushes this advice aside. "I can see it's a problem that I think of him and me as buddies. I hate when he's gone way off-road on his own and I have to come down hard as a parent. And I don't really want to let him know I've been snooping."

"Oh, but you really have to. He can't watch that stuff. Think of who he'll be at thirty if he does. You're going to have to have a talk."

"I hate when you're strict with me."

"You don't. You love it. And you know I'm right. As usual."

Someone driving an ancient Lincoln Town Car glides from the right lane across the middle lane, into the left-turn lane in one long move, then doesn't turn left, just slides back in ahead of a by-now-frantic reassembly of traffic. Cate lays on her horn, just to assert herself in a situation over which she has no control.

"Major drugs" is Neale's guess, which is always her guess about these sorts of drivers—extremely calm but totally clueless. Cate takes a quick left at the super-cheap car wash (and wristwatch outlet, if you count the guy with a few hundred of them pinned to the inside of his coat). Next door is her branch of the public library.

"You haven't mentioned Maureen today. Have you moved on?"

"Oh no. I'm actually kind of pinning my hopes on her." Cate hasn't mentioned Dana at the beach. Even saying Dana's name gives her a level of reality Cate can't bear.

"Really!?" Neale sounds surprised, and not pleasantly.

"I don't want to still be looking for a relationship at fifty in what are probably going to be reduced circumstances." What she doesn't say is what she found out on the dog beach—that it is still possible she could retreat into a life lived in someone else's back pocket. Going around with frostbite on her hands from making time-pressured love in the freezer at Toaster, haggard from nights of euphoric insomnia. Dana is Cate's narcotic. Huge highs. Crash landings where she finds herself alone in an empty room. Yet here she is thinking about Dana even as she's talking about Maureen. She has totally disconnected from this conversation. It's like she's speaking through a ventriloquist's dummy. The dummy sounds confident saying, "I think if I put in all my little details, the algorithm on any dating site would come up with Maureen as my best match." She pulls up in front of the library. "I just need to stop here for a minute. Maybe only thirty seconds."

The book she has on hold is a collection of letters Vita wrote to Virginia Woolf. Cate has read the current draft of the play. Also two biographies. The corkboard in her workshop is tacked up with photos of

+ Vita;
+ her girlfriends (Cate has found thirteen so far plus a couple of random guys);

- her diplomat husband, Harold Nicolson (also busily queer, conveniently closeted);
- her neglected (sometimes totally abandoned) sons in ill-fitting suits; and
- her garden (major).

The space she has pulled into is right in front of the library entrance, marked LOADING ZONE.

She punches the flashers, tells Neale, "If you see a ticket person—"

Parking enforcement, once a lazy, city-run revenue effort, has been sold off to a ruthless corporation based somewhere in the Middle East that conducts a reign of terror. Meter readers in Day-Glo vests troll relentlessly, ubiquitously. Everyone now lives in fear of huge tickets.

"Yeah, yeah. I'll take the wheel." Sometimes the smallest thing like this blooms into a nervous consideration of what would she do if Neale weren't there. To shift into the driver's seat and, of course, everything else. Cate travels with a sense of safety, that if a trapdoor opened beneath her, Neale would grab her before she went down.

Inside, she goes to the on-hold shelves, which means a journey that requires running a gauntlet between two long Wi-Fi access tables. Any time Cate has come here, every monitor has someone sitting in front of it. Some of these are regular people, but more fall into the irregular category. Irregular and often talking softly, as though they have a Bluetooth thing, but they don't. Or irregular in their intense smell. Today's smelly person is a huge guy with a tattooed neck. The tattoo, half-covered by his jacket collar, appears to be of

Daffy Duck. She catches a nice whiff off him as she passes to, then again fro, on her way back to the checkout desk. Not a urine smell. More like a bad egg. The patrons near him seem oblivious. Oblivious or resigned.

While she's standing in line to check out, Cate reads a few of the Vita letters. She is so happy to have a shot at this gig. Tons of possibilities for the sets. Long Barn, the Tudor country house where Vita lived during the 1920s, and Sissinghurst, a crumbling castle Vita and Harold restored in the 1930s, are going to be amalgamated into one interior. Serious surroundings for romantic treachery. Treachery because Vita had nothing beyond sex and flattery on offer for Woolf, or the others who came before, or the ones who followed. She didn't jettison them, just gently set them to the side and kept writing them flattering notes while she moved on to someone new. The teacup of jealousy stirred and stirred again.

"After their first night together," Cate says, getting into the driver's seat and tossing the book into Neale's lap, "Virginia went out and bought gloves. I think she felt her hands were now erotic elements and needed to be covered. Poor Virginia. All that genius, but she didn't see that Vita only liked beginnings."

"I see you're on a first-name basis with both of them now."

"Well, the whole thing *is* pretty compelling. Aristocracy and Bloomsbury and queerness. Historically, all that rustling in the back of the closet. All the codes and signals. The letters within letters, the pinky rings. Something delicious about all the secrecy. Now everything's so in the open, we're free from fear and oppression, but we've traded it for being commonplace. Queer's as boring as straight now."

"Oh, I think you still have a little cachet. You still have a bit of shadow. There are still places where you could get beat up."

"I love thinking of Vita getting Virginia into bed. Seducing someone so physically vaporous. So graceful and elegant, so inexperienced. Then add in the fragility from her mental illness. She absolutely needed someone to touch her. I like thinking of her being helped out of her long skirt and dowdy underwear. It's the first time in a while I've been so ramped up about work. Not since the last play I did for Adam. I'm thinking this will be sort of a fresh start for me."

shrimp platter

When she has turned off the ignition, Cate spends a few minutes lingering in the driver's seat, gathering herself up. During this short pause, the car cools and the shrimp platter, which has been bumping around on the passenger seat on the way up to Evanston, nice and close to the heat vent, now gives off a pale pink odor. A day in the refrigerator has brought a gray tinge to its initially vibrant pink. She sees that several shrimp have worked loose from their tight, military formation around the central cocktail sauce cup. She pries off the plastic dome, cracking it in the process, and tucks the deserters back into place. Which only makes them look tampered with. The whole display has now acquired a sullied aura. Also, it seems to have grown since she got it. Only now does she see on its label SERVES 8. She goes around and gently lifts it out of the car like it's plutonium.

———

"Really?" This is Ricky's response to the shrimp. "Did you win this somewhere? Like a shrimp festival?"

"I found it in the alley," Cate tells her.

Her mother puts the platter on the counter, just above, Cate notices, the slide-out garbage drawer. Poised for whisking. The counter is new, made of blue-tinted, polished concrete, banded with a matte-finish metal. She hasn't seen this before.

"I left a message on your phone," Ricky tells Cate. "I wanted to remind you to bring anchovies. I forgot to pick them up at the store." An essential component of the Caesar salad Cate makes for any occasion.

"I so didn't get that." She's on shaky ground here, as she hardly ever listens to her voice mail, just looks at the call log and guesses what the messages probably say. Then she looks around and sees the entire kitchen has been totally remodeled since the last time she visited. "Hey, this looks great." She wipes her hand across the cool surface of the counter; it's like worn rock in an undersea grotto. She looks down. "Wow. This floor."

"Repurposed basketball court." Ricky's beaming now. "It'll survive the nuclear winter." This house is her mother's masterpiece, constantly being revised and improved on. Her next-door neighbors hate her. Their children, they complain, have spent their whole childhood under a dust cloud, their hearing shredded by the din of power saws.

Cate thinks she was last here maybe a month ago. Ricky moves fast and efficiently when she wants something done. This is part of what makes her successful in her job.

"What's up with dinner?" Cate says. "Where are the simmering pots, the homey aromas?" This is a joke. Cate has to go back at least a decade to come up with a holiday dinner actually prepared in this kitchen.

"We got it from Stella Brown this year. Her menus are always interesting. Your Caesar, that can be our traditional element. I'm too beat from the Christmas ramp-up at the store. Nothing is going right, plus I think they're trying to edge me out, or at least over. There's a kid they've brought in from New York, from the flagship. Haydn. Right. So anyway, with the catering, I just have to warm up everything. It'll be fine. And then we'll be done and we will have gotten through another holiday."

"Well, when you put it that way, it sounds memorable. Moving, even."

"Why don't you go in the den and let Jason know you're here? He's only reading. Some giant book on tree grafting. He'd probably welcome an interruption. So he can rest his wrists."

"I'll wait until dinner." She never knows what to say to Jason. Although he is only a couple of years older than Cate, they inhabit different galaxies. He is her mother's third husband, a River North florist Ricky uses for special functions at the store. Although Cate is mildly creeped out by the two of them being together, she also understands that objectively, their pairing probably isn't all that ridiculous. Her mother, in her mid-sixties, is still attractive in a slightly sharpened way. And still powerful in the world of retail design. If she wants a new man, she can still pluck one from a moderately deep pond. Jason is the latest koi. Except for encyclopedic knowledge about flowers and plants, he is vapor. Even his vices are recessive. He's vaguely alcoholic. Nothing showy or embarrassing, just that he

always has a drink at hand and, as an evening wears on, recedes farther and farther into a quiet, comfortable niche. He is kind of hyp-
notic to watch. His eyes are heavily lidded. His hair is a pale color
that's neither gray nor blond, and it's thick, cut short like a scrub
brush. He has a calibrated amount of stubble. He's small, maybe
even a little smaller than Ricky.

They sit on high stools at the kitchen's island. Jason pours the three of
them such ample glasses of red wine that the bottle is nearly drained
on the first pass. Fiestaware serving dishes filled with catered food
slide back and forth across the concrete. They take trial-size dabs and
slices. Macadamia-crusted sweet potatoes. Seared duck breast with
Chinese plum sauce. Green beans with lemongrass. A berry cob-
bler topped with whipped cream. Ricky does her usual picking and
prodding with the tines of her fork. Once she told Cate about the
fashion models' trick of eating tissue paper to stave off hunger. That
plus hooking themselves up to vitamin drips so they could make it
through shoots. She related this, of course, as though it was horrifying. But on a higher frequency, Cate caught a note of respect. Jason
shows almost no interest in food; it's just a colorful accessory to a
drink—like a coaster or swizzle stick. Both of them do, however, take
heaps of her Caesar, the recipe they praise fatuously as world-famous,
but the joke did get started because the salad is quite good. Today she
put in extra Worcestershire to make up for the missing anchovies.

A second bottle of wine is opened. Jason uncorks like a somme-
lier. He offers the cork to Ricky. The two of them always drink excellent wine. Ricky knows the wine buyer for the store's restaurants.
She gets both the employee discount and good advice.

Jason says, "We meant to get down to see your play."

"It closed so fast." As she says this, Ricky scrapes, with the side of her fork, the slight film of plum sauce off the edge of a piece of duck.

"You dodged a bullet, trust me," Cate says. She doesn't mention the New York play. If the opportunity falls through, at least it won't be placed in the long failure column in her mother's thick ledger on Cate. Not that either of them acknowledges the existence of the ledger.

"In the theater, though, even if you get a stinker," her mother says, "I guess at least it's something new, a new challenge. As opposed to Christmas in the world of retail. All that red." She takes a deep drink of wine. "Not to mention the green."

Both of Cate's parents have careers in the profitable levels of design. Cate sees she probably should have gone some other route entirely—flight school, cardiology—so as not to be so continuously and unfortunately compared to them.

"You should have brought someone along," her mother says, looking at all the uneaten food. "A chum. Someone with a holiday spirit. Graham even." Ricky likes to bring Graham into the conversation. He's male, also the most financially successful person Cate has been attached to. Really, the most financially successful person either of them knows.

"Everyone was busy. Or not into holidays."

"What about the redhead?" Jason turned up in the lobby of the Evanston theaters a while back when she and Maureen were on an early date. He was alone. He likes to go to movies by himself.

"Redhead?" This information has perked up her mother's interest.

"Someone new. I met her in a cage fight."

"You should've brought her," Ricky says. Cate thinks Ricky and Maureen might even enjoy each other. They come at life with a similar ruthlessness, although Ricky's is aboveboard. She's trying to beat the world at its own game. Maureen is palming aces. But, of course, Ricky couldn't like Maureen, on principle, *her* principle.

"Right. You can't even look at my girlfriends directly, just sideways. Like they're solar eclipses or nuclear tests in the desert."

"Your sexual orientation isn't a big problem, just peculiar and a little embarrassing. Like some odd hobby I have to explain away to friends. Bavarian folk dancing. Like you're always lurching off to Munich for festivals." Ricky goes to the refrigerator and pulls out a bottle of sparkling water. "Plus, of course, it's sordid."

This last comment isn't part of their little sparring routine. It lies on the other side of a barely discernable line. Jason sees this, and takes the awkward silence as an opportunity to head back to the den and his tree book.

Ricky presses on. "Let's just say you're not what I was planning on. I wanted someone who would marry a lawyer and have a couple of interesting kids and then the husband would have an affair, but they'd get through it, and she'd get into local politics. She'd run for alderman—"

"At least you didn't have anything specific in mind."

Her mother moves along to the next station in this conversation. "I have some stuff for you. I was going through all the crap in the attic."

"Sounds promising. Crap from the attic."

Ricky goes upstairs, then comes back down with a small cardboard box. "In case you can use any of this in a play sometime. This is all from my grade school days."

Cate pulls out a turquoise transistor radio.

"Oh wow," she says, unfolding a felt skirt with a poodle appliqued on its front. "You could get good money for this on eBay."

"No, you take it."

Cate pulls a long piece of green gabardine from the bag. "I never saw this. You never showed it to me. What is it, a sash?"

"I know it must be hard for you to see me as a Girl Scout, but as you can see, I picked up quite a few merit badges."

"I see. Yes. Here you go. Swimming. Campfire."

"That's the symbol for camping. Making a fire was one requirement. But we also had to pitch a tent. The old kind, with stakes. String up food from a tree branch to keep it from animals. Dig a latrine hole."

"What's this?" Cate rubs a thumb over another embroidered circle.

"Pathfinder. You had a little map and had to find your way out of a place in the woods."

"That sounds a little risky. What if they lost a kid?"

"I think it was a small patch of woods. I don't remember any of the badges being that hard to get. But I was in, like, fourth grade. They were solid little accomplishments."

"Don't you want to keep this?"

"I'm all about getting rid of stuff now. I don't want to hang on to anything I can imagine myself fondling when I'm ninety in assisted living, showing it to my home healthcare aide. Telling her I was a little pathfinder."

"Yeah," Cate says, adding a little social awareness to the conversation, "while she probably arrived here in an overcrowded boat and worked her way up here through the Everglades, then hitching rides with truckers. Washing up in gas station restrooms. Sleeping—"

"Yes. I think we've got the picture," Ricky says. "The thing is, now that I have so much past, it's like I'm dragging it behind me and I want to lighten the load. Looking back turns out to not be all that interesting."

"Are you going to see your father for Christmas?"

"Just before."

"I hate when you go down there. I always think you're going to be disappeared. Your ear will come back to me in a FedEx envelope. And I'll have to be one of those powerless, cynical women. Like in an old Joan Didion novel. Drinking at the airport bar. Bleakly scanning the crowd for you."

"I know. I think about that every time I go. But really, nothing bad is going to happen. Dad picks me up at the airport."

"Is he still with the amazon?"

"Yes. They're a pretty solid thing. And she's not an amazon, just a powerful person."

That's all Ricky wants to hear about Seneca. "Can you get me some Ambien while you're there? I'm almost out. And whatever else looks interesting. Do you remember that yellow cough medicine you got me once, the one where you had to already be in the bed before you took it?"

Cate's single most important goal in life is not turning into her mother. Still, she takes her money.

When Cate is leaving, Ricky says, "I'm not going to have a day off between now and Boxing Day." She almost forgets the money, the thin, folded pad of fifties she presses into Cate's hand at the end of visits. Cate hates that she takes these, especially hates dawdling

around, as she is doing now, until her mother remembers and goes
to find her purse.

The heat in her car has rejuvenated a residual shrimpy aroma. She
sees a couple of texts from Maureen, who actually did want to come
along today.

on my way

Cate texts back, tosses her phone onto the passenger seat. She takes
Ricky's cash, hikes herself up in her seat to slide it into her back
pocket, then starts the engine.

On the drive back into the city, she thinks about the pointless-
ness of her relationship with her mother. They're like two people
who years ago had rooms in the same boardinghouse, a time neither
looks back on fondly. Visits like today's always shoot Cate into a black
hole. What lies down there emits no light. What always follows is a
slide of predictable brooding on assorted failures. Eventually leading
to sorrow for elephants. Specifically, the third elephant.

To start with, there were three elephants at the Lincoln Park
Zoo. Older females, friends from the circus/zoo circuit, a little past
their prime, settled for their retirement decades in a small space in a
cold climate.

Then Tatima died. Respiratory infection. Then Peaches died of
what the zoo claimed was old age, although she would have likely
had another twenty years left had she remained in the wild.

Which left Wankie. For the rest of the winter she was consigned
to an indoor space with a concrete floor. To keep her from being

lonely, zookeepers put an old television into the room. When the city understood what was going on at the zoo, a town hall was held, and the zoo was urged to repatriate Wankie to the nearest bit of wild, the elephant sanctuary in Tennessee. Instead, she was pushed into a truck bound for a zoo in Salt Lake City. She freaked and lay down inside the truck. Elephants can only lie down for a couple of hours before their weight crushes their organs. Somewhere outside Omaha, they tried and failed to unload her, and so the driver just kept going. When they arrived in Salt Lake, they took her out of the truck and euthanized her.

Whenever she is at her lowest ebb, Cate thinks about Wankie. Who is always available for imagining, not dead in the truck, but rather standing inside on a concrete floor, through a long winter, watching TV.

Sometimes we're not after money. Every now and then we just like to mess with people's minds. We scout a house and it has to be a nice one, with decor, someplace where the people who live there care about how things look. Then we come back a few times to get a line on their routine, and when we're sure they're out we slip inside. We pick the nicest piece of upholstered furniture. A big chair is best. Irene uses her box cutter to slash the seat cushion. Just once. And we don't leave any other disruption. We don't take anything. They find the slash whenever they do. It might be a day later. It's violence without a point or a victim or a context. We like imagining it creeping them out for a long time.

mulberry street

At least the middle seat is empty. Cate has the window. On the aisle is a thirtyish guy wearing shorts, an old Radiohead sweatshirt with the sleeves cut off, flip-flops. Flip-flops are his first choice in winter travel footwear. For December, on a flight between Chicago and New York. His toenails are thick and yellowed; his knees are hairy; one has a surgical scar across it. Cate has noticed more of these overexposed people on planes lately, like they were watching TV then went to take the garbage out to the alley then suddenly realized—whoa!—they had a plane to catch. Cate waits until he finishes reading the SkyMall catalog and settles into dozing. Then she bends as though she's taking off her shoes, and with her phone takes a close-up of his toes. She'll shoot this to Neale once she's off the plane.

She tries to read. She brought Woolf's *Orlando*, but she can't concentrate. It's been a long time since she has been this nervous, experienced the motion sickness that comes with being kicked up a notch, or kicked down; the anxiety is about transit. There's nothing more she can do, though. She is well prepared for this interview. She's read the working script of the play, plus a lot about Vita. Also two of her novels and a collection of her gardening essays. Although Cate loves Virginia Woolf, she'd never read anything by Vita, who appears to have been an industrious, pedestrian novelist and poet; a major gardener; a distracted mother; a reckless womanizer. Looked at one way, she was arrogant and slouchy and aristocratic; from another angle—ridiculous. She lived in a castle; she had a moat, also a mustache. The play spans a few years from the late 1920s into the early 1930s, during which she took up, then gently demoted, a series of lovers, most prominently Virginia Woolf. Their affair was a stepping-stone across a shallow stream for Vita, a small but deep pool of tragedy for Virginia Woolf, who had the bad luck to be bipolar before the arrival of lithium. She took to her bed when her mind went astray. Birds spoke to her in Greek. On the page it's a very good play.

Cate has brought one model and a few drawings of the sets she would like to make. This is not a minimalist play, or even an austere one. As much as it is about Vita, it's also about the cosseted life she lived in the rooms of castles and enormous country houses. Stone walls hung with massive tapestries abetted her seductions. The rooms are part of the story. As is her garden in nighttime. This is the vision she is presenting to Lauren and Molly. Dark opulence.

"We are so glad you've come to us." Molly opens the door and takes Cate's hands in her own. This gesture might have resulted in an awkward glitch, but Molly doesn't miss a beat as she notices, then pretends not to notice, Cate's shortfall of fingers. Smooth.

Lauren stands behind Molly. Although the three of them were once introduced at a wrap party for the Chicago production of *False Confessions*, Cate knows them mostly through photographs. Although one (Lauren) is small and white-haired, the other (Molly) darkly Latinate and broad-beamed, they share the same combination of success and age. Also, weeks here and there someplace warm has burnished them both. Everything they wear is either gray or black or putty. A dash of brown for holidays. (Graham told her this.) Their heavy wedding bands are rose gold. When they got married—in the ruins of the Greek theater at Taormina—theirs was the featured wedding in the Sunday *Times*.

Their apartment, on Mulberry Street in Little Italy, underlines the fullness of their lives. The living room is huge, especially for Manhattan. Floorboards run on the diagonal. The furniture is an amalgam of styles and periods (probably not by intention) adrift in a pleasant way on account of all the space around it. A lot of good art. What is probably their best painting, an Alice Neel portrait of Molly, gets its due high above the mantel. Beneath, a fire is lathering up, sparking red, orange, blue. Here and there are props from their iconic plays—the hull of a longboat hangs from the high ceiling, the anvil from *Smithy* has been repurposed as an end table.

"Something to drink?"

"If you have coffee."

Lauren heads back to, presumably, the kitchen. Then reappears too quickly to have done anything. "Marta will bring the coffee." They have help. Of course they would.

"Make yourself comfortable." Molly points with a flat, ushering hand toward an overstuffed chair upholstered in fabric that appears to have once been a carpet. As Cate sinks into it, she takes in a panoramic sweep of the living room walls. Propped on a primitive carved mantelpiece are framed photos of Lauren and Molly with other occupants of their stratosphere. Molly and Julie Taymor in conversation, small microphones clipped to their collars, sitting in front of the giant gold disk center stage at *The Lion King*. Lauren and Molly at a banquet table next to Caryl Churchill, all three laughing with heads tilted toward each other, like conspirators. Lauren playing checkers with Mike Nichols against a background of wood and leather, maybe a private club of some sort? Molly on a stage with Andrew Keates, regarding the London set of *Bent*, a set nearly as famous as its play. On another wall, shelves are layered with scripts. Those on the bottom have been there so long they look like brittle, flattened papyrus scrolls. There's a lot more to look at, but she doesn't have time to take more in, interrupted as she is by the here and now.

Her chair faces a huge, low wood table. On its other side, Lauren and Molly settle into a deep red sofa. Lauren sits with her feet tucked under her. Molly rests a hand on Lauren's thigh. Cate skips telling them how big a fan she's been. In her experience, although the celebrated love their fans, it's only in aggregate, fans as a single entity. As individuals, they are devalued. She's not sure why, but she has seen enough of this mechanism to never approach in awe.

"You may wonder why we are looking at your work, and why now?" This is Lauren. "The thing is, we travel a lot. We check out what others are doing. We loved Adam's work. Terrible about his death, so untimely. Not to mention brutal. In any event, we were in Chicago and saw the Marie Curie play. Your set was so clever."

"Well, most of my cleverness has been to disguise a lack of money."

Molly says, "You are accumulating a reputation in Chicago."

This takes Cate completely by surprise.

"We thought it might be interesting to see what you'd do with a larger canvas."

"Please, show us what you've brought." Lauren nods toward Cate's messenger bag. Cate pulls out her laptop and opens to the 3-D drawings of her sets, then angles the screen so they can all see them together. She also pulls her living room model from a canvas tote.

Cate clears her throat; she has rehearsed. "I'm trying to telegraph Vita's ballast, her weight in her world. As you show in the play, she traveled light emotionally. If she lived now, she'd just be superficial. Cheating wife. Neglectful mother. But she had a title and a castle. She dragged her family's past behind her like a train on a wedding dress. The play puts this across so beautifully. I'm just trying to underline it.

"As for the movement of the play, as I see it—well, Vita created a lot of commotion by standing in one place while moving everyone else in, then out. From the specs you sent, I'd have room to do two platforms. Sliding from side to side. Vita's easy shuffling of people is central to the play's intent. So as a scene ends on one platform, it's pulled back and the lights there go down while Vita walks onto the other, where the lights go up and—for instance—Virginia, in another situation, is waiting. I'd do heavy props, castle furniture. The two flats for Vita's bedroom walls will be painted, then added to with tapestries and ancestral portraits. Virginia's basement will only need masonry walls meeting at a corner, a high window letting in soft light. The garden will have only white flowers. She was famous for this garden. I'm trying for a sense of motion to counter the lack of physical movement. Motion is elision, between lovers, between rooms." Cate clicks between screens. "Rooms leading to unseen hallways leading to the basement where she and Virginia make out, leading to her garden, then to the train platform where she plays the timetables, putting one lover on her way to London, then waiting for another to arrive from the city—to save an extra trip to the station. The only stationary piece will be a high, perched platform to represent her writing tower. A Vita stand-in will sit, back to the audience, writing letters. Come-hither letters and farewell letters. This will be before the curtain goes up, and through intermission. A soft light on the desk, the words she's writing projected onto a screen above the stage. I've found a copy of her handwriting I can crib from."

Lauren looks directly at Cate. "Yes. You have it exactly right. Vita is interesting, just in who she was. But on a level beneath that, she was also a major player in a world that doesn't exist anymore. She worked the closet to her advantage. She shut the door and inside was a huge, darkened circus where she was on the trapeze, riding the zebra, springboarding to the top of the human pyramid."

The three of them inhale and exhale softly while they assemble their own versions of what the play will look like.

Then Lauren says, "Impressive." Cate picks up maybe a little nervousness from their side of the table. They are getting older, maybe wondering if their best work is behind them. Cate belongs to a newer generation, with all the threat implicit in that. Maybe they are trying to both give her a shot and at the same time latch on to some new energy, incorporate it into their work. She looks at them, tries to get a read on who they are to each other. These are women who at one time slept with each other, but not for some time now. Given the sexual metrics of the theater world, Cate gives one of them a treacherous affair a decade or two back that has left the relationship wounded.

The collaborative spell is broken by Molly's cell, which goes off now, taking up all the attention in the room. After peering at it as though it is a Magic 8 Ball, Molly takes the call and begins a muttered conversation.

Lauren forges on with Cate. "What about the lawn party at Charleston House?"

"I have an idea about that." Cate's voice sounds tinny in her own ears. Like she's a door-to-door salesperson with a revolutionary hairbrush. "I thought about taking the Bloomsbury gossips into the aisle stage right, gathering through the intermission, milling around with croquet mallets, glasses of lemonade. They'll be miked, of course, but initially speaking softly, then as the intermission winds down, they are audibly sniping about Vita and her pretentious poetry, and speculating on her relationship with Mary Campbell. They make fun of her breeches and mustache. All the good stuff you have in there already. They'll just amp up the volume, holding pipes or smoking cigarettes in holders. You could use vapes. One of the guys could wear a monocle. One of those guys *did* wear a monocle. And as the house lights go down, so would the light in the writing tower, and then Vita would appear tucked in an open doorway, briefly, to show her wounded at not being taken seriously."

Lauren, who has been attentive to Cate in a way that's unnervingly intense, now turns to Molly and says, "Can you get off that? Who is it anyway?"

"Rita. She thinks someone broke into her apartment. Wore her clothes then came in again to put them back in the closet." After she says this, she taps a forefinger at her temple, then presses the phone against one of her large breasts and stares at Lauren. To this, Lauren says, "Tell her the signal's breaking up. Come back to us. We're in the midst of seeing what Cate will do for the play."

Cate notices the "will" and says, "I thought I was only trying out for the job. I thought you were also interviewing others."

"That part is over," Lauren says. "We have chosen you."

In the miniscule bathroom of her tiny hotel room, Cate sits sideways on the toilet. Straight-on isn't possible for someone her height. Even in this unlikely situation, she knows this will turn out to be one of the happiest moments of her life—when she can taste pure joy alone, at a comfortable distance from its source.

She is nudging Plan C into place. She imagines the play will be a huge success, scooping up awards, including one for her sets. She sees herself in a better outfit than anything she currently owns, maybe a black tuxedo with a white linen dress shirt with a tiny collar buttoned at the neck. Lauren and Molly will unfold themselves from their seats to embrace her; one of them—she's not sure which—kisses her quickly but definitely on the lips. From there she sprints lightly onto the stage and grips her award and gives thanks to everyone involved. Her cell will be buzzing frenetically in her pocket. Maureen, thrilled in Chicago. (When Dana's number comes up, she will send the call to voice mail. There's no room for Dana in this organized, sensible fantasy.)

From there, she imagines she and Maureen live together in an apartment overlooking the lake. They get individual gigs, but also sometimes work together, as a design team. Their relationship blew past passion and went straight to sturdy. They care for and take care of each other. Cate works on bigger plays, no longer needs handouts from her parents. *Thanks, I'm good,* she says when they offer. She's no longer a small charity.

Further on, Sailor lives in a house with her and Maureen. He has a white muzzle now; this gives him a debonair charm. Graham lives with a new girlfriend in the apartment he bought for Cate. The girlfriend is way too young, just out of grad school, but she is, at least, not Eleanor. He has written and produced a new play, which is about surveillance, but by now everyone is paranoid, not just nutcases, and the play is a success.

Everything is smoother in this vision. Not so cliff-hanging. The craggy cliff is far behind her; grass tickles the soles of her feet.

Back in the here and now, Maureen is waiting at O'Hare. Cate sees that if they go on together, she will always pick her up at the airport. The luxury of this is overwhelming. Maureen will sit in the cell phone lot reading a biography of Liz Taylor or Esther Williams until she gets Cate's call, then pull up and help Cate wrestle her bag into the back seat, then kiss Cate as earnestly as she does now.

"Were they fabulous?" she asks.

marienbad

Maureen tries hard. Cate feels gratitude for someone making such an effort to win her. She wants to insinuate herself into the narrowest crevices of Cate's life. A piece of this insinuation is getting Neale to like her, and her strategy is getting to Neale through Joe. "I have a way with twelve-year-olds."

"Knock yourself out," Cate tells her.

Maureen sets up an outing for the four of them, a Sunday afternoon screening downtown at the Siskel Center. *Last Year at Marienbad*—black-and-white, enigmatic, French. Joe is a sucker for old movies that are inscrutable, doubly for anything French, like his father. His own French, after three years of it at school, is good enough that he almost doesn't have to read the subtitles. He and Maureen are riveted to the film's long silences and impenetrable dialog. Neale naps, sputtering awake from time to time. Cate uses this lazy stretch of time to think about the way Dana kisses, the way her lips soften two or three kisses in. She knows she should probably be daydreaming about kissing Maureen. She would like to feel less about Dana, so she imagines her home decor. She conjures up a random hodgepodge. A sofa in a trite color from a decade ago. The living room walls a pale blue from a Cape Cod cottage line of low-end paints. A couple of ill-considered chairs with high arms. A credenza made of pressboard covered with a mahogany veneer. This holds books, DVDs, also VHS tapes that lost their last player ten years ago. A Navajo-ish rug. Southwestern posters. A scented candle in a jar on an end table. Cate adds to this secular crèche piece by piece. Mental redecoration is her main form of snobbery.

On the drive back from the Loop, Maureen is perfect. Curious about Neale's work, offering a self-deprecating anecdote about how terrible she was at yoga the one time she tried it. Falling smack onto her head in her first and last attempt at crow pose. She agrees to listen to a clip on Joe's phone of his favorite noise musician, Merzbow, performing "Smelly Brain." After maybe thirty seconds, Neale makes him shut it down, leaving Maureen with an appreciative smile hanging in the middle of nothing.

She tells them about her new assignment, a whole new area for her. She is designing uniforms for staff at an indoor theme park going up in a repurposed indoor mall in Gurnee, a featureless exurb near the Wisconsin border. The theme park will be intergalactic.

"I'm working with materials I've never touched before. Stuff that's stretchy and shimmery. And military. I'm not sure why so many visions of the future are of a military state, but that's what they want in Gurnee. Uniforms with severe hats. When you come to the park you are subject to rules of the planet's government. You eat food that comes in cubes and squares. I think it's, like, brownies. Potato nuggets, parallelogram hot dogs. I don't know. You drink through a long thin tube leading to a softpack in a shoulder bag. There are space rides, but they're just part of the total immersion thing. Who do you think will come to this place?"

"Me!" Joe says, then laughs at himself.

All around, it's a really fun outing. But for all Maureen's efforts, Neale dismisses her out of hand. What she says when Cate calls her the next day is, "Joe loves her. I think they're getting married."

"Tell me—"

"She's fine."

"What do you mean, *fine?*"

"I guess I mean fine for someone. But probably not for you. Down the line you're going to want more from her but there's only going to be what she's already shown you. She's sunny and buoyant—"

"Oh, please."

"Lively, quite a bit of fun—"

"Stop."

"Okay. Also totally apolitical. Knows almost *nothing* about the hideous world we're living in. It's something unpleasant. So let's keep it at arm's length. Am I right?"

"This is about her and her sister, isn't it?"

"It's way not about her and her sister."

———————

Sex doesn't interest Irene. The sharp end of a needle, the cool glass tube of a pipe. That's all she wants to take in.

She doesn't want me to go without, though. She does what she can. She sets up dates. It's hard for me to get anyone on my own. My hygiene is casual and I have very little money, and I'm a little on the heavy side. These are not pluses with a lot of women.

So Irene picks up this or that woman—on the street, or outside one of the shelters. One time at the library. She promises drugs and a little party, and brings my date to the hotel above the Indian buffet and I meet them there. We don't bring a date home afterward. She shouldn't really know where we live.

The dates are all kinds of women. Once in a while they are even young and sort of pretty or you can see they were once pretty, but mostly not. It doesn't really matter. They all come with the same basic equipment and soon the three of us are high and in bed. Sometimes my date has even nodded off. Irene does this or that, she knows what it takes to make me hard and then she helps me in. This is not easy for me on my own. I am too big that way for most women, but Irene helps them manage it, and then I'm in for as long as it takes. If my date doesn't like this or that, whatever, Irene slaps her around a little to shut her up. That's as rough as it gets.

These outings are a nice part of our relationship. Something we can do together. It gets us out of the house.

puebla

Outside, the heat is brutal, doing a transparent shimmy above the highway asphalt. Inside the car, a new silver-blue Passat, Cate and her father are privileged in air that is dry and chilled, as though they are transporting something valuable and unstable. Infant lemurs. A replacement heart.

Alan, Cate's father, plays a jazzy game with the stick shift; the car is always in the perfect gear. When she was twelve and he was teaching her to drive, he showed her how to shift without using the clutch, that if you really pay attention, like a safecracker, you can feel when one gear is perfectly aligned with the next and just slip from third to fourth, then back down to third.

"Want to give it a try?" he says, pulling off, onto the sandy shoulder.

They switch seats. The shift is satin smooth. At a certain point she doesn't need the clutch, and rests her left foot on the rubber mat.

She's proud she can still do this. But she can only make it happen with a car like this one, on an open stretch of road like this one; in the city she can't hear the engine over all the ambient roar, can't find enough of a straightaway, plus she drives a small, utilitarian SUV.

Her father is an elegant man. He dresses like a golfer from the 1950s. Pants that sigh into light drapes on the tops of his feet. Shoes in pale leathers. His eyes, like Cate's, have light blue irises. They share the same pale complexion, and sharp, narrow nose. His hair is also like Cate's—black and dense. He used to comb it straight back off his face. Recently, though, there is more forehead, less hair, and he now sweeps what's still there into a forelock. People would know at first glance that they are father and daughter. She likes this.

He came here to Puebla for the job of his dreams: he picks colors for cars, interiors and exteriors. When he and Ricky met at art school, he was a painting student. He is excruciatingly sensitive to color, also has an impressive memory in this realm. He can match perfectly something here and now to something far back, or to the underside of a leaf in a floral-patterned sofa pillow in a home he has visited only once. As they walked around Puebla's zocalo yesterday, he showed off a little by pinning down the Pantone chip colors of the extremely vibrant churches. 17-1664. 14-0995. Like that.

Today they drove out of the city to the pre-Columbian pyramid at Cholula. He had to rest briefly as they climbed the million stone steps, the first time Cate has thought of him as old, as opposed to just older than she is.

Now they are heading out into the countryside, to a scruffy bar he likes.

She asks, as she always does, "How safe are we out here, alone on the road? I mean, I haven't noticed many other cars." Cate is thinking of photos she sees regularly in the news. Homemade Mad Max high-way tanks with revolving turrets. Dead women hanging in a neat row on the side of a building, their legs still encased in skinny jeans, feet in bright sneakers.

"Well, Volkswagen has a presence in the area. Nobody wants the plant to leave. I like to think that working for the company, driving a VW, is a kind of carapace we're traveling inside. And of course, it helps that neither you nor I are involved in the drug wars. Did you remember to move money out of your checking account like I told you? If you get express-kidnapped, they'll only keep you until the ATM runs dry." Statements like this are the closest her father gets to humor, *if* he's being humorous.

"Seriously," he says because he knows what she's thinking.

Cate gropes around for a snappy answer, but she can't find an offhand way to reveal (although she knows he probably suspects) that her checking account is her entire savings, an amount that would require only two or three modest ATM withdrawals to deplete entirely.

Cate sees her father at Christmastime and usually for a week in the summer. He and Ricky split up when Cate was a freshman in high school, a few years after the workshop accident. It could seem from the right distance as though her injury and his departure were unrelated. But the life of their small family thinned out after the mishap, the air in the house moved to a higher altitude, the noise of daily life became muted. This turned out to be the ghostly period during which her father was preparing for his absence.

The workshop project was just for fun—something she and her father would make together, a wooden silhouette of Cate to fasten to the kitchen doorframe. They decided to make it a foot taller than her current height. They made a best guess. The plan was to pencil-mark her height on the cutout as she grew. They were going to paint it with hair (black), face (pink), a blue-and-white striped shirt she especially liked, jeans, sneakers. They never got to the painting part. The jigsawed board was slippery with blood, then she never saw it again.

Because of the accident, because she had to live the last install-ment of her childhood without him, her father has become a some-what distant relative—attentive in her presence, happy to see her, interested in catching up, but the connection has become faltering, sputtering, a call between two valleys on either side of a high moun-tain.

At the bar, which is mostly outside, tables on dusty ground, he orders beers for both of them, then heads for the john, which stands at not quite enough distance to keep the smell discreet, its door hanging open. The waiter brings two Tecates, the bottles fe-verishly sweating. Cate takes a long drink and, in tilting her head back slightly, sees the monkey. He is sitting on a branch midway up a dusty tree at a near edge of the patio. He is eating a piece of tortilla with a rapid burst of munching.

"Hey. What's up?" she asks him. He cocks his head, which has a hat strapped to it, something like a fez. She checks out his situation. On the plus side, he probably has a steady supply of taco chips, and humans to amuse him. Still, there is the chain—one end wrapped around the tree trunk, the other clamped to one of his ankles, where it has rubbed away the fur around it. Mexico is, in general, a place with a lot of potential for an animal rights movement. She brings water to the thirsty, exhausted dogs that drag themselves around everywhere here. A metal bowl sits at the base of the tree, but it's empty. She gets up to ask for a glass of water at the bar, but her father, on his way back to the table, says, "You can't resolve this particular problem. I may have mentioned this before." He pulls out the metal chair across the small table from her; the tips of its legs scrape through the gravel on the ground. "There isn't enough water to satisfy the thirst of the dogs and cats, not to mention the monkeys in this patch of the world." Her father, she has noticed, has a slight deficiency in empathy. When he tries, it comes off as an impersonation.

"I can do a little." When she has gone up to the bar and come back with a glass of water, she pours it into the bowl beneath the tree.

Alan looks away. When he looks back, he asks her about the play.

"The playwright and director are kind of geniuses. The play is very good. If it takes off, a lot of people will see my work. Even better—they'll see what I can do with more than a twenty-dollar budget." She dips a taco chip into an earthenware bowl of salsa, bites into it, and her mouth explodes. After drinking the beer pretty much straight down, she's able to speak again, and then only in a crackle. "I suppose this is probably my big break. Of course, I'm trying not to frame it that way. I can scare myself silly."

"Has your mother dismissed it yet?"

"I haven't told her. As a general practice I don't ever tell her anything really good."

"Ricky loved you, you know. I'm sure it's hard to imagine now, but at the beginning she was enthralled by you. She used to sit you on her lap and inspect your ears, your toes. And she'd say to me, 'She's perfect.' And then everything else happened. Not just the accident, not just that you'd become imperfect in her eyes. The bigger problem was that you started having ideas of your own. Ideas different from hers. She had to punish you for that. And it was, of course, a losing battle."

Then why didn't you help me? Why did you just walk out? She doesn't ask these questions. What answer would be a good one? Instead, she sits trying, just for fun, to imagine Ricky enthralled by a baby.

Her father lives at the center of the old town. The apartment is vast, occupying the top floor of a four-story building with steps up to a roof garden. Cate hasn't seen all of it, even after many visits. There are corridors off hallways; everything, even the still, cool air, is dark. Every time Cate visits, the passage from hot to cool makes her grateful for air-conditioning until she remembers there isn't any, that the apartment's sepulchral coolness is the product of heavy shutters, lazy ceiling fans, and walls that are two feet thick. The building's stucco exterior is—her father tells her—painted the red of fresh rust (49-16-C) with dark green (638-7C) louvered shutters. She suspects he just makes up the color numbers, but she's not certain. The apartment, the whole building actually, belongs to Seneca, her father's companion. It has been in her family for generations. She is older than Alan, somewhere in her seventies. Physically, she is ample but with gravity rather than weight. She moves in a slow, smooth way, as though her tendons are silk cords. Her dark hair is shiny, almost reflective. She sits up straight and stands tall. Cate can see her as a girl, practicing with a book balanced on her head.

Cate thinks of her as Alan's companion because she is unclear about the nature of their relationship. It doesn't seem romantic exactly. They sleep in separate rooms. Cate sees their bond as adventurers in friendship. They shift deferentially around each other in these dark, cavernous rooms, then meet up at dinner, for which they dress. Whatever, it's clear the congeniality makes her father happy. Before they met, he was solitary in a way that didn't seem *un*happy. But he is very different now. When Seneca comes into a room, he looks like he has spotted her across a vast train station, after too long apart. He has told Cate that he feels so lucky to have found her, to be with her.

Today, they find her in her office, across a small courtyard from the rest of the apartment. Walls lined with dark wood floor-to-ceiling bookcases, filled with books in dark—ruby, evergreen, navy—bindings. She is at her desk, a stack of folders to one side. Although the stack is at least a foot high, everything is tidy, squared at the corners.

"Catherine." Seneca looks up, takes off her glasses. "How wonderful that we have you here. I woke up this morning feeling I had presents to open."

Seneca is a lawyer. The common thread running through her clients is that they all suffer from injustice or injury.

"Whose plight are you taking up this time?" Cate says.

"Miners. Silver miners. Very little has changed for miners since Orwell's *Wigan Pier* or even Zola's *Germinal*. Only the horses have gotten a break."

"What horses?" Cate sees her mistake even as these words are passing over her lips, requesting information she is not going to be happy to have.

"Beasts of burden. Pulling the carts. Their trip down was one-way. They worked down there until they died. Always dreaming of running across green pastures."

Cate doesn't say anything. She's afraid there might be more to the horse story. Seneca doesn't miss this.

"I am sorry I told you this. I forgot what a friend you are to animals. I am too distracted by the sorrows of humans. It's good there are others to concern themselves with animals." While this sounds sincere, Cate also catches on a small snag of trivialization. Seneca shifts her chair back to face the table she uses as a desk. Over her shoulder she says, "Maybe you are tired a little from your trip to the pyramid? Maybe you'd like to sleep awhile before dinner?"

Her father says, "Yes, take a nap. I have to go over to the plant. A short meeting."

"Is the meeting about a color?" Cate says.

"Yes."

"Is it about a blue?"

"No. It's about a gray. There are way more meetings about grays than about blues, but they are shorter meetings."

The nap is a fiction. In these suddenly busy days of her work life, Cate needs to steal every spare minute, even down here, to refine her sets.

Just a few years ago, if she were going to work away from her shop, she would have had to bring drafting tools and a tube of rolled drawings. Now she slips into her backpack a laptop thin as a magazine. Her ideas are now liquid, trickled into a design program, then shot into the cloud. She can work anywhere Wi-Fi hovers.

Seneca is late to dinner, then finally comes through the archway, placing a hand on the plaster in such a graceful way a stranger might not

notice she is steadying herself. She has suffered from balance issues
for years. At dinner she often wears a light caftan and heavy jewelry,
a rolled scarf as a headband. She moves slowly. Her approach is like
that of one or another of the three wise men.

As soon as she has made apologies and taken her seat, the door to
the kitchen opens for the cook, who bears a salad of nopalitos. Juana
is small and elderly in an extreme way. By now she has lost a hard-
fought battle with the sun. Her face resembles that of a shrunken
head. She seems to be done with speaking. Cate has only heard her
do so a few times, and then only the fewest possible words. Initially,
she interpreted this muttering as something ancient and important,
a blessing on her maybe.

Juana greets Cate the way she always does, with a violent embrace, which is a little awkward because Cate is seated, so the gesture winds up being a hug of both Cate and the chair. Juana then
takes Cate's bad hand and kneads it then rubs the bumps, which are
what remains of her lost fingers. All the while of this, she murmurs
something that's not Spanish but rather some indigenous language.
The first time this happened, Cate thought she was being prayed for
to some specialty saint. But when she asked about this, Seneca set
her straight. "Oh no!" Then laughed in a spilling way. "It's for good
luck. To rub any deformity—a hump on the back, the stump of what
was once a leg—is supposed to bring good fortune. You get a lottery
ticket on a day this happens. I'm sorry to tell you this. How can it not
be offensive? But she is from an older world than ours."

What Juana serves tonight is chiles rellenos and bread in the form of
soft, slightly sweet pads and a butter mixed with honey—all delicious.

Of course Seneca wants to talk about the political upheaval in the U.S. And of course Cate dreads this. It's one thing to go over (endlessly) with other Americans the huge wrong thing that has happened, but totally embarrassing to discuss with anyone in another country, particularly a country the new president wants to wall off to keep out mythical, rampaging rapists.

Cate gathers up all her resources.

"Apparently there was mischief from Russia. They picked the candidate they knew would be a useful fool. So he was their guy and they went to work for him with their massive hacking savvy. Lies and propaganda messages whirled out by the zillions by—"

"Bots," Seneca says. Cate didn't expect her to be so well-informed on this, but of course she is. And clearly seeing how uncomfortable all of this is for Cate, she pulls the rug out from under the subject and asks about the new play. But this is almost as difficult a subject. Cate doesn't feel up to explaining Vita and her crazy life. If Vita were a little more famous than a Bloomsbury footnote (by way of being Woolf's lover), Cate wouldn't have to keep relating her story to anyone who asks about the play. But that doesn't happen now. Seneca has, of course, done her homework.

"I have been reading up on your Sackville-West. A very good biography. Also a diary of a time early in her marriage. Dramas in hotels and Parisian dance halls for her, but her husband minded and the children barely knew her."

"Wow. I'm so impressed you did all this research."

"It wasn't a hardship. It's always amusing to read about the terrible things people did when they were young and run by their passions."

Cate says, "But the thing is, with Vita, age didn't completely subdue her. She didn't fly off to Paris anymore to ravish her girlfriend in small hotels and then go out on the town dressed as a wounded soldier. That stuff was over. Her affairs became more discreet. She stayed closer to home. And then eventually she got old and retreated to her castle. But even then she could spin a web for women who came around. One victim was a tourist she lured off the garden tour. The bus went back to London without *that* lady."

Her father laughs. He hasn't read up. All the Vita stories are new to him.

Seneca says, "All those passionate letters, all those walks in the garden in the moonlight. Then discarding one poor lover to take up with the next, then writing another mailbag full of love letters—does seem comic. Is the play a comedy?" Seneca always treats Cate cordially, politely, but it's clear she thinks Cate is postponing adult-hood.

"I think it's more a minor tragedy," Cate says. "Sorrow in the key of human frailty. Virginia Woolf's broken heart in particular, which she couldn't really afford on top of her mental illness. Those birds were speaking to her in Greek in one ear while Vita was whisper-ing in the other. She shouldn't have started anything frivolous with Virginia. Virginia should have been off-limits."

Seneca nods. "The play I would like to see is the one where Vita gets sent to the coal mines. Ah. Sorry. Perhaps miners are too much on my mind these days." But this is not an apology. It's tiny clipping—the sound of a single hair being cut. Cate doesn't take it personally. Seneca would like everyone to shape up, be more seri-ous. She wishes Alan did something more important than picking colors. It's difficult to take offense at Seneca's delicate prodding. She wears her erudition lightly, wages her battles against tyranny without fanfare. You can't dislike her; Cate has tried, but it's just not possible.

The scariest thing about Seneca is how she x-rays the vague, general version of Cate's life that she presents for inspection. She sees that much of Cate's movement through life has been thinly disguised stasis. If Cate, conversationally, positions herself at a crossroads, Seneca sees these would only be crossroads if there were actual roads crisscrossing the place where Cate stands. She comprehends, without really knowing, the slightly sad particulars of Cate's life. She can see the small pile of accomplishments, the reduced circumstances.

Cate's father has to work the next day, so Seneca offers to take Cate on a small outing.

"Something new since you were last here. A dream pool for you." This is typical of Seneca, this attention to the details that make up Cate. She is probably this way with everyone, which doesn't at all devalue it.

The pool is on the roof of a hotel occupying what used to be a water purification plant when this city was still a town. The redesign is all about architects at play without enough supervision. Everyone walks mincingly up and down staircases made of clear glass. The slate tiles in the lobby are set ajar, at slight angles to each other.

"I am an *abogado*," Seneca says. "These designers saw fun; I see lawsuits from all the late-night falls. Slightly drunken girls in high heels."

The pool is a more interesting bit of whimsy. It runs the entire length of the building, is a single lane, and has one side made of thick, translucent glass.

"Oh my," Cate says when they spot it as they come off the elevator. She goes into the ladies' room to change. She's childishly excited to get into this human fishbowl. When she comes out of the bathroom, Seneca has ordered them glasses of a popular red wine from Guadalajara. Incognito. They had it the night before, and Cate told her how much she liked it. Seneca doesn't miss many beats.

"Go on, now," Seneca flutters a hand urging Cate toward the pool.

"You won't come in?"

"Alas, I do not swim. I will do a little work here."

While Cate does laps so long she sometimes has to stop three-quarters of the way in disbelief that there can possibly be more water ahead, Seneca sits at a high table making phone calls. Her forehead rests in the palm of her hand as she talks, as though the conversations are burdens she bears. When Cate gets out of the water and is toweling off, Seneca puts her phone facedown on the table and smoothly redirects her attention.

"How do you know about this place?" Cate says. "If you're not a swimmer."

"I know some of the masons who worked on the crazy renovation. They are plain men and found the architects' mischief hilarious. All the glass floors, the crazy tiles in the lobby, as though an earthquake has passed through. When in fact earthquakes do pass through here on their own, shuffling tectonic plates without any artistic intentions." Then, upshifting her tone, "You had a very nice swim?"

In this single moment, Cate sees the position she occupies in Seneca's maternal life. Her own children, a doctor and a lawyer, are deeply serious adults treating burn victims, representing indigent clients. The daughter has an autistic child. They have chests filled with the medals of responsibilities firmly met. Seneca doesn't dismiss Cate as Cate has assumed until now. She sees her as a child who is still playing out her childhood, someone she can still spoil.

At the airport, Cate changes for dollars the pesos her father stuffed into her backpack when she wasn't looking. She minds this less than the money her mother gives her. She thinks of her father's donations as minor installments of penance, for his carelessness at the tool bench.

Waiting at the gate, she watches elephant videos on her cell. She has to be careful. Eventually the uplifting stories, like that of the friendship between Tara the elephant and her best friend, Bella, the small white dog, lead to those which involve happy reunions like Shirley and Jenny, but with backstories of why they needed to be reunited, some tragic twenty-year separation as they were shuffled from circus to zoo and back again. Or Raju, the elephant who is so amazingly happy he's weeping because he has finally been released from fifty years of misery and beatings in a cage. How will anyone be able to make that up to him?

visitors

Cate has finished her articulated drawings and sent off the files to Lauren and Molly. Now she waits. After a crush of too much to do, she suddenly has nothing pressing. She calls Neale and asks if she can tag along to yoga.

"I can even pick you up. I travel with four-wheel drive."

"Oh, that's great. I don't and I was fishtailing all the way to the Jewel and back. I thought about canceling on account of the snow, but I got calls from people in the hood, women with cabin fever. So I'm going to run a limited schedule. Come soon. I just have to put away my groceries. You can get me there for Level One."

Now, after her big offer, Cate is running late, which is bad, but when she pulls up in front of Neale's house, Neale is not waiting outside. Cate calls her cell, but gets sent straight to voice mail. The front door has been unopenable for the past couple of weeks since Joe played a trick on Neale with crazy glue. He was thinking about the crazy part, not enough about the glue part. Although at twelve he usually seems twenty-five years old, every once in a while he seems eight.

She drives around into the alley and puts on her flashers. As she gets out of the car, the DJ is saying, "New song by Neko Case, right after the weather—" Turning off the ignition annihilates the rest of the sentence. Cate loves Neko Case, and if she's quick, she thinks—in a very small thought—she can get back in time to hear the song.

She heads in through the back gate, along the gangway by the garage, then the small patch of snowed-over vegetable garden. The back door is ajar, Neale's key ring like a crappy charm bracelet with swipe tags dangling from the lock. Tapping into some vein of instinct, Cate moves quietly into the mudroom. From there she can hear someone talking, loud without quite shouting. A woman's voice, abraded, punctuated by a stuttery cough. Cate thinks, well, maybe a neighbor.

"She's just your type," says the voice. "And look. She's not fighting all that hard, she's just teasing you."

Not a neighbor.

"Hey mama." A higher voice, but definitely a man. "I can't get in."

Cate understands that what she is walking into will be horrible. She presses her back against the cold masonry wall and moves slowly up the short flight of stone steps. Halfway, when her head is level with the kitchen floor, she sees Neale pinned to it by a large man, too large, his back to Cate. He's wearing a hoodie, bright blue with a low tide of grime around the bottom. He has Daffy Duck tattooed on the side of his neck; he's the guy she noticed in the library. Neale is squirming under him. He is trying to get her cooperation by slapping her head one way, then the other.

"You don't simmer down, we might need to do a little dentistry." He pulls a pair of pliers from a pocket of his hoodie. Warm saliva slides up the sides of Cate's throat. She swallows hard. This is it. The moment underprepared for.

Scattered around on the linoleum are a bag of chips, some peaches, a block of tofu, a box of spaghetti, a box of doughnuts, a plastic bottle of V8. Neale's purse with glasses and wallet and a small pack of Kleenex spilling out. A roll of mints. All of this detail Cate registers pointlessly, as though she's been asked to play an old-fashioned party memory game.

Then she sees the woman, pacing, skinny in jeans with jeweled back pockets, cowboy boots with pointed toes. She is fiercely agitated. She comes over to help subdue Neale, who is twisting harder now. To remedy this, the woman kicks her casually in the side of her head—casually but hard.

"Simmer down, cunt."

yule log

Cate and the detective are the only people in a large room crammed with rolling chairs and beat-up desks, one of which is buried beneath the ruins of an office Christmas party—a desiccated Yule log cake; a crumbling tower of unspooling lunch-meat wraps; a large, clear plastic bowl nearly drained of punch. This room is an opposite of the office in *CSI: Miami*; the only colors are bad ones—tan and wheat and beige and off-white and gray, and a dirty pale yellow. An atmosphere of failure in keeping up with the bad behavior of humans. The detective sees her looking at the cake.

"Yeah, happy holidays, right? The truth is there's always a surge in bag-snatching, small-time burglaries, muggings just before Christmas. People want to get presents even though they can't afford them. I think they also resent the gap between themselves and people who can afford gifts and turkeys and trees to decorate. They start thinking about evening up that score." He shifts around in the chair and groans a little through clamped jaws. "Crappy back," he says. Three red-light buttons on his desk phone are blinking; every once in a while, he looks at these, but doesn't press anything, or pick up the receiver. It occurs to Cate that landlines are no longer conveyances of important information.

"I'm not sure I can be of much help. A lot of what happened is kind of static in my head."

"So when you go through something like this, your mind can wall off the mess for a while. I mean, you did a lot of damage in that kitchen, considering that the fire extinguisher was your only weapon. You hit them hard and fast. Were you in the military at some point?" He nods toward her partial hand. Cate sees that the cop is imagining her to be a very different person. The kind of person for whom danger and violence are routine.

"No. Childhood accident." She rubs the two knobs of bone where fingers used to be. Even her memory of them as full fingers is lost by now. "Actually, I don't think I've ever been in any sort of violent situation before, unless you count a table saw.

"Is he dead?" she asks. The last she saw of him, he was being wheeled out of Neale's kitchen on a gurney, little oxygen pods stuck up his nostrils. "Did I kill him?"

"The gentleman is down for the count. They've got him on a ventilator, but when they pull the plug, they don't expect him to go far on his own steam. We're still trying to figure out who he is. Guy carried zero ID. Maybe living off the grid. We'll find him, though. He probably lives near your friend. With break-ins, the perps often live nearby. It's just a casual, walk-by bit of business. They saw the door ajar as a pleasant opportunity. They surprised her. They went in to take some stuff and then decided to mess with her."

"When he dies, will I be charged with murder?" As though they're talking about an episode of a crime show.

"Oh no, lady. You're the hero in this, not the bad guy." He shifts in his chair again. He could really benefit from a little yoga. Then she tries to picture him in yoga class.

He pulls her out of her mental drift. "You sprayed the woman with the fire extinguisher. Can you see that? Maybe you're starting to remember, even a little would be a big help. Could you help me build a rough picture of her?"

Cate shakes her head. "I'm not sure I even registered what she looked like. It all happened so fast." She is so tired. She doesn't want to select noses and lips to make a composite. She wants to disconnect from both of them, the huge guy and the crazy lady. The detective isn't interested in Cate's reluctance; he turns his monitor to the side so they can both look at the same time, and clicks the mouse to call up a selection of face shapes. Cate watches as the photos flip onto, then off the screen.

"No."

"No."

Shakes her head to indicate no.

"No."

Then, "Do you have a category for really crazy-looking? That was her look, like someone escaping from the asylum."

"See. Even that's helpful." And then he switches back to eyes. "Any of these look familiar?"

"Maybe smaller."

"Was she white or black or Hispanic?"

"White. But dark."

"What color was her hair?"

"I'm not sure. Brown? Maybe black. Dirty. Everything about her was dirty. Kind of caked in."

"Short or long hair?"

Cate shakes her head. "She had a hat or a cap on."

After reshuffling the component images a few times, what they wind up with prompts the detective to ask, "Was she Hawaiian?"

"I think maybe we've reached the limits of this technology."

machine burgers

Joe looks so small in the chair by the hospital bed. The chair has a back that's high and straight, upholstered in teal vinyl. Framed by it, he looks like the boy king of a bleak country. His eyes are closed and he's wearing earbuds, putting himself inside his noise music. It's cool in the room but he looks sweaty, even in just a T-shirt and jeans. She puts a hand on his shoulder and he jumps a little.

In the bed, his mother looks startlingly bad, worse even than she did when Cate got separated from her by triage in the ER. Her affect, though, is peaceful in a doped-up way. The two sides of her face don't match. The right side is Neale, but the left is several colors and misshapen with swelling. An ice pack is strapped against the left cheek, connected to a whirring machine on the floor next to the bed. One small stitch has escaped from under the pack, which hints at more. They've put her into a nightgown patterned with tiny evergreens. Cate watches the tree line along Neale's chest go up slightly, then down. Her right wrist is held by a splint. And then Cate can't look anymore. She loves Neale so much.

Beauty is so fragile. Neale's isn't just about her face, it's part of the whole easy, open way she is in the world. Maybe everything will come back together in time, but Cate imagines from here on, fear will be part of who she is. Boldness will have to be summoned from a past, remembered place.

Joe pulls out one of his earbuds, leaving it to dangle, touching his chest, leaking steel-mill noise into the quiet room.

"I'm so sorry about this, honey." She doesn't know what to tell him. She can't even think where to begin. Where to stop. The best she can come up with is, "Are you hungry? Is there any food around here for you?"

"The cafeteria part is closed. There's a machine in the basement. It has a dead apple, a flat cheeseburger. Weird candy bars. Lucky Lady. I think they might be from another country. I didn't have money anyway."

"Sometimes machine burgers can be pretty good." She pulls a wad of crumpled bills from her jacket pocket, tries to smooth them flat, then hands them over. "Also, we should probably try a Lucky Lady. I'll meet you down there after I talk with your mom." She stops as something occurs to her. "How'd you get here?"

"Mrs. Pappageorge. I went over to her house when I came home and saw the kitchen and couldn't find Mom—" Cate hates that he saw the kitchen. Also hates that Mrs. Pappageorge, Neale's next-door neighbor, was his designated driver. She is well into her nineties. She drives a huge, ancient sedan, sits on a phone book to peer over the steering wheel, has wood blocks glued to the accelerator and brake pedals. She wears thick black plastic wraparound elder shades. A few months ago, Cate saw her run a red on Ashland, totally blow it and keep right on going.

"They're going to have to pry her license from her cold, dead hands."

"Yeah. It's like being on a ride. You know, like at Great America."

When he's gone, Cate bends down to Neale and kisses her softly on the mouth, something she has never done before, but anything else seems too little to convey the amount of emotion she's holding about life and death and love and friendship. Neale's eyes open a little. She nods slightly, toward Cate's bloody clothes. "Nice hoodie."

Cate takes her free hand, the one without the IV needle punched into the back of it. Neale sees Cate's bandaged palm. She looks at Cate.

"Yeah, I cut it up a bit with the extinguisher handle." She pulls three pill bottles from her pocket. "He might've been a junkie, so I have to take these until his HIV test comes back. Apparently they're horrible. You get gas and the runs for days. They promised the lab results will come back fast, though, and hopefully he won't be infected, and then I can stop taking them."

She sees she is talking to someone who has fallen asleep. But when Cate moves to get up, Neale says, "Hey, you know. Thanks."

"Anytime."

Neale lifts her head as far as she can to say something in a low voice. Cate puts her ear to Neale's mouth.

"He didn't get in. I'm telling you so you don't have to wonder. There was a problem. He was too big."

"Yeah. I saw it. Well, thank God for that, I guess."

Neale says, "So much smell."

"I know. It was like a zoo. They were like hyenas. I couldn't bash him hard enough. And then I couldn't stop."

"The woman—?"

"She kicked you in the side of the head, maybe you don't remember. Anyway, that's the first thing I saw and I didn't care for that. From there I can only remember pieces. I don't think I was scared at all while everything was happening. I was in too much of a rage."

"Joe." She's tired now, drifting off.

"We're going to my place for tonight. For as long as you're in here."

"Tell him what you can. Maybe a G-rated version. You know him. What he can stand to hear."

"Hey. You know. Here's the big thing. We're alive. We're going to be okay." What Cate doesn't mention is the strong breeze rushing through her, pushing her a little aloft. This is about knowing that what just happened will bring the two of them so much closer.

On her way down the stairs, she thinks, *Maureen*. Shit. Cate was supposed to get together with her after yoga. Yoga seems so long ago, a country from which her ancestors emigrated, someplace on a folded and refolded map. As she calls, she imagines Maureen's phone dark and silent on the nightstand, Maureen glaring at it. When she answers, Maureen sounds alert as a sentry. Cate abbreviates, condenses, although that's not easy, given how much has happened.

"I'll be right over."

"What I need more is for you to go over to Neale's." She gives

Maureen the address. "My car is out back. The extra key fob is inside the armrest. I know, I know that's stupid." Then, "Can you drive it over here?"

In the corner of the dead cafeteria, Joe says, "I heard you killed the guy."

"I *tried* to kill him. I don't think he's dead yet. I didn't have a very good weapon. I grabbed the fire extinguisher on the way in. I don't remember everything that happened. Big chunks seem to be missing."

"Yeah, I saw the floor." He's eating his third microwaved machine cheeseburger. Cate gets one for herself, and a Coke. The two of them are alone in a room that has a desperate level of cheer to it. The murals are an underwater world of colorful cartoon fish.

"Let's get going, what do you say? Come home with me. Maureen's picking us up. Graham will be at the apartment. And Sailor. I think if I put you on the sofa, he'll sleep with you. I know there's a lot to think about, but tonight we all need to get some sleep. We'll deal with everything else tomorrow."

She's a little surprised when he says, "Okay."

Downstairs, in the teal hospital lobby (walls, chairs, carpet, even a tealish air-freshener) next to a giant statue of a saint who appears to have hammered things, Maureen is waiting. She pulls Cate into a crushing hug, then reaches to put a hand on Joe's shoulder. She doesn't bother to say anything. What, really, could she say?

Cate is so happy to see her. Maureen has apparently gone through some efficient progression of steps, probably taking a Lyft to Neale's; rescuing the car; bringing it here. Cate is so happy and then she's crying. Maureen looks so fresh. Nothing bad has happened to her today. From the car, she calls ahead, and so Graham is waiting for them when they get there. Also, Sailor. As usual, he's standing right in front of the door. So to get in, Cate has to push his nose with it, softly. Graham is dressed for company. Jeans and a white shirt. Socks.

"I have some wine open. And pop in the fridge. If anybody's hungry, I'm cooking a snack in the oven." Cate smells lobster and sherry, which means there's an ovenful of Dean & DeLuca soufflés. Something nobody wants at three in the morning.

"We had burgers," Cate says.

"Yeah, I'm good," Joe says, patting his stomach. Maureen and Cate pat theirs.

"We'll definitely have a glass of wine, though," Cate says. "Even Joe. Half a glass. We'll pretend we're a French family."

"Well," Graham says, sounding so agitated he's kind of scary, "you're all safe and sound now. That's the important thing."

They make camp. Sailor gets a walk with Graham and Joe. Then Joe gets a sweatshirt, a comforter, a couch, and a dog across his feet.

"I'm trying not to move," he tells Cate. "So he'll stay."

It occurs to her that everybody tries to keep a sleeping dog in bed with them. Like it's an honor.

In the bathroom she hands off her bloody clothes to Maureen.

"Just so you know, these are going in the trash. Even if we

washed them on some super After-Killing PermaPress cycle, you'd never wear them again." She takes the hospital bandages off Cate's hands, then gently pushes her into the shower, then gets in with her. Afterward, she recleans and rebandages the scrapes on Cate's palms. When they are finally in bed, she pulls Cate into a full-body embrace. "Wonder Woman."

Embarrassed, Cate says, "Everything about me is sore."

Then Maureen says, "Do you want an Ambien? I have some with me. Xanax, too." Maureen is definitely who you'd want to help relax you through Armageddon. Her bag is filled with necessities for almost any bad situation.

"Maybe. I'm so tired I thought I could sleep standing up, but now that I'm horizontal, I can see I'm probably going to jitter through the night. I can't stop my mind. I never in my life thought about killing anybody."

Maureen is out of bed, tapping a small festival of pills out of an amber prescription bottle, into her palm. "Here." She plucks out a skinny pink tablet. "Take this. I'm sorry for what you had to go through today. But you saved your friend. As a bonus, you put a piece of human garbage into the dumpster."

Cate takes the pill, washes it down with the glass of water Maureen has put on the nightstand. And she thinks, *I guess.* Then backs up a little. Maureen's judgment seems too summary, made from a position already held. Although she supposes you could say the guy was human garbage, Cate wouldn't frame it that way. She doesn't have a frame on him big enough to make any sweeping assessments. She hates what he did to Neale, and she hates what she had to do to stop him. She hasn't had time to assess him and his place in the universe. All she can do just now is close her eyes and roll away before Maureen says something else, something that might make Cate like her a little less.

Half an hour later, Cate is still awake. Even as she gets groggy, her mind is too busy trying to herd thoughts into some corral. She has a vague ringing in her ears, not really a ringing so much as an extremely tiny voice of Linda Ronstadt singing "Poor Poor Pitiful Me." She's surprised she remembers the words so well.

She rolls over. Maureen's not asleep either; rather, she's on her side, watching a YouTube clip on her phone. Linda Ronstadt.

"When she could still sing, before the Parkinson's, she could *really* sing. Nothing will ever take that away from her. Does the music bother you?"

"No. It's okay. I think the pill is kicking in." This is a total lie. There isn't a pill that could subdue her heart; she can feel it as a muscle, even now pumping blood through her at a level necessary to heroics.

The next morning, in spite of being in an apartment overstuffed with an ex-husband, a boy, a dog, and a girlfriend, Cate wakes shivering and sore everywhere, also massively alone. She understands she has arrived on another side of everything. No one is over here with her.

crosswinds

Everyone, of course, weighs in on the matter. When Cate calls her father, he and Seneca put their phone on speaker and listen together and almost simultaneously insist she come down to Puebla for a break. She can't now, she tells them, and they ask if she needs them to come up there for a while, stay with her. This brings her to tears, ducts fill and empty. An unusual occurrence for her. But she's okay, she assures them.

Her father offers to call Ricky with the news, which pleases Cate to no end—Ricky having to find out secondhand. When she calls an hour later, Cate lies to her, on principle. "I was just about to call."

At first Ricky seems properly empathic, but then she quickly segues into fatuously confusing the fire extinguisher with a Crock-Pot. The perpetrators she categorizes as hoboes. Assembling a version that's slightly cartoonish.

"Well, I didn't get a choice, really," Cate says. "I didn't get to pick

light saber and Armani underwear model for my weapon and victim." She's pretty much done with the conversation at this point. Her
most immediate preoccupation is how sick to her stomach she is
from the antiretroviral meds, another crummy aspect of the whole
thing she doesn't want to present to her mother.

"How's Neale?"

"Banged up. Her cheekbone is fractured. She's going to have to
have surgery. Her wrist is sprained. I'm not sure exactly how that
happened."

"Did he—?"

Ricky's slightly gossipy inflection further softens with a velvety
tone of concern that makes Cate decide she doesn't have to answer
this essential question.

"And of course the whole thing will now be distorted into heartwarming. Like you're the crossing guard who saved some kid from
a hurtling truck. And now you're taking him to Disneyland because
that's always been his secret wish."

Cate waits, hoping Ricky will dial this down a little, but she
doesn't.

"And it's a shame they brought your hand into the story. Here.
Wait a minute." Cate sits through the giant crackle of a newspaper
opening and folding. "'In spite of her disability—'"

Cate presses the red hang-up icon. Later, she'll say the call got
dropped and she really should change networks.

A few days later, after the nameless guy has died and Cate is officially
a killer, another local TV station asks if she'd be up to doing a news
feature on home invasion, "a sort of DIY piece," what someone can

improvise when their home is invaded. This is put to Cate with a feminist cast, and she's persuaded her story might be of help to other women. How it turns out, though, is her sitting on one of two low sofas, around a coffee table, with two morning show hosts and another guest, a guy who sets a bear trap by his back door every night before he goes to bed and how this paid off big-time when a couple of robbers jimmied the door open one night. He sits with the bear trap in his lap throughout the segment.

"That's it," she tells Neale. "I'm getting off the parade float. If other people want to murder their intruders, they can find their own crappy weapons."

Graham comes at the event from a completely different angle. She comes in to find him at the kitchen counter, fiddling with a small piece of electronic equipment. She doesn't bother asking what he's tinkering with; she's too tired. His paranoia now seems ephemeral and elective. Like her own worries before. Before.

"The lab called. They said you can stop taking the meds."

"Great! That means he tested negative. If HIV is the worst thing in the world, the pills are the second worst. I won't go into detail."

"Can I get something for you? Espresso?" A new, Italian machine has found its way onto the counter. Nice, but she hopes not a sign of him settling in.

"What's toasting?"

"Cranberry crumpets. You can get them from this place in London. Frick and Frack. You know. Crumpeters to the Queen. Something like that." Since he's been living here, Graham has become expert at ordering expensive everything from everywhere.

"You know, when T. E. Lawrence was eight years old, he became convinced his destiny was to save a captive people. That seems unbelievable, but I do think some people have a clearer path than the rest of us. Along those lines, I think what you did was inevitable, a moment all your previous fine moments were paving the way to. You were there for a reason. Because you could take care of it."

"Graham. I mean thanks, but I don't think anything about it was foreordained."

"Remember when we were first married? That heat-wave summer the temperatures were in the hundreds. The power was out? And you were bringing bags of ice up to old people in high-rises?"

"Are you kidding? Everybody was doing that. And truthfully, that's one of the things in my life I feel worst about. I only got up fifteen floors. I've always worried somebody on sixteen died of heatstroke."

"Well, that's one way of looking at it. The penitent path. Go sprinkle sand in your sheets, put pebbles in your shoes. You're still my hero."

"So, I'm not sure I want to ask, but are you still seeing Eleanor?"

"She's been in Fort Lauderdale doing that new *Doll's House*. So we just Skype."

"Often?" She's hoping for once a week.

"Just at night."

Not a good answer.

"Do you want me to put some guava jam on your crumpet?" he says, changing the subject. "It goes great. With the cranberries in the crumpets. There's this guava orchard in Honduras. You can only get it in certain months. And only one jar per year."

night shift

Quarter to three in the morning. She's pulling in Spotify on her cell phone, playing all the Lorde they have. She is at her drawing board. Before she took over the lease, this workshop belonged to a cabinetmaker. He left behind a huge, work-worn table he probably made here, with no thought to ever getting it out through the door. The thick legs are inset deep into the top, further stuck with adhesive and bolts. She added a tilting top for drawing.

Waiting for the heat to kick on, she shrugs into a stray sweater, a shape-shifted maroon cardigan once worn by the evil Cathy Ames in a teen-outreach production of *East of Eden*. Its current shape is that of a large rag. A tide of designs and models—her own and those of students, also props she hangs on to because the next play won't have them and she doesn't want to have to go looking again, the stray piece of some costume—all wash up in this workshop and have to continuously be beaten back, like sand from a desert hut.

She is trying to use work to confine her mind. But her mind is not interested in confinement, not at all. Rather, it wants to leap around madly, go forward, then circle back again to the scene of the crime, to see what more it can pull loose. She pushes aside the small set she is working on, pulls over a notebook with an articulated drawing of Neale's kitchen, showing where the players were. Laying a grid on chaos.

She is caught between two immovable and large pieces of her life: what happened in Neale's kitchen and what's happening in New York. Her worst event and her biggest break. In a reasonable life, these wouldn't be juxtapositioned. She should be able to have a minute to take a deep breath. In her recent past there have been months-long stretches of underemployment when she could have easily fit in killing someone, then curling into some PTSD fetal position for a while afterward. After the Vita play, she has two shows on her schedule—one in April for Handlebars in Milwaukee, one in Chicago in July when school is out. A reasonable schedule.

(The heat has come on. Wet meets dry, and the memory of carpentry releases a sigh of wood and glue.)

It's the New York play that's putting a thumb on the scale. Now is a time she really shouldn't be away. She called Molly Cracciolo to let her know what had happened and how she needed another week or so at home, to find her footing. And at first, Molly was notionally sympathetic. She returned Cate's call right away. Then how terrible, she told Cate, she and Lauren had their own experience along these lines, a recent robbery at their summer house in the Hamptons. Their entire collection of nineteenth-century French dolls, precious things, so articulated. Tiny necklaces of real diamonds and lapis lazuli. Lauren cried off and on the whole night they found out.

Fuck your French dolls! Cate screamed internally as she sat silent on her end of the call. But she does not want to lose this job and so she let Molly condescend to her—informing Cate that with the play only weeks off now, there was really no time for anyone involved to have a life, especially not a horrifying one. And so she is looking forward to seeing Cate on Tuesday. The change of scene will do her good.

The drawing of the kitchen suddenly pulls a bad lever and she's through the trapdoor.

> the terrible odor like a bad zoo, a roadside repulsion. neale, squirming under the fat man. "help me here, mama," he says, and the woman with silver-toe cowboy boots skitters over and places a neat little kick to the side of neale's head. a thin, dark red seep begins. there's no time to consider anything, to weigh options. there is no options list.

This is how it goes. No matter how hard she tries, she can neither hold back her memory nor force it. What she gets are short clips like this one. Important chunks are still missing. She doesn't know what she's hiding from herself. It can't be that she's too frightened to look at these pieces. She's actually weirdly unfrightened. But she's another person now. She has been tested and, in a fumbling way, has passed. She has always lived on an easy island. Plenty of bananas, breezes over her hammock. The odds were against her ever having to save someone or, even less likely, kill someone. But she had to, and she did.

The night sky crackles softly with pale, distant lightning. She goes to the front of the shop and opens one of the casement windows to watch. Sailor jumps up beside her, paws on the sill. Together they read the strangely tropical wind. A storm is on its way. Warm weather is smashing into what had been a grim cold snap. Cate is working through this night because all that has happened to her in Chicago this week won't matter in New York: the machinery of the play is in fourth gear and she has to catch up with it. She puts away the notebook and tries to put her energy to the task at hand.

The play now has a title: *Blanks*, in reference to a terrific quote by the architect Edwin Lutyens, a friend of Vita's mother. Cate has the quote push-pinned to her corkboard.

> *The only thing is to know and realize that Vita has got blanks in herself and these blanks are blank. If I find a blank, I get a plank and bridge it and I don't look down, lest I get vertigo.*

Presumably the blanks were the dead spaces in Vita's empathy, particularly for those she seduced and abandoned. Cataracts occluding her view of the marriages she wrecked along her way. Damage and collateral damage along a potholed country road, a treacherous garden path.

The work Cate is fiddling with tonight is something small and manageable: drawing the front of the newsstand for the train platform.

Outside, the storm has broken free of the clouds and the rain is hammering down. She Googles the font for British train signage, which turns out to be Gill Sans Light. She types:

SEVENOAKS

then inlays a background of a worn, yellow/gray/white to print on sign stock.

A sweep of light brushes across the surface of the drawing table. Tires crunch through gravel. Sailor rushes to the window. Dana. Cate doesn't even have to look to know. A text hisses from her phone.

like what, you weren't going to tell me?

The TV interviews. She's gotten calls all week. At least it saved her the embarrassment of having to tell the story again and again, to find a posture to take around it. And now, she sees through the open window the air shimmering above the radiator, and beyond that Dana sitting on her car hood draped in a clear plastic, disposable rain poncho. Cate can't think of a snappy response.

Dana lifts the overhang of the plastic hood and peers up at Cate, then puts her head down and they restart the conversation.

are you alone in there?

no

are you counting that dog as company?

fuck you, Cate texts, then goes to open the door.

Sailor gets there before her, poised at the threshold, shuffling his butt on the floor, getting ready. It's always a good time for company as far as he's concerned.

"You stay. No jumping." As Cate opens the door, he jumps up on Dana, then licks her face on both cheeks, as though he's French. Then, to make a further impression, he does his "spin," his easiest, default trick. He has only ever seen Dana that one time at the dog beach, so he can't have a scrapbook of fond memories of her. Then he's back for some more kissing. It's becoming clear he's not going to be much of a guard dog.

"Graham and I are trying to train him to not do this," Cate says, pulling him off. But then he's standing again, paws on Dana's shoulders. She can't remember if she told Dana about Graham and Sailor staying with her. Dana rubs her cheek along the side of his head, thumbs the inside of an ear. "Who are you, the make-out king?" She laughs in a way that's particular to her, a rollout of delight. Always appealing.

A serious shot of lightning crashes and bleaches the sky. Sailor rushes into a corner. Dana turns to look outside, then turns back to Cate. "Shouldn't it be, like, *snowing?*" She brushes the water from the poncho in sweeping gestures that cause droplets to stipple Cate's jeans. "The thing is, I knew before. I knew that afternoon. I knew something bad was going down." The crazy thing is that Cate believes her. Because this is how they see their connection. Like a deserted power station, mysterious and huge; darkened, but always active, sudden orange running sparks skittering through the air inside. This example will be tacitly added to the Myth of Them. Since this turned out to be a belief system of extremely limited value, Cate doesn't think it warrants any acknowledgment. She goes into the small bathroom to get a hand towel, then gives it to Dana, who wipes her face only a little. She can't help this.

"How are you here? Shouldn't you be slinging your hash?"

"I can't stay long, but I had to come by." Dana spins around. "Where'd the couch go?"

"I got rid of it when I stopped seeing you. Now all I do here is work."

"I always fucked you on the table. You should've gotten rid of that instead."

Cate opens the mini-fridge and pulls out a couple of beers, pops them open. Dana takes one, then sets it on the windowsill as she rubs her wet hair with the towel. She has such thick hair that any gesture involving it carries a small erotic payload.

"I just had to see you. See that you're all right. And Neale. Is she a mess?"

Although they only met twice—when Cate brought Neale to Toaster for breakfast—they clicked right off the bat. Of course they did, because Neale could see how perfect she and Cate were for each other. Although really, she'd probably like any girlfriend of Cate's who was politically progressive, with a blue-collar background, a degree from a culinary academy instead of a college.

"They did a scan, to see if the concussion was serious. It wasn't. But the woman kicked her in the face and her cheek is broken. There's going to be a surgery around that. She also has a sprained wrist. *And* the guy was trying to rape her. So of course she's flipped."

"Jesus. I guess I figured that was probably in the mix. How long is she going to be in the hospital?"

"Two more midnights. I got that off the wall chart in her room. I guess that's how they measure time in the hospital. Regular night and day must get mixed up inside. I have to tell you something else. Today I looked at the menu on her tray table. She's on soft foods because of the broken cheek. For breakfast she can have pureed waffle. I hate to say this, but I'm kind of glad you came by so I could tell you about the waffle."

"That's hilarious. But you can tell me the bad stuff, too. *Your* bad stuff. Maybe that'd help?"

"So. The thing is, I don't have a solid memory of a lot of it. I don't have a full picture. I was just operating on impulse. You know. Something bad happening. Stop it. Smash smash smash. I can see this part all over again if I want to. And then when he stopped moving, I rolled him and his flopping dick off Neale. Jesus. I can see any information about this is kind of TMI. But also NEI, not enough information about the whole thing. Patches are still blacked out, like with a Sharpie. I supposedly whooshed a rather large amount of spray from the extinguisher at the woman, got her in the eyes. But then what? Where did she go and how did I get to the guy while he was still gettable? I think I'm censoring my own mind."

Cate's cell buzzes its way across the table. She looks to see who it is, then lets it buzz on. "Private caller. No idea. I mean, I always thought it was you. But you, as you can see, are here."

"It *did* used to be me. Are you in something new? I thought you were seeing someone on the up-and-up."

"I am. And it's something I'm hoping goes somewhere. It has a lot of promise."

"Yeah. I've seen her. Very presentable."

"Where'd you see her? You mean from half a mile off at the beach?"

Dana doesn't say anything.

"Oh, please don't be stalking me."

"I'm not stalking. That would imply hiding. I *want* you to know I'm still close by. Walking the perimeter." She pulls Cate in by the front of her sweater. "Especially now." Cate feels her shoulder getting damp with tears. Dana is an easy crier, but even so, Cate's moved. She stands still, but inside is trying to back up. Really trying.

"You have to remember we've entered a new time frame. We're *not* close anymore. We're supposed to be going on with our lives without each other. Shouldn't you and Jody be getting married? Now that it's legal?"

"I don't want to talk about weddings." This is exactly the part of conversations with Dana that she hates. Sidesteps out of the way of pointed questions. Like now. Does Dana mean she hates flowers and dresses with trains? Handel? Or the weddings of friends, how corny they can be? Or is she saying she and Jody, on the other side of an opaque barrier from Cate, have already gotten married? Cate doesn't want to ask, because that would indicate she cares about the answer, and she does not want to indicate that. She'd like to keep her distance from Dana's real life, as though it's a play and she has a seat in the last row of the balcony. Between scenes, she can hear the shushing of pieces being pushed around while the stage is dark and the events to come are fine shadows made of dust, reassembled into new, colorful items, already in place when the lights come up again. But still, far, far away. She tries again to get this across.

"Every time I see you, you seem to be operating on the assumption that I'm still waiting for you, that nothing has changed with us. When in fact everything has."

"Unfortunately, for me anyway, not enough has changed. I still think about you way too much. You, too, maybe? Your hand is shaking. Your little half-hand." Dana takes it gently, by its two fingers. "Oh, baby."

"I've got too much going on now. In my life and in my head. I can't get back into it with you."

"Maybe now is exactly when you need me. To understand where you are." And then she's pushing Cate against a wall, wiping her wet hands through Cate's hair, holding her head as if it needs protection. Then, instead of saying any of the things anyone else would say—how sorry she is that this has happened, how traumatized Cate must be, how brave she was—she puts her mouth over Cate's ear and says, "You must feel so fucking powerful."

No one else has guessed this.

bludout

She knocks on the back door. "It's me," she says to it. Sailor adds a couple of paw scratches. He's here too, is what he's saying.

"Hold on. Joe will unlock it for you." Neale's voice from the other side is faint. Cate can barely hear her.

Joe opens the door but doesn't say anything. Sailor stands to put his front paws on Joe's shoulders. The two of them stand like this for a while, Joe rubbing his forehead against Sailor's.

"Did you get creepy questions from your friends?" Cate asks him, lifting Sailor from under one of his front legs and setting him back to ground level.

"We're on Christmas break so I've only seen Kiera and Theo and they'd never ask a creepy question."

A piece of memory is sliding into place.

he makes a terrible sound. his hands go to his head, which has started leaking blood. she twists the opposite way, then smacks him much harder with the extinguisher, this time with a backhand. there's the slightest cracking sound, like that of an eggshell. then just mush.

"oh no, no." he says this mildly, almost politely, as though there has been some mistake. more blood rushes out, a lot of it onto cate's hands. he sways a little, then collapses sideways, onto the floor. she looks at daffy duck on his neck. the tattoo makes everything a little worse, she's not sure why. lying still on the floor, he looks big, but now soft. his chin is recessed into fat, babyish cheeks. the rain jacket, although filthy, has hung onto its price tag. now he's still. she's not sure if he's alive, dying, or dead. a new smell has come to the fore, warm, and bad. what the inside of humans smells like. for good measure, she bashes his head a couple more times. she started out just wanting him off neale. now she also wants to make sure he's dead.

She refocuses on Joe, who is grabbing around on top of the refrigerator, for doughnuts that aren't there.

"I'll get some this afternoon."

Neale is sitting on the kitchen floor with a rag and a can of a product called BludOut, rubbing in a hopeless way at a faded but stubborn stain on the linoleum. Banged up and dressed for bloodstain removal, she looks like an extra in a war movie. Her cheek is still swollen and bruised. Cate realizes that of course all of this is superficial and will dissipate. Her surgery is scheduled for next week.

Joe says, "I can walk over to the Seven-Eleven. Not a problem." He seems relieved at the idea of getting out of the house. Weirdly, he looks older, even though it's only been a few days since Cate last saw him.

"No way you're going by yourself. Cate killed one of them, but the other is still unaccounted for."

And so Cate drives Joe the two blocks to the 7-Eleven. Their easy, oblivious days are behind them. Now they must protect themselves.

When they're back, Joe takes his doughnuts upstairs and Cate opens two cans of diet ginger ale, then drops to the floor next to Neale, thinking how could you be closer to someone than saving them? This horrible event has brought them to a new place, past the ordinary configurations of friendship, which now look like preliminaries. Of course, she can't bring herself to say this.

Neale says, "The other thing I feel bad about is that, although I am totally grateful, what you did was really too much for any friend. The whole mess itself was too big, then your response had to be so huge, so way off the edges of anything. It's hard to put everything back to regular." Then, after a bit more worthless rubbing at the stain, "Do you think they had our house staked out? Like for a burglary? It's kind of hard to imagine."

"Maybe they weren't looking for lucrative, maybe they were just roaming around, looking for something easy. They seem like people who might've had a lot of free roaming time. Maybe they tried this and that gate and they were all locked but yours wasn't. The bigger problem was the keys dangling in the door. Maybe the door wasn't even open—"

"No, it was open. I was just back. I knew I was running late, that you were going to be here any minute, and so I was a little frazzled, I was yanking stuff out of bags. I remember thinking if I could just get the frozen and cold stuff put away I could leave the rest until I got back. I keep replaying those first minutes. I see the two of them coming through the back door, but this isn't even remembering. It's only imagining, because I never actually did see them come in. My back was to the door. I was putting a couple of Leans into the freezer. I didn't even know they were there until the woman coughed. The cough was the scariest moment in my life.

"And now I'm frightened she'll be back with one of their friends. I don't even know how to picture them. I think maybe they're junkies? The police weren't able to ID the guy. He just slipped away, like a spiky line melting into a nice, smooth anonymous one."

"Do you think you should see someone professional?" Cate says. "Or do you think *we* should?" Cate would like to fold her arms around Neale, but the two of them have such a withering view of hugging there's no way they could just start that sort of thing up now.

"The hospital brought in a counselor, but she used words like *penetration*, also *ejaculate*. As a noun. *Journey* as a synonym for life."

Sailor is busy now, sniffing the floor with a little too much enthusiasm. It goes beyond sniffing into a snuffling that implies prey. A squirrel in a bush. Or with the new influx of urban wildlife, a rabbit. Or in this case, traces of blood from a large man.

"Hey, buddy." Neale rubs her thumb over the sharp angle of bone above his eye. "Everything is over. All is said and done."

He casually licks the bruised side of her face. He's a visiting nurse.

"Maybe Joe and I should get a dog. I think we could use a canine presence in the house."

"We could look on Petfinder," Cate says, but she can tell Neale has drifted away somewhere. "I wanted to be the one who brought you home, but Mrs. Pappageorge beat me to it."

Neale revives a little to say, "We were at a red and when it changed, she jumped like a jackrabbit in front of the oncoming traffic to turn left. Laying on her horn the whole way. It was a heartstopper. When I mentioned that it was a little scary, she told me this was how she learned to do it in driving school. That must've been a driving school in Athens. I imagine it has more aggressive traffic, more done with honking." Cate looks around. The kitchen is not its usual mess. It's not even just clean, it's sanitized. Maureen called in a crime scene/dead person cleaning service, which did a great job with the exception of the intractable bloodstain, which is now the only sign of a large event having taken place here.

"Let me text Maureen. Tell her you've already tried this stuff." Right away a reply buzzes in.

bludout worthless. do you have any magnesium chalk around there?

Instead of replying sure, cases of it, Cate texts back: thanks!, clicks her phone off, and slips it in her back pocket, then turns to Neale.

"Let me help you up." Using her hands like blades, she awkwardly hoists Neale by her armpits. This proves to be a difficult negotiation. "Getting down on the floor might have been a bad move for you so soon."

"Fuck," Neale says when she's up, rearranging herself over her feet, shaking one foot out of sleep. She's missing a tooth, far enough toward the front to be noticeable. Cate hadn't registered this before. "Little Billy Bob thing you've got going here." Cate taps a finger against Neale's cheek.

"Cold." Referring to Cate's fingertips. Meanwhile, Cate is adding up the damage Neale has sustained.

"Oh man. So much happened before I arrived. If only I hadn't been running late—"

"Oh, please don't get into *if only* thinking. There's no end to that. You'd have to go back to if Ricky was using her diaphragm that night, she wouldn't have had you and you wouldn't have been there to help me. Things might've gone *worse* if you'd been on time. They might've been facing a different direction. The way it went down, you had the jump on them. The element of surprise."

"I was just so furious I didn't think to be afraid. I was Liam Neeson in those movies where he's always rescuing his daughter from international sex-trafficking operations."

"There was more than one of those? How could his daughter keep winding up in that same situation? She'd have to be pretty unlucky."

"I think his wife gets taken in the next one. I think it's a business that's hard to get out of. Oh, I have to tell you. Ricky's embarrassed by the whole thing. She would've preferred a gun, maybe a dagger. Something dramatic and avenging, but also neat and clean. Maybe a fencing sword. She referred to my weapon as a Crock-Pot, to make the whole business sound a little goofy. Maybe rural."

"You can always count on Ricky. She always comes through."

Cate sees belatedly that she's going to have to open Neale's can of pop for her. "Sit down. In this chair. Not back down on the floor. Do

you have any straws? I think you're going to need one to drink this."
She rummages through a few drawers and comes up with one still in
its McDonald's wrapper.

"I have to keep the studio open. I can get somebody to sub for
my three classes, but to make up for that extra salary, I'll have to be
over there most of the time, manning the desk, and that's going to be
it for a few weeks, maybe longer. They say the wrist is going to take
its time. I hate that he did this to me. Put me out of business."

A queasiness floats up. Cate identifies it. "I don't like that knowing him is something we share."

"But we don't really share any of what happened. First it was my
experience, then I was out cold while it was being your experience.
I knew him when he was alive. You knew him while he was dying."

"Okay" is what Cate says, although this is not the response she
was hoping for. The assault is the worst thing they have ever shared,
but also the most significant. As circumstances arranged themselves,
she rescued Neale, but if their positions had been switched, she
knows Neale would've done the same for her. For Cate, saving Neale
has eliminated whatever thin space was between them. Neale has had
a different response. She has the look of someone at the end of her
own private dock, looking seaward toward a fogged horizon. When
she pulls back into herself, she is looking around what used to just be
her kitchen. Cate tries to help. "You don't have to stay here. You could
move to a blander neighborhood. Or even just a frumpy one. West of
Ashland. No one will think you're a wimp if you get out of Dodge."

"You know what I hate most? I hate that from here on this will
be the centerpiece of our friendship. That we used to have a regular
friendship and now we have this thing with weights all over, dangling from it."

This is so not how Cate sees things. In the first place, she has never thought of their friendship as regular. She thinks of it as way big enough to accommodate what happened. Nothing in this conversation, though, is reinforcing these assumptions.

Neale is fixed on the matter of the house. "I don't think I have what it would take to rehab someplace else, and I won't get enough for this place to buy anything but another fixer-upper. I'd have to look at all those listings that say, 'tons of potential.' I wish that house all the best, but right now I don't have whatever it would take to help it realize its destiny."

Cate gets stuck in a long pause, then pulls her random, sorrowful thoughts into some sort of action. "What do you say we go get the magnesium whatever for the floor and pick up some Vietnamese sandwiches on the way back. You and Joe and I can eat spicy sandwiches here and start reclaiming your kitchen, the way trees take back abandoned parking lots."

Neale disappears for a few minutes, then comes back with two bathroom rugs, drops them over the offending patch of floor. "All right. Rock and roll." When they get to the door, she shouts up the stairs to Joe, "Don't open the door for anyone!"

breathing room

The Tuesday Molly insisted Cate come to New York turns out to be Christmas Eve, and the important meeting turns out to be drinks with her and Lauren at a bar in the Village. Nothing gets discussed that couldn't have been handled over the phone or through email, but it's not until Cate is back in her hotel room that she realizes the meeting was really just a command performance. A reminder that Cate is in their service.

In an unexpected way this summons turns out to be a blessing. Instead of heading back to Chicago right away, she lies to Maureen that she needs to stay through the holiday to do some complicated measuring while the theater is dark. What she actually does with her Christmas is sleep through the morning, then scour Yelp for a restaurant that's open and has a turkey-dinner special. From there she walks south through the short afternoon, and through a lower Manhattan that's on pause. This allows her to be a rare sort of alone. She's purchased a bit of freedom from everything that's just happened and whatever complications might be rolling in.

auld acquaintance

A middle-aged guy dressed as a New Year's baby is walking up Halsted in a sash and a diaper under an open down coat. It's not even 5 p.m.

"No problem," Cate says.

Paint cans and pans rattle in the back as they drive. They pass an antiabortion billboard on Ashland that says AT 9 WEEKS BABIES HAVE FINGERPRINTS.

"Doesn't that seem a little early to worry about that?" Neale says. "I mean, considering they can't really get out to commit crimes."

She and Neale and Sailor are planning to use the long, last night of the year to obliterate the current version of Neale's kitchen. They are painting it red and yellow and blue. These are the colors of Frida Kahlo's kitchen in Mexico City. Neale saw a feature in a decorating magazine and kept the pages.

They'll have the house to themselves for the project. Joe is on a three-day family Caribbean cruise with Kiera and her parents. This is their present to him, distracting scenery and all. Neale resisted at first; it seemed too lavish a gift, but when they told her how cheap the cruise was, she caved.

"Apparently it's almost cheaper to be on a cruise now than to live your regular life at home," she tells Cate. "The boat putters around the Caribbean for four days from one formatted fun place to another, beaches set up for snorkeling and parasailing. At night, the disco has teen dances. Although Joe pretended he was too cool for that sort of thing, I could tell he was really pretty psyched."

Maureen is dressing up and taking herself to a big LGBT charity dinner dance. She wanted to take Cate, but Cate is still a long way off from dancing, even from dinnering. Maureen did not take this view, not at all. Apparently in her world New Year's Eve is a big deal. She wouldn't speak to Cate for three days. Finally she blinked. She's coming by after the ball, or whatever. Her giving in, weirdly, disappointed Cate.

"I thought she'd be tougher," Cate tells Neale, then, "I can see I'm starting to think of her as I don't know, like a hobby. Which is so wrong. Because it's clearly a bigger deal to her than that. I thought it was going to be a bigger deal to me, but that hasn't happened. And now she wants to take care of me like I'm a wounded bird. She wants to feed me with a little eyedropper, nurse me back to who I used to be. But I'm not sure I can go back there."

"This is about Dana, isn't it? She's back and wants to take care of you, too, doesn't she? What's the difference?"

"She doesn't think I need recuperating. She thinks I did something important and that I'm a new, slightly better version of myself for having done it. She says—"

"What? She says what?"

"'That she has to find a more important way to fuck me.'"

"Ah," Neale says.

Coming into the painting project, Neale is handicapped by her wrist. It's still in a splint. She's been told to do as little as possible with it.

Cate tells her, "You can still paint all the lower cabinets with your good paw. Just sit here on the floor. Start here. I can pour you more paint when you need it. Weird reversal, me being the one to lend a hand."

"Ah, I don't think you're supposed to stand on the top part; that's not even a step really," Neale says. Cate is on the ladder to tape off a wall from the ceiling.

"Balance is my strong suit," Cate says, then after a few minutes, "Does anything seem normal to you yet? I'm just checking in. Do *we* even seem normal to you—you and I? Doesn't it seem like we're in a play about our life? We have lines but they're anodyne. It's a quiet play. Like we're in act two: 'Painting the Kitchen.' I say something. You say something back, but it's too quiet around us. Right outside the theater, though, bombs are going off. Do you think we need to talk more about what happened—to dilute it, or wear it out, maybe?"

"I just want it all to go away. Talking about it gives it a little chair where it can sit right next to us. And you might want to rehash it because you have a heroic role. But I'm the flaky broad who leaves her back door open in a sketchy neighborhood. Then forgets all those practical moves we learned in that self-defense class years ago. He was so big, and he got me from behind, and I know there was probably a tricky move to get out of that hold—something that KGB wife would use in that TV show you like."

"*The Americans.*"

"Right. Like she'd grind her heel down hard on his little toe. Reach around to pinch some little thing in his neck. Instead I was confused and powerless. And now I'm a victim, a survivor. I *hate* that. I mean, of course I'm grateful you came along, but why couldn't I have done him in *myself*?"

"Well, yes. That would've saved me quite a bit of trouble. But that's not how it went down. You got sandbagged. I had to step in. That's it. I don't want you jumbling all the credit and debit around anymore. Everything has already happened. Forward is the only direction. I don't know if it's helpful to look back. When I do, it's a giant ball of horror in my head. How crazy they were, the terrible smell, just the wrongness of them being in this room. It's not like I had a tactical plan. I didn't have any time to sort things out. All I could do was improvise. And there's a hundred details I still can't remember. Like after I sprayed the woman, where did she go screaming? When the cops arrived, I told them they should look around the house—upstairs maybe. Or in the basement. I thought she was still around somewhere. But she'd gotten away. Even bashing him. I can only remember it in a very general way. I was just a crazed basher. I made a huge mess."

"I forgive you for sullying my kitchen in order to save my life."

"Yeah, yeah. You hate being the victim? Well, it's not all peaches on my side. The culture has co-opted being a hero. I'm in a cheesy category. That stupid TV show they got me to go on. And this week

I got an invitation to join a Facebook page called Women Who've Killed."

"New friends!"

The only way midnight—in this case the shift from one year into the next—is signified in the kitchen is the inconspicuous guitar chord notification tone indicating a text coming in from Dana. Cate ignores this. They go on painting.

They are nearly done with the walls when Maureen comes by around one in the morning. She's way too bright and shiny. The glitter of social life clings to her. She's wearing a dress that's about seven leagues more fashionable than anything Cate has worn, or ever will wear.

"Wow," she says, appreciating it. Maureen is not drunk, just tipsy enough that her general volume is way too high for the room. She doesn't see this, of course.

"I know. It's ridiculously expensive. Who would actually pay this much for a dress?"

Cate understands this to mean Maureen has "borrowed" the dress, probably from Saks, her favorite lending library, one aspect of her lightly comprised system of ethics. She rushes to cover this statement, although Neale has probably taken its meaning. "What's that you've got? A goodie bag?"

"*Excellent* goodies." She pulls from a tote covered in fake jewels an extra, extra-large Ziploc (brought from home) filled with crab Rangoons and bacon-wrapped breadsticks and tiny quiches. Chicken wings. She arranges these, crushed and bruised and stuck to each other, as decoratively as she can on a plate she grabs out of a cabinet.

"Come on. Time for a break. Smashed appetizers from my mother's purse when she came home from parties were some of the highlight treats of my Hollywood childhood."

She sets the plate on the kitchen table next to a roller pan filled with tomato-red paint, then ushers Cate down from the ladder, says, "Pretend it's midnight," and gives her a way-too-lingering kiss. She hauls out and pops the cork on a bottle of sparkling something, then goes looking for glasses.

It occurs to Cate, not for the first time, that the planet Maureen lives on might be too many solar systems away. But while it's okay for Cate to think this, it's not okay for Neale to look in a slightly withering way at Maureen for trying, however ineptly, to blast a little cheer into this muted scene.

"Yes!" Cate pops a crab Rangoon into her mouth and holds up a juice glass of champagne. Sometimes, in a small way in a particular instant, you just have to take a side. And even Neale—ordinarily kind, currently wounded—can be a jerk.

moonachie

This simple trip is made long and annoying by a tight budget. Her flight was the lowest fare she could find among the inconvenient-hour departures. Six thirty-five a.m. out of Midway, with a stop in Tampa, as though Tampa is on the way to New Jersey. The rental car she picked up in a strip mall ten minutes down the road from the airport has fuzzy cloth upholstery steeped in cigarette smoke from an ancient civilization. Ninety-five thousand miles on the odometer. Engine rattle when she tries to push it past sixty-five. Although this play is a huge career opportunity, it is nonetheless even lower paying than some of the productions she's worked on in Chicago or Milwaukee. The off-Broadway pay scale is absurd; she's heard this before and is now experiencing it. But off-Broadway is, of course, adjacent to Broadway.

So she rattles onward, from the Newark airport to Moonachie, a remote New Jersey location where the sets for *Blanks* will be constructed. She's here today to start things off with the fabricators. The shop is in a retired candy factory. A caramel aroma drifts vaguely out of the corners. Everything is in forward gear. Cate loves the energized scent of wood and metal and sweat and, of course, caramel.

It turns out to be an all-woman shop. No-nonsense women. Five of them. One has an injury much worse than Cate's—her right foot has been replaced with a high-tech prosthesis. This is, she tells Cate (part of a universal private conversation among those with missing parts), from a previous career in chicken processing at a plant unbothered by concerns for worker safety.

Most of the afternoon gets used up working out details from drawings and images Cate throws from her laptop onto a pull-down projector screen in what was once the candy baron's office lofted above the factory floor.

The carpenters want to know does the stage at Ropes and Pulleys have tracks for platforms?

Cate says no, but they've okayed installing them.

The painters are doubtful the walls of the basement scene can be done to Cate's specification with just paint.

Cate says, "The writing room Virginia has there needs to be already old in the 1920s. Old cellar is, I think, a special color, a particular mix of gray and decay. I've brought along Pantone chips for this mottling." She doesn't say she got the specific colors from her father. "I've also brought an old British fuse box I ordered off eBay. That basement wall needs something for Vita and Virginia to bump against. A romantic nuisance."

Someone wants to know how much greenery will be needed to create Vita's garden.

"Bushels and then some. Vita's writing tower will perch twenty feet above the stage and needs to be covered in vines. The garden backdrop is going to require its own floral tonnage, also climbing roses over the pergola. Basically we'll need fill for everything that isn't walkway and French-door entrance."

Someone has already started painting the wall of books that is the backdrop for Vita's living room. The books, she sees, are life-size. Cate hates to start off a project by correcting the mistakes of others, so she frames a correction as a collaboration.

"I've had to do this before," she tells the painter, "I think the books look more substantial from a distance if I go to one-and-a-half size. Can I borrow your tape measure?" She pencils in a line three inches above and just under two inches wider than the first book, then does this for the next few books What do you think? Let's paint them in this size then back off and see how they'll look to the audience." Part of what she's become adept at is asking the opinions of people who will not really be concurring so much as following her orders.

By six, the crew is ready to order materials and begin construction, and Cate heads out. She gets a breakfasty dinner at a steel-sided diner. (Holding her cell under her newspaper, she takes a surreptitious picture of the grill, which appears to be from the beginning of the twentieth century. She shoots this to Dana. But, of course, why is she shooting anything to Dana?) She finds a cheap motel for the night before heading into New York tomorrow. Cheap hotel rooms in Manhattan are way too scary. What she finds on the outskirts of Moonachie is the Loch Lomond. Hers is the only car in the parking lot; all the other guests have trucks. Her room is both depressing and agitating—a pageant of plaid. Bedspread, drapes, and small, tragically decorative pillows on top of the real ones. All the plaids are different tartans. The walls are hung with prints of fox-and-hound events, and of Bonnie Prince Charlie, who does not appear to have really been all that bonnie. The carpet is clean, there's that. No bugs scatter when she turns on the lights. In the corner across from the bed, there's a full-size refrigerator. She's not sure whether to count this as feature or flaw. A flat-screen TV is mounted high on the wall across from the bed. She opens all the windows to get a breeze going, to dilute the air in the room, which is thick with loneliness. There's a ten-dollar deposit for the remote, which Cate declines; she has a copy of a good play with her, something she saw years ago, early in her career. *Gross Indecency: The Three Trials of Oscar Wilde.* She remembers the set allowing a lot of agility on the part of the actors. Reading scripts, imagining (or remembering) them up and running, is one of her great free-time pleasures, a busman's holiday.

She showers and gets into yoga pants and a long-sleeve T-shirt, crawls into bed.

This is their second design meeting, and so the initial butt-sniffing is over, and they are now going forward with a tacit agreement that they can work together. Dan Tennent, the lighting guy, like a lot of lighting directors, thinks the set is a corpse his lights can bring to life. He may be a problem, but Cate decides not to worry about that yet.

Saya Arai is doing costumes. She's really good. Cate knows *how* good by the fact that the couple of times her name has come up, Maureen has had something negative to say about her. Saya is ethereal in her presence, thin in a way that implies an internal focus, a diet of lichen. She is extremely quiet. She didn't talk much at the first meeting, only took furious notes in a slender gray notebook. Cate isn't crazy about having notes taken on everybody else by someone who's not putting out her own ideas.

Jenny McAdam is the stage manager, an old pro, a security blanket for Cate. She comes with an air of capability and crisis management. She and Cate were friends back at RISD, so she's a known among unknowns. Cate could even stay on her sofa to save the hotel bill, but she did that once and found out Jenny keeps ferrets as pets. They live in the hall closet amid a circus of hammocks and exercise wheels, but slither in and out through the night under its door.

Oliver Palmieri, the company's dramaturge, is the last to arrive, and takes several minutes to negotiate getting out of his coat and sitting down on one of the folding chairs around the table. He weighs probably 350, and is a short man to start with. His butt cheeks overflow the seat of his chair, and the closest his stomach will allow him to get to the table is about a foot away. Cate used to enjoy watching extremely fat people—imagining what they eat when they're alone, how they manage sex. But now that small, crummy curiosity has been corrupted. Now corpulence tugs a grimy cord inside her.

Ty Boyd gets up to stretch. He's singular looking. Dramatic, with a white shock of Beckett hair, heavy glasses with thick lenses behind which his weak eyes swim. According to Graham, he's asexual, which gives him a subtle aspect of outlier. Along with this, there's a (Cate suspects deliberately) random aspect to the way he dresses. Today it's a varsity swimmer's jacket and dark green work pants. Hiking boots.

He was here before everyone else. He catches Cate's eye and points to his wrist, although he has no watch, to say Lauren and Molly have yet to arrive. They always show up a little late for everything, to let a small flutter of apprehension gather up among those who await them. At the twenty-minute mark, Ty goes to the single window in the rehearsal space, opens it, sticks his head out and looks down the street. He pulls himself back in and shuts the window. "I guess we should just begin." He's clearly not convinced this is the right decision. Confirmation of that comes another fifteen minutes in, when Molly and Lauren swirl in, see the meeting in progress and don't say anything, either of them.

They arrive just as Saya is suggesting—her first entry into the general conversation—that Vita be in skinny jeans for at least the garden scene. "The way Sofia Coppola put those Converse high-tops in Marie Antoinette's closet. A little anachronism. You just know Vita would have worn Levi's if she were around today."

"We'll think about that," Molly tells Saya. This is her version of no.

Throughout the rest of the meeting, maybe forty-five minutes, Molly and Lauren are chilly.

No one will start a meeting before they arrive again.

Cate booked herself on the last flight tonight to Chicago. She wants to take a couple of hours to be a tourist. On these recent trips, she's inside the play more than she's in Manhattan. She heads up to MOMA, which is open until eight.

Down in the subway, a train must have just come and gone. The platform on her side is empty. The air is sweet and sour with urine. She's cold, but it's also nerves that make her shuffle a little from foot to foot, flicking glances toward the passage she's just come through. She needs to know who will come out next, into this echoing tunnel with no visible police presence, only videocams to record whatever happens down here, the footage valuable only afterward. She hates that she thinks like this now. It's not fear. Neale bought all the fear available from what happened. Cate's fallout is a constant readiness. She hates that she's so ready. Being always ready is quite fatiguing.

December has pushed into January, the light staying longer, the sharpness of winter growing dull. The air—because it's New York and not Chicago, also because of the changing climate—has a balminess to it. She gets out a couple of stops early, stops in a shop called Black Hole that sells jeans so heavily dyed you have to wash them by themselves not just the first time, but forever. She buys a pair, decides to wear them to MOMA, stuffs the old pair she's wearing into her backpack. Might as well be modern herself.

Inside the museum, instead of being absorbed by the art, she stands alone and outside everything around her. This is a new bad feeling. Not a panic attack exactly. More a heightened awareness, hearing sounds from a higher register, picking up something drifting in on a chilled wind.

She catches a cab to the airport. Inside, she presses Dana's number on her contacts list, which she has obscured as T. Oaster. She's in luck. Dana answers. It's too early for her to be at work, so she's probably at home.

"Just tell me I must have the wrong number. I'll call you later at work. I'm just having a bad moment. I want to hear your voice is all."

"Sorry. I think you have the wrong number."

tiles

Cate is in such a tumble of departing and arriving these days that she worries Sailor is confused about her. So this morning, before she has to go downtown to teach the first class of the spring semester, she takes him to the beach, where he wears himself out with a pack of younger dogs.

Which makes her slightly late for class. She has fifteen undergrads. She sees that what's trending this semester in terms of hair is two chroma colors in addition to regular hair color. These kids are color-ful, but silent as little monks. She breaks the ice with an old-fashioned parlor game. Each of them has to write on a three-by-five card three facts about her/himself—two true, one false. And the class asks ques-tions to try to trip them up on their false fact, which, since it is false, they don't know enough about. By the time they've gone around the table with this, the atmosphere has warmed enough to begin class.

Their first project is to design a set for Lillian Hellman's *The Little*

Foxes. She has found this to be a successful assignment. First, they've never read the play, and so this forces them to do that. Second, it requires period furniture, so they have to go rummaging around in the past. One class she goes with them on the el up to Belmont junk shops to measure and photograph pieces they might use. Every once in a while, one of them sets a play on another planet, or after whatever apocalypse, which is nice, a little off-roading, but it's still good for them to have a basic grounding in the way things looked historically.

Only one of the students recognizes her from local newspaper stories. It was a bit of luck that Cate's newsworthy fifteen minutes took place during winter break and most students were home, out of range of Chicago news. This student, though—a girl wearing a cocktail dress and Doc Martens—comes up after class to say, "So. Are you okay?"

This seems way too intimate but for the fact that when your personal life makes the news, it's no longer off-limits for strangers to mention.

"I am," Cate says, reflexively, then wonders what okay would be now.

After class, she drives up to see Neale, who's recuperating after surgery on her busted cheek. She finds Rose and Arthur in the living room. With a little conversation she also finds they are not just here in a post-op way, but in an open-ended residence. Well, of course, they *would* be staying here. Activists take action. They're wired for it.

"Cate, sweetheart," Rose says, briefly holding her phone away from her, "we're adding home security to the cable package here."

Arthur reads aloud from the Comcast site on his laptop. "'Check your home even while you're away. Use your mobile app to monitor your property inside and out.'"

"Sounds a little Orwellian," Cate says.

"Except in this case, *you're* Big Brother." Occasionally Arthur will speak to Cate as if he needs to give her a boost up the learning curve. Everything about him is aimed at the greater good, but in matters of personal kindness, he often comes up short. This gives Cate permission to look a little too long at his abundance of protruding ear hair. Both he and Rose, who are a few years younger than Cate's parents, look a decade older. Probably because they have been working for the good of others since their youth, thereby pretty much skipping their youth. Their brows have permanent furrows, their gaits are arthritic from years of marching and shuffling at demos and on picket lines. They've never had a citrus peel or microdermabrasion, or, like Cate's father, an eye lift.

Cate has brought three excellent bagels from a deli on Seventh Avenue. For her and Neale and Joe. Three is definitely the wrong number of bagels for five people. She leaves them in her messenger bag.

"Joe-Hill is at his friend Kiera's house." This is the name Neale, in a weak moment, promised her parents she would name her baby, but in practice, only Rose and Arthur use it. Joe himself shrugged it off years ago. "Nealy's upstairs resting," Rose tells Cate. She hasn't heard Neale's mother refer to her daughter as Nealy since junior high. While she's thinking she'll have to ask Neale about this new level of parental attentiveness, she senses over her shoulder that Rose is following her upstairs. What's this about?

"Hey," Neale says from her bed. She's not in any sort of invalid mode. She's in jeans and a sweater, reading a new novel by Elizabeth Strout. She loves Elizabeth Strout.

She looks better than Cate expected, or at least no worse.

"Little titanium plates," she says, tapping her bandaged cheek. "My first step toward becoming bionic."

"Now you can go to Bionic Hair."

"I need to go somewhere. I'm stir-crazy."

Rose says, "I think you're supposed to get bed rest just now."

Cate knows that Neale will not respond well to this directive cloaked as a suggestion, and indeed she is grabbing her jacket off the bedroom doorknob before her mother has a chance to try again. Instead, Rose turns to Cate and clears her throat, which means she is about to deliver a preformed message. "We're so lucky you were here to help that day."

This is not the first time Cate has seen Neale's parents since the assault, and she is getting tired of being thanked by them. Hero is a single-dimension entity. She'd like to go back to being Neale's friend with a million aspects and reference points and a long history with their family. She knows Rose and Arthur are traumatized by what happened to Neale, and she could probably help by giving them a version with a pastel filter. They would probably see through it but maybe be comforted nonetheless. But she can't come up with any version of those events, not even the true one, because of the redaction of her memory. She suddenly needs to be out of this house as much as Neale does. She asks her, "You still want to go look at tiles for Frida's kitchen?"

This is the last step in the renovation/obliteration of Neale's kitchen, finding the right floor tiles.

When they're in the car, on their way to Home Depot, Neale says, "What about Tile City? Wouldn't they have a bigger selection? I mean, doesn't their name suggest a stronger mission?"

"They might. But what they don't have is a woman who's in charge of the floor-covering department. She's helped me before." Neale smiles. It's the first time Cate has seen her smile in a long time.

"You're so cute. Your little lesbo map of the city." Then, a few beats later, "Look. I'm not telling my parents about this." She pulls a small automatic out of her backpack.

"Oh, Jesus."

"I know what you're thinking. That people like us don't have guns. But now I'm part of a new population. People like us who've been attacked in their homes, where their kid also lives."

"Do you even know how to use it?"

"I took a lesson at the gun shop. I have four more to go."

"I know I need to talk with you about this, but not just yet. I don't think I've ever felt so far from your thinking."

Neale slides the gun back into her bag, then tacks away from the gun and starts talking tile. "I think we want a pattern."

"How much do you think about it, about what happened?" Cate says.

"An easier question would be how much do I *not* think about it."

"I keep trying to put it in a small box. I have to close the box and sit on the lid, but it keeps thumping underneath me. There's our whole lives before, then ten minutes in your kitchen, now the rest of our lives. Those minutes were totally anomalous to everything else. Unless we go through a third world war or an antibiotic-resistant plague, nothing like that is going to happen again in our lives. So it wasn't a learning experience. All I'm hoping now is that it doesn't color us, and I'm beginning—what you just showed me—I'm beginning to feel that's what's happening."

"Well really, though," Neale says. "How can it not?"

"Who do you think they were? Sometimes I try to imagine them in their life. Maybe it was so hard it bent them. Maybe they were terribly abused as kids."

"No, no. You need to get off that train of thought. That's the train that takes you to second thoughts. Rue. You don't need to muddy up things with rue. You don't need to think maybe you could have just knocked him out so he could have come to and gotten into prison counseling and back on the straight and narrow. Because what if he came back to consciousness? He was quite huge, as you might recall. You were only able to kill him because you caught him from behind. And by surprise. I just don't let my thoughts branch out. Marlene says I need to keep my thoughts on it circumscribed by those minutes, that room, that for now it's best to confine it."

"Does Marlene know about the gun?"

Marlene is the therapist Neale has started seeing. An old friend of Neale's mother. She ran Rose's consciousness-raising group in the '70s. Cate knows she should want Neale to get professional help, but in fact she resents the fact that Neale is talking to someone about what happened, but not talking about it to her.

In Home Depot, Neale points to a small square of tile on a thick page filled with samples. "What about this?"

"There's multicolored, then there's dog vomit."

"Yes, this one here is called Trip to the Vet." This is the salesperson, Darlyn. She's amused by the idea of a dog-vomit palette. The three of them are in a tight huddle over the sample books, and Cate can feel a dry heat coming off Darlyn, just wafting around in the confined air. She finds this comforting because it's something she'd notice in regular life, her life before. Darlyn pulls a big sample book out of a slot and opens it. "Here are some confetti patterns in circus colors. And here's one with yellow-red-blue."

When they're back in the car, Cate asks how it's going with Rose and Arthur in residence. She's sure Neale has some anecdotes about their oppressive presence, but all she gets is,

"They're being great. Well, a little overbearing, but—"

Then Neale is quiet in a sinking way. Then she is saying, "The thing is, I think I saw her."

"What? When?"

"Last week. At the Aldi. On Broadway."

"Aldi?" Aldi is a budget supermarket on Broadway in Uptown. Cate has only gone there once. They didn't have bags at the checkout; many customers were taking their groceries home in suitcases.

"This happened last week and you're only telling me now? Did she see you? And why were you at Aldi in the first place?"

"I don't know. It's so close. Their yogurt is really good. I'm not absolutely sure it was her. She was buying candy. I didn't do very well with the situation. Basically, I just left. I was afraid if I called you, you'd make me call the cops."

"Well, yeah?! Didn't you think you ought to do that?"

"I don't know. The thing is, I'm not really sure it was her. I don't think I could pick her out of a lineup of scraggly old women along that stretch of Broadway. And I guess I don't want to bring it all up again. Maybe she has friends—you know, bad company. Maybe the guy was her husband or her brother. Someone she loved. Someone whose death she might want to avenge. I don't want to draw her attention."

"But she already knows where you live. She can find you any time she wants. But you could have followed her home and found out where *she* lives, told the cops her address."

Neale doesn't say anything for another long time, while Cate starts thinking she might make a shopping trip to the Aldi.

When Neale says the next thing she's going to say, it's, "Anyway, pretty soon our defenses are going to be even more bolstered. Claude's coming back."

"Claude? He's coming back from India? *He's* going to help *you?*"

Claude is the most self-absorbed human Cate has ever known. He's literally a navel gazer. She has seen pictures of him in Pondicherry, in the ashram, in a loincloth. She can't imagine him helping anyone. He'd step over an old lady collapsed in the middle of the street. He wouldn't take her cane, he's not wicked. He just can't be bothered with the inconvenience of other people. Cate thinks the only reason Neale married him is that beautiful women like her are in an elite class that attracts handsome men who in turn blind everyone to their underlying character. Claude looks like Jean-Paul Belmondo in *Breathless*. Also, Neale wanted someone to give her the baby who turned out to be Joe.

"Joe told him about it on Skype. So Claude's Mighty Mouse, coming to save the day. I don't know. I think it's the right thing to do. Put a little more male presence in the house. Just for now. Get my parents out of my hair."

Pain slams Cate hard in the chest, as though she's been whacked with an oar. Nothing big happens, she's beginning to see, without knocking around the adjacent pieces.

girls kissing

At the rehearsal space above a Korean restaurant, the actors are bouncing their characters off one another. The room has heavy fragrance—body odor and sizzling beef.

Today, the actors playing Vita and Virginia have come in to work out logistics for the basement scene. Gladys Banner is the exact right type for Vita; it's easy to see why Molly and Lauren went against the advice of their casting director, who doesn't think Gladys is up to the job. But she's British and casually wields both a Received Pronunciation accent and an imperious manner. Most important, she is famous for starring in a movie and two sequels about an icy detective seeking justice in a ruthless world of the future. Molly and Lauren are hoping Gladys's presence will sell a lot of tickets even before the reviews come out.

Virginia is being played by Ruby Pepper, who, though she has a stripper name, also has a long list of stage credits for having played one or another sensitive artistic type. Her part in *Blanks* is smaller. Vita's affair with Virginia occupies only the first act. Act two moves Vita through the destruction of Geoffrey Scott and her subsequent philandering through a short list of lesbians working at the BBC, where she and Harold give their talk on "the happy marriage."

Today Molly lays out the challenge of the scene in which Vita has come to the basement of Virginia's London house, to the small writing studio. She's ostensibly on an afternoon social visit, which will include tea, small sandwiches, and London gossip. Virginia's husband, Leonard, may be around. So they make an arrangement, a letter inside a letter (*"You'll be nice to me, won't you? And I'll be nice to you."*) to meet half an hour early so they can make out a little in the basement. This is the scene for which Cate bought the old fuse box.

Molly delineates the action for the two of them. "This is a subtle sex scene. Virginia is often portrayed as fragile, but in this relation-ship she is also slightly the aggressor. She's forty. She's had very little romance in her life. Vita's offering her that opportunity and Virginia's interest is piqued." Molly pushes and pulls Gladys and Ruby into an embrace in one corner of the room. She steps back to see how they look, then comes in for a little rearranging. "Okay, so Virginia's bril-liant as a writer, but she faces a steep learning curve in flirtation and seduction. You know what? I think I need you to reverse your posi-tions. Vita should be against the wall of the corner stage left; she's the catcher. Ruby, I want you to stand with your right foot between Gladys's feet. Gentle but pointedly invasive." She turns to Cate. "I need you to make sure these walls, onstage, are firmly buttressed, sturdy enough to have some passion pressed against them."

Both actors are straight. Ruby is professional, Gladys is tiresome. She needs to put her heterosexual watermark on the scene, giggling into and out of the first practice kisses. Asking Molly, "Is this right?" As if kisses between women operate on a different mechanism, like a language with a glottal stop.

"Perfect." Molly brushes the stupidity aside.

Cate goes off to take measurements on a chaise Gladys says is too short for her to stretch out on seductively. She wants to be out of earshot when Gladys says, "Oh this feels so weird!" Or whatever.

While this run-up has the usual urgency of every play ever mounted, its machinery is more oiled than Cate is accustomed to. The Babes, as Cate thinks of Molly and Lauren, are totally in control of the production. Also, because one of them wrote the play, it's a living organism, adapted as it goes. Underlines and italics can be added and removed, weak lines cut, new ones added.

It's only been three weeks since the assault. It feels both like ten minutes and a year. At first Cate thought, no way she could do this play. She'd have to give it up. It was Neale who pushed her, but the sporadic separation has not been good for their friendship. Cate missed Neale's surgery, her gun buy, her parents' move-in, and Claude's imminent rescue. But for Cate, the job and its thousand details help keep at bay the replay loops in her head. During the days anyway. Nights in Manhattan, she's on her own.

long-term dating

found a place west on montrose.
not cuban. some other island, near equator.
in the back of a little grocery store.

This is Maureen arranging an activity for the two of them. She still does this. Cate is to a place where she doesn't need an activity to justify the two of them getting together. But Maureen still likes to create a little honeypot, as though she needs to lure Cate into seeing her.

She mines every area of common interest they've turned up. Along their short way, they've found a mutual love of restaurants located in one or another obscure corner of ethnicity. This one is cozy. It smells of plantains and salty fat and coffee. The tables are covered with frantically patterned oilcloth. The menu is not in English, not in Spanish either. They order by hunch and the color photos on the menu.

The food arrives. Cate surveys her plate. "Mmmm. This thing—it's a root?" Whatever it is, it's puddled in an orange oil. "And these spongy greens. It's like a little hillside, a knoll maybe. What you're having looks better."

A small patch of silence as they poke and taste. Cate pushes the oily root (now it seems more likely to be something from the ocean floor) to a distant region of the plate. The fronds are aromatic in a medicinal way. "I think I may have moved into a land beyond edible. At least without a period of cultural assimilation."

Maureen's dish is probably chicken, but could be rabbit. (Cate tries not to think "bunny.") She gives Cate a piece along with the slice of Wonder bread and a butter pat that sit next to it. When Cate doesn't eat either, Maureen says, "You're right. Your selection was a step too far. Let's drive down to Oak Street. We can stop at the fancy Norwegian frozen yogurt place. You've earned some vanilla."

Next to the yogurt place there's a rarefied clothing store.

Cate says, "These shops. How do they make money? They only have six pieces of clothing in here. I always think if I even walk in, I've made a commitment. I'm going to have to justify my presence by buying a two-hundred-dollar T-shirt in size two. Their version of large."

Minutes later, sitting across from each other at a smaller, this time steel, table, eating small dishes of cloudberry frozen yogurt, Maureen voices a complaint.

"Sometimes I feel I'm losing you to this terrible thing that happened. That you're never going to get past it."

"No. Really. I'm not only traumatized. I was also surprised by what I was capable of doing. I'm kind of exhilarated at my competence."

"Yeah, well, that might be another problem." This crankiness is turning up fairly often. Of course, she has a perfect right to it. Maureen is stuck in an annoying set of circumstances. Instead of a blossoming romance, she's getting Cate in random pieces scattered between her travel to New York, her trauma, and her taking care of Neale. If she could hold off being cranky at least until Cate is full-time back in Chicago and can sort out a few things. But she can't.

Even if she doesn't know all the specifics of Cate's distraction, Maureen perceives the general inattentiveness. She's also unhappy about the social engagements Cate slides out of, particularly getting together with Maureen's friends, of which she has quite a retinue. Keeping these friendships lively entails dinners and reciprocal dinners, brunches (a meal Cate sees as a sucking time hole with eggs), a subscription to Hubbard Street Dance with Ingrid and Patty (an ex of Maureen's). The list winds on. Maureen takes defection from any of these as Cate rejecting her social world. Cate, for her part, feels beleaguered trying to stay in step with Maureen. It's like dancing on broken pavement.

apocalypse beach

Maureen is still asleep when Cate wakes up. She looks deep in there, definitely a couple of hours shy of getting out of bed. Then she will awaken refreshed, having missed out on the pageant of her own sputter-snoring, her twitching legs, her strangled nightmare screams. She's like a road hog—passing on the right, tailgating, tossing hamburger wrappers out the window as she goes. Of course, she doesn't believe any of it. "I sleep like a baby," she says.

This is by now an inside joke. They are starting to have inside jokes. Every step forward with Maureen feels like it's toward the edge of a cliff. She knows she should sit down and take a closer look at this feeling.

Every morning Cate has to put on her shoes with the obstacle of a dog's cement-block head in her lap. Sailor's excitement is never tamped down by the predictability of his walk. Sunny or inclement outside, he drags in one of her shoes every morning at 8 a.m., even this deep into winter, when 8 a.m. means not long after daybreak. He's never off by more than a few minutes. This morning the shoe is being pressed against her forehead and pops her out of a dream about hurling herself down stairs, taking them a flight at a time by swinging around on the newel post and throwing herself feetfirst in a springy way down onto the next landing. This is the way she takes stairs in her dreams. Her dreams are filled with stairs.

"Okay, buddy," she whispers and looks down at Maureen, lying like a fallen fighter, her fan tattoo soft across her shoulder blade. The scent coming off her warm body when Cate lifts the cover is dry and autumnal, like a burning pile of leaves (or a couple of cigarettes). Even though Cate moves as delicately as possible, *shh-shh-shhing* Sailor backward so she has room to get out of bed, Maureen stirs.

"It's early," Cate tells her. "Go back to sleep."

"No, I have to get going. I've got a breakfast meeting. Barry Shriner." She is presenting a portfolio of costume sketches for a musical version of *Dr. Zhivago*. Maureen is dying to get this job. The play has both ballroom dresses and the rough clothing of the revolutionaries. By her own estimation, she is a master of peasant fashion. She can tatter and sully a shirt like nobody else. Pencil shavings are her trade secret; she rubs them into the fabric. They add the most believable dusting of historic urban dirt. There are a lot of tricks like this to her trade, and of course to her entire life. The way she borrows clothes from Saks and Neiman Marcus, and a small rotation of Near North shops. Tomorrow night she's going to a Jeff Awards benefit. Which means today she will find the perfect dress, then wear it to the cocktail party very carefully (drinking only white wine or vodka).

At home afterward, she will steam the dress, refold it inside the store tissue, refasten the price tag, if she's been able to get it off. Later this week, she'll return it with a limp excuse. It didn't match the shoes she had in mind. Or maybe when she sat down, it felt a little too snug at the hips. When she explained this little routine to Cate, it wasn't with any shame. She was showing off. Maureen sees herself as crafty and savvy. Her justifications are collapsible and expandable. The implication in this matter is that women who actually *buy* fancy clothes for this or that occasion are spendthrifts supporting shops that she can then use to her own small advantage. When Cate misses the beat where she's supposed to nod and laugh or come up with a similar anecdote of her own, Maureen sidesteps. "You know, the store usually gets a dress back in better condition than when they sold it to me."

Maureen enjoys detailing her guerilla agility. And passing it along to others. Cate overheard her on the phone telling a friend whose car had been T-boned on Ashland to get the car out of the shop and over to CarMax fast, to beat the accident report, in case there was anything gravely wrong with it. Even though she has lived an entire life within the roped-off area of upper-middle-class privilege, she maneuvers like a new immigrant, as though she needs to climb her way up through an unwelcoming culture. It's a game she plays, maybe to add a little burr of friction to her smooth life of ease and plenty. Cate hasn't confronted her on this sort of stuff; she hasn't yet been able to find a way into that conversation. She's never had this dilemma before. Questioning someone's ethics isn't something easily brought into any conversation. Any talk along these lines would be big and damaging. For now, she's waiting for other shoes to drop.

But really, what if they do? She's going to point out to Maureen that she's ethically challenged? And who is Cate to judge? She doesn't have gray areas herself? Although when she tries, she can't really come up with any of these sorts of tactics in her own behavior. Or, for that matter, in the behavior of anyone she knows besides Maureen. But are these sorts of shabby edges reason enough to break up? It's kind of the same as Maureen's affair with her sister. Although initially shocking, if she looks at these pieces from a few angles, gives them time to wear down, they begin to seem more like quirks. And addressing any of this would imply the existence of a totting-up. No budding relationship could survive that.

It's way too cold for humans at the dog beach. Not too cold at all, though, for the two other dogs whose humans were able to rouse themselves and dress in layers and layers plus two hats, plus boots with heat packs stuffed in the toes.

Cate sits on one of the broken benches scattered around the beach, facing the brutal, steel-colored waves. And in an instant she has left her current circumstances behind, sucked back and down.

she's statue-still on the mudroom steps, frozen, the big guy kneeling over neale, who is unconscious. his butt emerges as he shrugs down his sweatpants. two pillows of flesh fall away from the center furrow. she does not look at the furrow. the exposed flesh is gray, patterned here and there with small patches of angry red rash. this mass jiggles as he shifts around flat on neale to position her, set her in place.

the fire extinguisher. one step up from the one on which she's standing. she picks it up slowly, to avoid the grating of metal against cement. there's some sort of wire ring, a safety latch that needs to be removed. when she pulls this loose she uses her bad hand, which unfortunately doesn't have enough fingers to keep the ring from falling onto the concrete with a small but definite ping.

the woman hears it and turns. her stare is fierce with calculation. no time to think. cate just rushes her with the white fog billowing out of the extinguisher, which sets her screaming like a frozen wire and zigzagging around the kitchen. cate loses track of her. she has to stay on the move. the big guy is turning around and trying to get up. she can't have that. she starts spraying him, but too little is left. it's then she starts swinging the can by its trigger, smashing his head wherever the metal lands. she doesn't have a strategy.

She comes back to find herself hunkered over her knees, positioned against the slicing wind. Sailor is blissed-out, the air rippling through his fur like an invisible brush. He tries to get a rumble going, first with a terrier, then with a malamute. Since no other dogs are available, the three of them—in spite of their large discrepancies in size—gamely try to box and roll each other over, then set up a race. In between rounds, Sailor comes up and sinks his head into Cate's lap.

"You're the most handsome dog in the world. And you don't even know it. Which only makes you more handsome." She kisses and kisses the soft fur just above his eye. "And *I* got you. Imagine that." She's trying to let him know she's still there for him, even though she's a slightly different her. He has sniffed out the change.

And then he's off again.

One of the changes is that she's lost five pounds in the past month, without trying—part of the morphing, as though the person she's turning into needs to make a lower weight, maintain a more agile vigilance. She suspects this isn't temporary, that she's made a permanent move to this interior neighborhood, some unincorporated area of aftermath.

She can't really talk with Neale about this stuff, about how different she feels. Neale is on a mission to forget. And everyone else Cate knows still lives in the old neighborhood: they're stumbling through the middle years of their lives in a familiar place, which they find tricky and difficult enough, filled with small, ultimately solvable problems. Their innocence fatigues her. She looks back with nostalgia at a sepia-tinted time when she thought Maureen's affair with her sister was a big problem. Or Graham's inability to resist the siren call of Eleanor. (He's been spending the odd night over at her place lately, but in a tapering way.) These look like play problems now.

She knows anyone would advise her to see a shrink, but she hasn't been able to bring herself to that yet. She thinks anyone worth seeing would cut through the counseling platitudes and start poking around in soft spots and sensitive areas, and Cate isn't yet up to opening herself—particularly her new self, with whom she's just making first acquaintance—to the judgment of a professional stranger.

She had long thought her bad thing already happened, down in her father's workshop. This relieved her of a lot of luxury fears. She didn't bother worrying about exploding stoves or falling safes. She allowed herself to take on small bits of daring. She still sometimes throws her feet forward and takes the last three steps onto whatever landing, a real-life version of her staircase dreams. A childhood trick she probably should have given up this far into adulthood. Now, though, a further bad thing has happened to her, adding random-ness to bad. The treaty she thought was in effect has been violated. She has been tossed back into the general risk pool. Also, she has the extra worry of a new encounter with the woman whose darting eyes she sprayed with fire retardant. If there is an encounter, Cate wants to be in charge of it.

On *The Americans*, Elizabeth, the undercover KGB killer, does most of her disguising with glasses and wigs. So Cate got some cat's-eye frames at a thrift shop on Belmont, then found a long, blond '90s wig at Elim Wig and Hair on Broadway. She wore these with old jeans and a drab peacoat from the wayback of her closet. Assembled in all this, she looked in the mirror and hardly recognized herself. It was a little amazing.

The Aldi itself is also a little amazing. She has been there twice now. She puts on her disguise in her car, then wanders the aisles with a cheesy straw tote. Most of the store's stock is of brands that remind you of regular brands. Savoritz crackers. Chef's Cupboard soup la-bels with a definite Campbell's graphic to them. Other brands seem part of a fictional shopping neighborhood—Millville (cereal bars) where you'll find Friendly Farms (milk) down by Crystal Creek (chardonnay). But there are also weird outliers, brands that seem to have been born out of a fundamental unfamiliarity with language or concept. Like the scary cans of Gridlock energy drink.

She's not sure she will recognize the woman's face, but the jittery way she moved, she's pretty sure she would be able to spot that. So far, though, she hasn't seen anyone like her. She doesn't know how long she's going to keep coming back, or what she will do if she does see her. Tail her home, then call the cops, but what will they be able to do? Cate's flying blind, but does not like the idea of the woman being out there, on the loose. On the loose and possibly keeping an eye out for Cate. Or going back to Neale's.

She feels warm, beefy breath, then a slip of a tongue on her lowered forehead. She sits up and looks around to see Sailor has lost his small cohort. The two of them currently make up the entire population of the beach.

"Okay," she says, "you've definitely got a point." They walk together toward the car.

hypothermia

"Now?" Cate is pressed against a cold metal wall between stacks of boxes of eggs, coffee, cartons of half-and-half.

"Not yet."

She and Dana are in the cooler at Toaster. Dana has one of Cate's wrists pinned next to her head, part of an erotic strategy.

"Can you hold off a little longer?"

"I don't think so. I'm too close."

Dana pulls her hand out but only a little. "You can stop if you really try."

Both of them go completely still. Then all it takes is the slightest flicker of Dana's fingertips and Cate is there.

"Oh."

"There you are." Dana presses her forehead against Cate's collarbone. "Now you have to leave. Any second now, Felipé is going to come busting in here looking for coffee beans. He wouldn't care but he's a terrible gossip. And by terrible, I mean he tells everybody everything."

When they've gotten themselves together, just before Dana pushes the red ESCAPE button on the closed door, she looks unblinking at Cate. "I understand it might be hard for you to see. You have to come at it from a slight angle, but what I'm trying to do with you is honor this as something important. And I know I'm not doing a great job. But I can do better."

This is how Dana makes her crazy.

In spite of the back-and-forth to New York, Cate is trying to maintain the pieces of her life at home. Maureen is a piece. Sailor. Neale, even if she no longer wants to be an important piece. That Dana is even a piece at all is absurd, but there you have it.

Cate and Sailor spent last night at Maureen's. They cooked from a service that FedExes a box of gourmet, premeasured items along with instructions for making a dinner for two. This is like eating in a good restaurant, only you do all the work. Maureen thinks it's a fun thing for the two of them to do together, and it is undeniably a touching bit of domesticity. After dinner, they cleaned up the kitchen, then watched a movie with Sailor draped across both their laps. He's so long he's a laps dog. When Cate was on the sofa, under Sailor, snug against Maureen, both of them in plush "TV Sweaters" Maureen ordered off a commercial (as a joke, but still, they're wearing them), watching *Ben-Hur* (so Maureen could ridicule the costumes), everything seemed in its place. But then this morning, Cate pretended she had a 7 a.m. flight back to New York. She dropped off

Sailor at her apartment, picked up her travel bag, then told the Lyft guy to go down to Toaster, where Dana was at the change of shift and the two of them had maybe half an hour together before Cate ordered another Lyft, this time actually heading out to O'Hare in time to make her flight, which is actually at eight-thirty.

Here she is, finally pulling her life together:

She's a hero in a crisis.

She's working on what might be the biggest play of her career.

A fabulous dog has come to her out of thin air.

She has a real chance of making a relationship with an adult, also with a future.

Everything lately has been narrowing the space between who she is and who she would like to be. Yet with all this, she is nonetheless currently huddled in the musty back seat of a Lyft that smells as though a large animal has recently defecated, the event then masked with a spring bouquet spray. And her teeth are chattering hypothermically from twenty minutes inside a cooler with a woman who will never leave her girlfriend. Jody has Dana in every real-life way, while Cate and Dana are confined to small vignettes they've become adept at creating and decorating. What bewilders Cate is the potent distillate of emotion generated by these small pieces of time. She has little direct observation of Dana in the world. She has to study her small remarks and references. In the cooler, for instance, she asked if Cate was going to the Women's March.

Yes, she told her. The one here. With Neale and her mother and Joe. Did Dana think it was going to be big?

She thought so, and she was hoping it would make every person feel part of the bigness. The way unions work.

"I don't want to wear the pussy hat," Cate told her.

"Hat not mandatory," Dana said, and pressed a wrapped sandwich into Cate's hands. It now rests inside her backpack, on her lap,
inside the Lyft. Cate knows it will be egg salad made with duck eggs,
aioli, capers Dana pickled herself. Bread baked in an oven in back
that looks like the entrance to hell. The sandwich has to stand for so
much, there is such a burden on it.

flat white

Rooting around in an antiques shop in the Village, Cate has found a gnarly gilded picture frame. Perfect for Vita's living room. She can fill it with a portrait of some ancestor. Ancestors were something Vita wasn't short on. Cate really shouldn't be bringing this in herself. She has a prop master; this is technically his bailiwick. But sometimes she goes a little off-road, lured in by a thrift shop window. Cumulatively, over the years she has been extremely unthrifty in thrift shops.

Due to a small schedule snag, they have the theater for a luxurious two whole weeks before the play opens—now down to a week and a half. And after today, they will see how the sets hold the actors without confining them. That's always Cate's first priority.

Lauren spots the frame as Cate brings it in. She thinks it's possibly too ornate.

"We like your idea of the living room being overstuffed. But we want to stay shy of distraction."

Molly comes over. Cate assumes she's going to weigh in personally on the frame. Instead, she looks briefly at Cate and blinks a question to the surface. "Could you run and get me a coffee? A flat white?" It's a wonder no one has killed them by now.

Still, they are inarguably talented. Molly will give her opinion of the frame, just not right now. Their attention to detail is impressive; this is something Cate really likes about them, and might be a reason they picked her. She enjoys watching them roll the pieces around. Tiny, wobbly balls of mercury that attach to each other as they go, obtaining critical mass. This is the way they assemble plays that will be remembered, and win awards and get produced again and again. In this effort, they appear to have abandoned small courtesies that might siphon off their focus. They let everyone else recede to a pulsing blur, a blur emitting a soft gray noise. It's kind of hilarious how everyone is a gofer to them, fetching whatever while the two hold their vision aloft. Well, except for Gladys Banner, who, being a huge movie star, could have taken the play or left it. The play's success is not reliant on her, but her name on the marquee will pump up advance ticket sales. Gladys is not asked to run errands.

When Cate brings the coffee back from Hssss, an espresso shop around the corner, ferrying it with the enormous amount of balance necessary to not disrupt the skin of micro-froth on the top, she sets it on the binder resting semi-precariously on the arm of a fourth-row seat next to the one Molly occupies. (A few hours later, when Cate leaves the theater, she'll notice the coffee still in place where she set it down, the foam intact.)

They've loaded in the sets today. Two—Vita's living room and her garden—are already up on the gliding platforms. The less elaborate ones—the train station platform, the basement, Persia (two taxidermied camels; a large, shallow sandbox; a stationary sunrise at a horizon) await transfer. This afternoon Cate will time the stagehands switching the sets to see how the scene transitions might be speeded up. One of the pitfalls of multiple set changes is the collective blinking of cell phones lighting up the darkness so audience members can check the time. When that happens, you've broken whatever spell you've managed to create.

Cate is looking at the camels, which are a little more threadbare than she was hoping for. She'll have to find a rug to cover the bald spot on the worse one. Persia would not have given a diplomat's wife a mangy ride.

Cate is not going to have the luxury of being a creative diva on this production. She runs even the smallest adjustment past Lauren and Molly. They are her masters. If they want changes, even drastic ones, she nods and gets to work. Nonetheless, by the tiniest increments, they seem to trust Cate more, now leave small and middle-size choices to her. She can bring in a frame or a fuse box now, relatively unchallenged.

She sits down on a seven-step staircase, stairs to nowhere. Eating a bag of chips. Waiting for the arrival of one of these revisions, a change she herself suggested. Cate thinks Vita needs to be reading on a long sofa rather than on the love seat originally planned. A sofa is sexier, even if it's not being used for sex. A lot of the aura of this play is sex and its treacherous power, power derived from its societal suppression.

The metal grate of the elevator door screeches as it's pulled open, revealing a heavy, blood-red velvet sofa with slightly ragged fringe at the bottom. This will provide Vita a place where she can both sit and recline. She's going to be sitting and reclining with a number of girlfriends throughout the play. (One actress, Alex Shields, will play each of these women in turn. Her specific talent is taking on a character, vanishing into it. Here, she can disappear deftly into these characters with only wigs, hats, dresses, and voices.) Cate gets up and goes over to inspect the sofa. She asks Gladys to try it out. She's a little thrilled to be ordering around a megastar. Who takes the order, bounces onto the sofa, stretches out full length, then sits up with her legs crossed.

Ruby runs the same test, then turns to Cate, who left her bag of chips and a Mexican Coke on the steps behind them. "Might I have a crisp?" she asks, pointing. Ruby is in full costume as Virginia Woolf—long, nubby sweater, narrow tweed skirt, sturdy shoes, her hair "bobbed." She speaks in a high, reedy voice she says she has found in a rare recording of Woolf. She has dressed and spoken this way through every day of rehearsal. Like she's Daniel Day-Lewis on the set of *Lincoln*. Another piece of this verisimilitude is that she inhabits 1927. If you try to talk with her about something in the here and now, she looks at you with fake bewilderment. This makes her impossible to talk to or be normal with in any way. Cate doesn't even try. In this particular instance, she understands that Ruby is asking for a potato chip.

"Thanks awfully," Ruby says to the offered package, then pauses as she eats two chips. The pause is long enough that Cate is afraid she might be about to start a conversation, but then, mercifully, she walks off, twiddling her fingers next to her head. "See you on the morrow."

Cate moves through the shadows at the back of the stage, then climbs up into the lighting grid to get a bird's-eye view of the sofa, see how it works in the scene about to be rehearsed—a conversation between Vita and her husband, Harold. Their marriage is, at this point, purely companionate.

Judd Shoemaker, playing Harold, is a good physical match—a slight man, given heft by brogue shoes, a thick mustache, and a pipe. Before this, Cate has only seen him in movies. Onstage he has to project. He's skillful, though, and by now, toward the end of rehearsals, he has blended into this role. He smells of cherry pipe tobacco and tweed.

Harold has just come into their library; Vita is at a small writing table, intent on a note she's writing, scratching away with one of the fountain pens Cate found at the used-desk store.

HAROLD

Who's the favored recipient of that letter? Mrs. Campbell?
[Mary Campbell is a new interest of Vita's.]

VITA

No. The recipient is Mrs. Woolf.
[Vita is arranging the assignation with Virginia when Vita goes up to London. She will arrive half an hour early to meet Virginia in the basement. The scene lays out the terms of Vita and Harold's

philandering. Harold takes his pipe, knocks the ashes out of it into a
standing ashtray, and leaves it there. He sits on the arm of the sofa.]

HAROLD

Perhaps, between kisses, you might tell her I've a notion to
do a book on George Curzon, his postwar policies. I'm thinking Hogarth might be interested.

When Vita says nothing, just keeps scratching away with her
pen, he falls gracefully backward, onto the couch. Molly, in the front
row with Lauren, holds up a gnarly hand to stop the clock, then
hoists herself out of her seat and totters up the steps to the stage.

"Judd, I'd like you to do something a little faggy here. Just to
underline. Vita doesn't really have to do anything but look butch
and commanding. I think it would be good counterpoint if you did
something small that a straight man mightn't."

He gets up, goes back to the doorway, repeats his lines, falls
backward onto the sofa, this time crossing his legs at the ankles, as
he props them on the sofa arm.

"Perfect," Molly says. The scene moves on.

HAROLD

[*Stares at the ceiling.*]

Your silence, is it cloaking something we ought to talk
about? Is it, in fact, speaking volumes?

VITA

Well, perhaps one. A slender volume. You're going to scold
me now, aren't you?

HAROLD

I'm just saying you have to keep in mind that you don't have *la main heureuse* when it comes to other peoples' marriages. And you might want to be particularly careful with Virginia. She's really too mentally delicate for your hijinks. You wouldn't want to tip her over her edge. You might not see her advancing toward that, given there is so little in the way of edges for you.

VITA

No. I *do* think about that. But she's more the seductress in this than I. And for my part, it's such fun bringing romance to someone who hasn't had much of it before. I think she's surprising herself. And—

HAROLD

And—?

VITA

Well, I suppose part of *my* attraction to *her* is that she's a big silver fish. A prize.

Lauren interrupts from the third row. "Gladys. You're reading that line as though you mean it, which Vita doesn't. She's thirty, beautiful, titled, a popular author of her time, more popular than Virginia. So let's go over that line, and give it a reading that's blithe and slightly insincere."

Lauren knows exactly how she wants every line read. She wrote them and can hear them in her head. The cast is filled with terrific actors; the only weak link is Gladys, whenever called on to act queer. Which is kind of a big problem, in that she's the lead. The next day, Cate gets up some nerve and asks Molly if she and Lauren have a minute, that she has a small idea.

"Of course. We encourage our people to come forth with better ideas." The tone in which she says this indicates they never encourage this. That no idea could be better than theirs and that if it were, they wouldn't want to know about it. But now Cate is out on a limb and there's no way to scurry back down the tree.

Surprisingly she isn't put off to another time. They all three sit down on the red velvet sofa.

"The quick scene in the basement, where we project that flirty note above them? *'So I'll see you tomorrow, in the basement, and I'll be nice to you and you'll be very nice to me, won't you?'* What I was thinking was maybe the scene could be played without dialog. There's only a couple of lines before they kiss, and having total silence in that small space might increase the tension. Then Virginia, who wants this more, just moves her hands inside Vita's open coat, like you already have her doing, but neither of them says anything. They start to move in. Then, just as their lips are about to meet, the lights fade to black. The audience never sees the kiss. They're left in a state of anticipation, which is something like arousal, isn't it? The tiny pause just before something delicious."

Molly looks at Lauren in a telepathic way, then says, "Interesting idea. We'll try it out."

Cate is not accustomed to elation. She almost doesn't recognize it. At first she mistakes it for indigestion.

Later in the afternoon, she gets a glimpse of how Lauren and

Molly finesse suggestions that don't interest them. She is in the wings, working with two stagehands, packing a large trellis with fake white roses and five boxes of plastic greenery. Onstage, a read-through of a revised patch of the first act is happening at a collapsible (and slightly collapsing) table. Gladys is pitching a small, muted fit. She can't feel the line she is supposed to say at this point; she thinks the line is unnecessary.

"Would Vita directly tell Virginia she's busy with Mary Campbell? Wouldn't she couch something that would be so upsetting?"

Lauren says, "Yes, well, we all have our jobs here. You especially, your job is to be a perfect Vita. Mine is to write as near-to-perfect a script as I can. You are Vita as I wrote her, not as the person who lived. You'll need to keep that in mind as we move forward. Now, can we start with that line and go from there?"

Cate hopes to never be scolded like this.

Ty Boyd walks her back to her latest hotel. This one is plaid-free, but goes wrong in another direction. Two really old guys—visible through the door—are asleep on the lobby sofa.

"They must've cropped them out of the TripAdvisor photos," he says. "You can come back home with me. I have one of those blow-up beds."

"Thanks. I'll just take an Ambien and block out the room."

"You have my number if things get hairy at three a.m. Like if the walls start dripping blood. I know this play isn't happening at a good time for you, but life is so wily, so always out-of-order. Your situation is a lot like everyone else's, just kicked up a few notches. And you're doing fine here; Molly and Lauren are crazy about you. Sometimes a newcomer has the advantage. New York theater is a tight community, but sometimes a breath of fresh air is welcome exactly because of that. Sometimes we're all a little weary of each other.

"If you're interested, there'll be more work here for you. Even though you're a murderer. Maybe *because* you're a murderer. I think that gives you a certain stature. You're a little scary."

Cate senses she and Ty are at a tipping point. He appears to be pursuing a friendship. She has by now been to his apartment (a quietly dramatic scheme of gunmetal gray and Chinese red filled with hard-to-find pieces of low-end Americana—in other words, a temple in her religion); met his cat, Chris; eaten what he says is his best dinner offering, fish tacos. From here, the next steps would be small, then larger personal revelations, trust, a gossipy alliance. But she can't do it. She is by now too far outside almost everything and too low on social energy, and is not looking to be let in anywhere new.

"I'd better get up to my lovely room and hop on eBay," she tells him as a way of slipping free of their conversation. "I have some accessorizing ideas for Vita's living room."

She thought this hotel—slightly above her price range—would be better than the plaid hotel, but it's really just a different spin on awful. Everything in the room has either a scary sheen or a burnish. The color scheme (flamingo pink, gray, and mauve) and artwork (pinky-orange sunrise, or possibly sunset; it's hard to tell) suggests modulated grieving. The bedspread is a slippery grayish beige. Greige. She has folded it and put it in the closet.

She sits cross-legged on the bed with her laptop and a small plastic carton of couscous salad and shuts out the room around her. Instead she pushes her thoughts inside the play, which is the best thing she's worked on since Adam died. Once in a while, despite the antiquated nature of theater—all the fakery happening in the same room as its viewers—a really good piece can use this propinquity to intensify the audience's experience, make them forget where they parked their car. This is that play. Vita's serial womanizing could easily have been played for laughs, a sexual farce, but that's not what Lauren had in mind. Vita is just a vehicle for the confusion that comes from not being able to firmly stake an identity. And the pain that comes for those who lend their emotions to a shadow that lengthens, then recedes. This is not the story of damage done by a reckless lover, but by a society with ignorant, vigorously enforced conventions.

Once the furniture was loaded onto the sets today, Cate could see that Vita's living room—the biggest set, using both sliding platforms at once—could benefit from a few more details underlining who she was. A substantial stack of manuscripts, books by writer friends. Souvenirs from globetrotting. Definitely Persian cushions on the sofa. A hookah. A cheesy painting of the Grand Canyon, where she set one of her novels. An ashtray and cigarette caddy on the coffee table. She texts these to the prop master to see what he has, what they have to order. She is so grateful for something preoccupying to work on just now. Her thoughts these days are not her friends.

Which doesn't keep them from stopping by, particularly at night when she is too tired to fight them off.

A text coin drops in. Maureen.

start spreading the news . . .

(followed by an emoji of can-can dancers). Today Maureen has been firing off lyrics. It's a sort of thing she does.

you're leaving today . . .

Cate types, hoping a single reply will end this small dialog. She's too tired to get perky and creative just now, which isn't to say she doesn't appreciate the contact. Early on, their calls developed a hollow ring. Texting goes better. With texts they can steer around what Maureen clearly finds an unpleasant subject. She is beginning to tire of Cate's PTSD. ("I hate that you suffer from something that already has an acronym.")

And Cate can't really blame her. Enough repetition can flatten even a harrowing narrative. Maureen wasn't in the kitchen. She's sorry it all happened, of course, but mightn't it be time to move on, particularly with their relationship, which Maureen probably still hopes is spreading strong, sturdy roots beneath it? On this matter, she has moved a step or two beyond Cate. Sometimes Cate likes this. Other times she wishes she could stop Maureen until she's had time to catch up.

The texting does offer a jaunty flavor to the bad place in which Cate still too often finds herself. Sometimes, like tonight, she wakes up at two-thirty barely hanging on to a slippery rung above a space narrow and bottomless, where she finds, usually, an already-worn memory, but sometimes a whole, fresh, stinking scene being served up to her consciousness for the first time.

she's down on the floor, making the call to 911, at the same time trying to wipe blood off neale's face, which is already start-ing to swell, particularly around her left eye. she notices her own hands, the right in particular. the side of it along the thumb is caked with blood. the skin looks rusted. her palms are shiny and raw with a web of small cuts. half of one of her fingernails is torn off; she can't look at that. she goes very still, listening for the possibility that the woman is still somewhere in the house. she gets up and pulls a knife out of the block on the counter, then crouches next to neale, waiting for whatever comes next.

She pulls out of this, but can't lose its oily, metallic aftertaste. She calls the one person with whom she still (ludicrously) feels an open connection.

"Let me go back to the storeroom. We've only got one customer. A gentleman who has mistaken my restaurant for Starbucks. He's been on his laptop for an hour now. One cup of coffee." Then a few footsteps and the squeaky hinge of the swinging door to the kitchen, then its rubber flaps thwacking behind her, and she's back. "So, black thoughts again?"

"You think I only feel powerful. But I also feel smeared by the contact with him. Like now I'm soiled."

"I think it's probably hard on a person, being a killer. If you're a regular human, it pushes you out of any space you're used to. And

probably into a space the people around you are uncomfortable with."
She stops to take a drink from a bottle of water; Cate can see this
exactly, the way, when she's finished, the bottle drags away, tugging at
her lower lip. Then, "Honestly, I think all this drift will eventually go
away. But in the meantime you should definitely keep talking with
me about it. You really can't call me too much."

martinis

Cate backs up to get a distance perspective on the overstuffed bookcase flat. Looking good. She pulls on her down jacket. She goes out by the stage door, leaving only the ghost light on. The ghost light is never shut off, an old, old tradition, to give the ghosts who inhabit the theater light to put on their own shows.

She lets the metal door slam shut behind her, then looks both ways up and down the alley. She no longer moves into any new space without calculation. She checks directions on her phone and heads out to the bar. She's been summoned by Molly. The bar is called Dean Martini. It's not particularly close to the theater or to Cate's hotel; there's an Uber ride involved. Odd-hour phone calls have been part of her job description for the past couple of weeks, but until now, late-night drinks have not. Tonight Cate is in New York, and Molly needs someone to talk to. She and Lauren have batted something around too many times. They need an outside opinion; can Cate meet her?

———

Molly sits still as a Buddha in a red leather booth near the back of the bar, under a blowup of Dean Martin in a tuxedo with his black tie undone. He's rakish. He's on the sound system singing "Baby It's Cold Outside." She is sitting behind the remains of a straight-up martini, wearing some delicious cologne that smells like lilac and woodsmoke. Cate had kind of forgotten about cologne. She might have to revisit that. Molly does older well—stylish but with little old-fashioned touches. Her watch is a rectangle with a dark yellow face, brown leather band about to tear at the buckle. Very 1940s. Of course, just wearing a watch at all is pretty twentieth century.

She makes a swishing motion for Cate to slide in across from her, then orders for both of them by signaling the bartender with two raised fingers. Cate's not much of a hard-liquor drinker, but the martini moment seems to be at hand. When drinks arrive, Molly takes her speared olive and drops it into Cate's glass. A flirty gesture, but inconsequential. Cate supposes Molly has dropped olives into the martinis of many women along her way. In forward motion, she seems much younger than her seventy-plus years. She's a dynamo. But at the end of what has been a long day directing, she is weary. Her color is slightly drained, her cheeks sag into slight pouches at the sides of her mouth. This makes her more human, definitely less iconic.

"Houston," Molly says, "we have a problem."

"Gladys." It's not a wild guess.

"In almost every respect, she's doing a great job. She's command-ing, but also blockheaded. Her Vita is totally heartless and oblivious.

But when sex comes into the picture, well, you can see she's playing Vita like an old letch. I actually caught her wiggling or whatever her eyebrows. Like Groucho Marx. She just needs a cigar to wag. Wiggle and wag. How do I make her stop? I can't just bully her. I think of all those tickets bought on the basis of her presence in the play. I can't afford to have her leave in a huff."

Cate takes a sip of her martini: it's vaguely but not unpleasantly medicinal. She thinks for a few beats. "Gladys is straight. It might be simply that she's not a good enough actor to imagine herself into the role and doesn't have a model for the kind of seduction Vita was wielding. Assertive but not aggressive. Maybe you could ask her to think about removing testosterone from the equation. Also to think about sex between two people who already know what's in the offing, who don't have a gender wall they can hide tricks behind. They have the rabbit and the hat, not the rabbit *in* the hat."

"That's good. That's very good. That might be a path. All this reading I've been doing, I'm starting to think Vita was more concerned with flowers and houses than humans. That fucking country house. Three hundred sixty-five rooms and a deer park. Why did her ancestors need all that space? Maybe they had a lot of company?"

Cate says, "They didn't want to have to haul out the blow-up bed in the family room."

"The house was her true obsession, but it went to her cousin Eddy. First male in the line. But really, couldn't he have given her maybe fifty rooms and her own entrance? She could have mowed the lawn in exchange? Okay. So. Gladys. Tomorrow after rehearsal you should take Gladys out for drinks. I'll tell her it's going to be the three of us, then I won't show up. I'll text you that my thumb is sore, or my dog is puking. Then you'll be alone with her and roll into your argument about the difference with same-sex seduction—"

"My argument is definitely brilliant, but I think you're the one who's going to have to make it. I'm the set designer. I can order a longer sofa because Gladys's legs are overhanging the chaise. But you're the director. So I'm afraid you're the one who has to direct her out of her misery." Cate loves that she can talk to Molly like this. "Just tell her she can lean back a little. Her Vita will still get the girls."

Molly's thoughts move on a little. "I'm more than a generation older than you. My coming out was made quite difficult by the general ignorance that prevailed back then. Some of it happened in dyke bars that still had peepholes in the door. You know, knock three times. A lot of dykes hid for their whole lives inside marriages of convenience to men. Or shared apartments and their lives with *roommates*. I came into my sexuality in shadows that were dissolving, but they were still there. Shadows of shadows. Vita was even farther back, my grandmother's generation. She was bold, but she still had to toe the line. She was an aristocrat, she had a small title and a famous garden. She had the Queen Mother over for wine and truffles, for crying out loud. I hate that this conversation with Gladys falls to me, but Lauren's wary of busting her chops anymore. And you, you turn out to be a total chickenshit."

It is kind of satisfying to see that even when you are Molly, you have to deal with people who are more arrogant than you are. It's something to keep in mind. Cate watches her drain her martini. Her eyes water a little as she does this. The gin has entered her central nervous system. But also, Cate can see, the two of them are inching toward a camaraderie.

Molly says, "By the way, how are you doing?"

"How do you mean?"

"Well, didn't you just kill someone in Chicago?"

polka favorites

Graham puts a finger to his lips as Cate comes in. He points—
dot dot dot—to his phone and computers and the ceiling; she
always takes the last to mean the satellites roaming the stratosphere,
scooping up private data. Cate isn't impervious to his paranoia. By
now she has a tiny paper circle taped over the camera in her laptop.
She texts with an encrypted app.

He puts on a new CD—*Polka Favorites*—to white out whatever
conversation they're about to have. He seems alarmingly alert today.
He's wearing a gray gas station suit like the ones on the characters in
the play he's writing.

"How's it going in here?" A question Cate feels obliged to ask but
is afraid to hear answered. Most striking, he's cut his hair. It's basically gone, except for a military, flattop buzz cut. She tells him, "I'm
having trouble processing your hair. I'm going to need a little time."

He doesn't want to talk about hair. "Do you remember, in *1984*, how Winston Smith can only escape the camera in his apartment by slipping into a far corner of the living room and that he can't stay there, out of sight, for very long or he will draw suspicion? That's where we're heading. A few years ago we thought, Oh cool, all the information in the world at our fingertips. How easy, how *convenient*! We can trace the movements of criminals, find our high school friends, do a little light stalking of old lovers, store our credit card information, get the results of our latest cholesterol test. We were so innocent and happy. We weren't thinking about the reciprocity, that we were also giving ourselves over to whoever was interested. And I think some people don't mind that, and most people mind a little but have no idea how to shut off the spigot and a few people, like me, are a lot bothered by it and are looking for ways to short-circuit the worst of the prying. And finding a place to be unwatched. A place bigger than the far corner of the living room that the camera can't see."

Cate sits down on the floor, next to Sailor, who pushes his long nose into her armpit.

"I understand your concerns, I really do. But I'm not sure anyone's going to be able to stem the information flow. It's worrisome, but so are the depletion of the oceans and the melting ice caps. The lunatic weather and how it's being ignored for short-term profits. The perpetual wars. And in the middle of everything scary and tricky, I'm trying to live my one life. This is the place and time in the world where I came in, and sometimes there's too much to deal with. And now that too much includes my post-traumatic flippage. I'm not in here with you that much, and I worry that you're in here all the time, sinking under the weight of your massive knowledge. Come out with me. Get some fresh air. We can take Sailor, open the windows. Go down the drive, then swing back up. We can hit the drive-thru at McDonald's and get him a cheeseburger. Half an hour, *max*. Does that sound manageable?"

"Okay," he says. Then, "Not today, though."

Maureen has given Cate the name of a therapist for Graham— expensive she says, but good. Cate raises this possibility. "It would just be someone for you to talk with. Just small air holes punched into the top of the box."

"I talk to you every day. And Lucille Rae, and Ed."

Cate doesn't ask who Ed is. Why, really? He doesn't mention Eleanor. She doesn't know if this is good or bad.

"Two years ago you would have thought someone living your life was terribly depressed."

Sailor has been sitting up between them, his head turning from one of them to the other, as though he's watching a tennis match. But now he goes under the table. He doesn't like it when talk gets a certain kind of serious, sharp at the edges. They think his previous home contained a lot of arguments. Also a lot of salads. If any salad is left on the table, he eats all of it, then licks the carton or bowl. They've tried to extrapolate his previous life from clues he gives them. From the salads and the arguments, they think his former humans might have been corporation lawyers. Shitty corporation lawyers who left him off in the exercise yard by the shelter, closed the gate, and that was that. What did he think, watching them drive away? Until then, he thought they were his best friends. Cate can't hold on to this image for too long. All the time people send her videos of rescued dogs and how happy they are now. Like a dog so frightened by his past that he stands facing a yellow wall, his nose an inch away. He just stands there. Then he's shown in his new happy home playing with another dog. *Isn't this heartwarming?* the sender will say. But all Cate can see is the dog staring at the yellow wall.

"Let's talk in upbeat tones," she says.

"Okay. Here's the thing!" Graham says, in the voice of a balloon-making children's entertainer. "I'm just not all that interested in what's going on outside. Taking Sailor for walks fills my need for the out-of-doors. AND SAILOR IS SUCH A GREAT DOG! I can see that you still find things to go out for, but I'm not there anymore. I'm someplace way elsewhere."

"That kind of thinking is agoraphobia."

"I've already been to the agora. It's always the same stuff on sale. The same people walking around. It's repetitious. Maybe if the agora was in Morocco. But I don't want to waste my time being outside just for the sake of appearing normal. I have too much to do in here." He gestures. "Just to keep up. I'm falling behind."

She stops and imagines how much fear-inspiring material must exist stacked in the corners of a billion spare rooms and basement offices, files within files within files on laptops, also in shaded corners of the web itself. It would be so easy to get lost in there. The other day she was doing a little research for the play, looking up the destruction from bombing around the countryside of Kent during World War II. Which led her to the small vials of prussic acid Vita and Harold kept in case the Germans prevailed. The hope being they would never have to catch that final whiff of almonds. Then from there to the cyanide capsules given as the war was ending to German citizens who didn't want to face the rough justice the Russian soldiers were going to mete out. Women who didn't want to be raped a hundred times. Then it's just a hop, skip, and a jump over to "Hitler: The Missing Years, 1945–1965." Time to close the box. She can do this, but for Graham the box is always open, beckoning.

She hopes that a year from now he won't still be in here, with four instead of three desktop monitors. That he'll be on to a better phase of his life, not underbathed and buzz-cut and still sitting in her spare bedroom.

pussy hat

Cate is not going to wear the hat. She is extremely unhappy with the new president and fired up to be marching in protest of his election, and thrilled with the size of the crowd they join coming up out of the el at Jackson, but she's not going to wear the hat. She thinks it brings the symbolic discourse down to his level. She doesn't want this to be a problem between her and the person who knitted the hat for her, but it has started them off on the wrong marching foot. And then there is also this person's—Maureen's—sign to contend with. It features the president groping the Statue of Liberty. While its message is sound, its graphic is a little, well, graphic. Cate walks a short way off, to distance herself from the sign.

two-flat

The two-flat is in Bucktown. It belongs to Dana's aunt. She owns the building, lives on the top floor, and spends the winters in Tampa. Dana checks the apartment to water the African violets and goes down to the basement to make sure no pipes have burst or pilots gone out. This is the first time she has brought Cate along. She has shut down Toaster for the night, but hasn't told Jody. This is unprecedented and carries a certain amount of risk, which Cate takes note of.

They have until morning. Cate has ducked out on Maureen, who was planning to fix cacio e pepe and put *Mad Max: Fury Road* on her giant flat-screen. Cate loves cacio e pepe, really loves Charlize Theron, and of course especially loves her with a phantom arm. She has replayed quite a number of times on YouTube the part where Charlize undoes the leather straps of her prosthesis and lets it drop onto the postapocalyptic sand. She basically thinks *Fury Road* is a masterpiece, so this was an extremely generous offer considering

Maureen does not like violent movies and thinks Charlize Theron is too hot (whatever that means). So Cate feels bad about saying no, but opens up a big box of lies anyway. She'd love to come over but can't. Her mother is throwing a work party up at her house, to launch the spring season. Although the spring season in retail does start in January, the party is imaginary.

Cate and Dana are both shy coming into the small foyer.

"Wow," Cate says, craning her neck, taking in as much of the hall and living room as she can. A recliner facing the TV. A medium-size Arc de Triomphe, also a Leaning Tower lamp so large it could only have been bought in Pisa and dragged back here. There's more. A poster with LOVE spelled out in blocks. A kitten dangling from a clothesline with HANG IN THERE typed across the bottom. "Your aunt, it looks like she's cornered the global market on cheesy souvenirs and bad Pop art from the sixties and seventies."

"Oh no you don't. No professional snobbery here. This is borrowed decor. We're not here to give it a rating."

The evidence suggests Aunt Vicky is a woman deep into creature comforts. She has a giant bed facing a second giant flat-screen TV. She has also managed to fit a whirlpool into the house's small bathroom. The tub has a terry-covered plastic pillow suctioned to one side. Several slinky Polynesian-print robes hang from hooks on the inside of the door. On a shelf above the toilet sits a complex machine that plays ambient sounds while it heats herbal oils.

In the whirlpool, Dana grabs hold of one of Cate's toes and says,

"How's it going with you, mental-wise? I worry maybe you're getting exhausted just trying to hold it together."

"It comes and goes. I'm fine, fine and then instead of fine, I'm freaking out. And then I'm not freaking out but I'm very sad that people like them exist in the same world as Neale. That their sort of wicked foolishness can take down a really good person."

"Oh, I think you won the round. And I think Neale's going to be okay only *because* you won it."

"But really, nobody was a winner coming out of that kitchen. I'm made of something different now and it's not just stronger, it's way bleaker. And Neale, I can see her folding in on herself, and I hate that. And I can't help. I know she loves me and appreciates my taking time out of my busy day to save her, but also I'm the only witness to her humiliation. If I weren't around, she could put it all away more easily."

"I think your friendship is so much bigger than what happened. I think you just have to give it time to recuperate."

And then Dana is quiet. This is one of the things Cate likes best about her, that she doesn't have to fill pauses. She can sit inside them.

After a while of letting the water roil around them and the aroma machine pump out little blasts of vetiver, letting Dana's cell phone stream Nina Simone's cover of "Here Comes the Sun," Cate says, "Let me take you to bed. A giant bed."

They have plenty of time for everything. Sex and foreplay and after-glow. Now they are searching for small scars and the stories behind them. Dana inspects Cate's finger stumps in detail, then comes up with a way Cate can put them to use. They make love naked. Naked is rare, given their usual opportunities where even horizontal is a bonus. With her clothes off Dana is impressive. Thick in a way that's about muscle gravity, like a gleaner in the Millet painting. Cate closes her eyes and trails her fingers over hard calves, little trapezius bumps at the top of Dana's shoulders. But it's not so much about parts as about the whole, the way Dana occupies herself.

Dana says, "You miss the traction of those potato sacks under you."

But Cate has lost the ability to see their connection as light-hearted and storeroom-specific. "I feel too much in this. I'm emotionally ridiculous. What we have is totally concocted. Stolen moments. Midnight meetings. Sex that has to carry all the freight because we don't have any regular everyday connection. We're not building a history together. Affairs don't have a history. They're on the calendar in invisible ink."

Dana considers this. "I don't think we're an affair. If we brought this out into real life, had the time to go grocery shopping together and plug into each other's families, go through old photos, if we had all that, it would just be surround to a center we've already created together—that we've made ourselves known to each other. I've never done that before. I've always held back something. This is new to me. So of course I'd like to see more of you. And I'd like to not be worried that this takes something away from Jody. But I'm mostly just so happy that someone gets me, that I've been able to show myself and you've shown yourself to me. I think we already have that foundation."

———

Later, when they get to thinking about food, Dana goes into her aunt's kitchen and makes them burrata salads with heirloom tomatoes. She brought a stocked Igloo cooler.

"Oh yes," Cate says. "Cream stuffed into cheese. Like the upscale version of the deep-fried butter at the Kane County Fair."

"This kitchen is tragic," Dana says as she goes through her aunt's cabinets. "Her spices are seasoned salt and garlic powder. Look in her freezer—she's got a bargain bucket of strawberry ice cream. Frosty Fun. And a summer camp–size package of hamburger. She didn't even break it into smaller packets she might be able to use. It's just a meat raft in there. I need to come over here more when she's around."

They are wearing just their shirts, butts sticking to the vinyl dinette chairs around the small, yellow Formica-topped table. Ciabatta crumbs drift down on Dana's breasts as she tries to explain her life with Jody.

"I don't know how it all happened so fast. We moved in together. We got two cats."

"Salty and Pepper," Cate says.

"I hate that I ever told you that. The thing is, you'd like her if you two met."

"It doesn't matter whether I'd like her. I'm never going to have that opportunity. I don't even want to drag you out of your relationship with her. I feel bad enough seeing you behind her back. What I want is for you to have been free and clear when we met."

"You can only see this from your side. From your perspective, things aren't moving fast enough, but toward what? What makes you think if we had each other free and clear it would be better than what we have now? What if what I give you is the best I've ever given anyone? Why would a conventional relationship necessarily be better? Maybe we put so much value on this *because* of its limitations." Then she gets very quiet, then takes Cate's hand and leads her back upstairs to bed.

"Lie exactly on top of me. Press me down." Then, "This. This is it."

They stay this way for a while, pancakes on a plate; then Cate pushes herself up, away from Dana, looks down on her. "I know this is important to you. I get that. And that nothing stays the same. But doing it this way makes me feel bad about myself. The higher I feel when I'm with you—*stoned in paradise,* you know, like the song— the lower I sink in my own esteem. I have to stop."

"Yes. I know," Dana says as she reaches down around the backs of Cate's knees and pulls them apart, slowly.

Cate's phone makes the coin-drop sound. Maureen.

how's the party going? send a pic.

Cate rolls off Dana, then sits cross-legged on the bed, stumped.

A pause, then the phone rings—Maureen deciding she needs to communicate more directly. Cate and Dana watch as the phone keeps ringing, which is to say, as it keeps playing "Danny Boy," the special ringtone Maureen put on so Cate will know it's her.

"I can't answer," Cate says. "There's supposed to be a party in the background. I hate this new personal-surveillance state. More and more, I'm starting to think like Graham."

"You have to go to the last line of defense. Say your phone ran out of juice. That'll give us until tomorrow, then call her back."

"I know I have to do something about this. Maureen was part of my Plan C and I seem to have tossed that plan over the side. And I don't think there's a Plan D. I have to let her know all this. Just not while I'm sitting naked next to you in your aunt's bed."

Then they watch silently as the phone winds its way through the ring's last notes—*and down the mountainside.*

symphony

They—Cate and Neale and Joe—are at the symphony. It's intermission. Neale has gotten tickets to the premiere of an avant-garde cello concerto featuring extraneous sounds piped in along with the music made by the orchestra. Maybe, Neale is hoping, these sounds will qualify as noise.

They are in the top balcony, but the front row of it. So, pretty good cheap seats. Joe sits between Neale and Cate. As soon as the intermission began, he pulled out his phone to watch an obscure French movie. Since what happened to his mother, he cloaks himself in silence; it's a hoodie cloak, with earbuds. He's not available for comment. His people will talk to your people. Later.

Something new has moved into the space between him and Cate, and she suspects it's her attachment to his mother's assault. It doesn't matter that Cate's part was stopping it. She was there. She saw it. It's stuck to her. She's dirty by association. She hopes this is a phase

they will pass through, that there will come a time when her presence doesn't carry the smell of the kitchen that day when he walked
in, after everything was over, onto a stage littered with props from
the previous scene. The spilled groceries, eggs drooling out of their
shells, milk carton busted. A plastic bag of fun-size Snickers torn
open with the candy bars scattered along with some empty wrappers. Meaning they ate candy while the whole thing was going on.
They fucking ate candy.

"Going to the john," he says as he climbs over their knees.

Cate puts a hand on Neale's. "I've been going by the Aldi."

"Have you seen her?"

"Not yet."

"You should stop. If she was going to come back at me, she
would've done it by now. It's over. Don't keep it alive. We need to
move along. On our merry way."

isle of mull

She and Maureen have perfected the rituals of dating but haven't really moved beyond them. And lately Maureen has dropped mentioning hypothetical moves forward in even the middle-distant future. Maybe she has grown wary. The only event they've pinned to their horizon is the trip in May to Scotland. They sit on the floor this night in February looking over travel magazines and guidebooks opened and scattered across Maureen's coffee table.

"Look at this castle on Mull!" Cate tries to pin an exclamation point on this sentence, hoping to convey excitement, but doesn't quite pull it off. Their tickets have been bought; they've booked a small cabin on a small ship run by a company specializing in educational tourism. Maureen's news tonight is that she has upgraded them to a bigger cabin on the ship; the theme park costumes she's designing have turned out to be a bonanza for her.

Maureen does not look at the castle. Instead she says, in a tone that applies a sympathetic overlay on exasperation, "By May, you'll probably be in more of a vacation mood."

"I know *yes* would be the best response here, but the truth is I don't know what kind of mood I'll be in a couple of months from now. Or even tomorrow. Too much is going on. In my life, but also in my head. Do you remember that carnival ride? I don't know why I'm reminding you about old carnival rides. Your father probably built one in your backyard. So it was a cylinder and you strapped yourself standing against the inside wall. And then it started spinning and then it started tilting—"

"The Round-Up!"

"Exactly. But you don't fall forward off the wall. On account of centrifugal force. That's me. I'm spinning, but the spin is what's keeping me from peeling off the wall. That's kind of why I don't want to see that therapist you recommended." Maureen has therapist recommendations in the same way she has a stash of pills for every minor mood problem. "I'm sure she's brilliant, but I know she's going to want to slow down the ride. And I'm afraid that's when I'll fall off."

Maureen doesn't say anything. Cate wishes she would say something indicating she gets it. But she doesn't. Her mouth is moving around a little from side to side. As though she's sucking on a small, intensely flavored candy. Cate tries to wait this out, but in the end, blinks first.

"Do you think we should sign up for the day tour of the famous whiskey distillery?" These sentences are so difficult to form. Her dread of the trip moves sluggishly through her veins. She's not sure if it's the trip, or the implication it holds that she and Maureen will still be together in a distant May. What so recently looked like the stable, portion-controlled life she was aspiring to now comes with a sense of suffocation.

Maureen has been maybe three of the four pushpins holding Cate's Plan C to the wall. She rounds up a few doubts and tries to give her the benefit of them. So her ethics are a little sketchy. So for a while she was going steady with her sister. So what, really? Nobody's perfect. She still often enjoys Maureen's company, and if she's circumspect, she could hang on to that without giving up the small, secret piece of Dana she has. She just has to keep Dana in a back pocket. As soon as she has formed this thought she's ashamed of it. If she were the truly decent human she'd like to be, she'd be honest about what's going on. Which would be the beginning of the end of her and Maureen. But she's not there yet.

She doesn't know what to hope for. A bittersweet breakup in April? A quarantine put on all the Hebrides, Inner and Outer, on account of some species-jumping sheep pathogen? Maureen helpfully moving on to someone else? Maureen catching Cate sneaking around with Dana? Even that would be better than Cate having to introduce the matter of breaking up in some quiet conversation in a private place, a conversation begun with throat clearing. Tonight would be a perfect opportunity, but she just can't do it. Tonight will not be even a slim chapter in her autobiography: *Profiles in Courage.*

Then it's Maureen who clears her throat. "I feel terrible about this, but the thing is I'm not going to be able to come to New York for your opening night. ZordorWorld is opening that weekend. They're freaked out about costume malfunctions. There will be a hundred and eighty employees rigged up as intergalactic functionaries, and so they figure something will for sure go wrong, and I need to be there when that happens. I'm so sorry, honey."

Here is where human life gets ridiculous. After all her internal distancing, instead of being relieved in this moment, Cate finds herself a little miffed that Maureen is blowing off her big moment.

opening night

Usually Cate stays with a play through the first or second pre-view night. If everything is going smoothly, her work is done. With *Blanks*, though, she wants to see the impression it makes on the opening-night crowd, spot the critics, count the curtain calls, duck the champagne corks popping at the after-party. It's a beautiful, fragrant nocturnal flower. She wants to be there when it unfolds.

An hour before the theater doors open, she's double-checking the tech they're using to project Vita's letters of seduction, passion, and eventual dismissal onto a sepia screen above the writing tower where Vita (her body double is Ally Wilber, a totally unfamous actress with a long, bony frame) sits at her desk, her back to the audience, writing on an iPad. Ally is in place now, fooling around, writing, *Fuck you and the horse you rode in on*, over and over.

"Whatever size you have now," she tells the tech guy who's running the projection, "Double it." Then, "Yes. Perfect."

From there she goes onstage to unnecessarily fuss with some
fake clematis climbing the tower wall. She's just burning off nervous
vapors, like everyone else. Backstage, the air is alive with hope and
vanity. Molly and Lauren are in a tight huddle with Judd Shoemaker,
working on a small dialog revision for Harold Nicolson. Costumes
are checked back and front. Ruby Pepper tries to engage Cate in a
silly bit of conversation.

"I've just rushed down here by the tube," she says in an annoying
impersonation of someone out of breath.

"Right," Cate says. She seriously doubts the London Underground even existed in Virginia Woolf's time. She waits until Ruby
is gone, then Googles it, and unfortunately finds it opened in 1863.
Still, she has a hard time picturing Virginia hanging from a strap
next to someone eating "crisps" from a bag.

When she sees Gladys coming out of her dressing room in fit-
pitching mode about something or other, Cate decides to get up out
of the oncoming fray and climbs to her reliable perch, the fly gallery,
to watch the audience settle in. She's not expecting to see anyone
she knows. Maureen is at the amusement park. Neale is feeling too
fragile to navigate crowded airports. This seemed reasonable when
she announced it, and Cate said she totally understood, but really,
she doesn't. She took it as one more piece of the distance Neale has
been throwing between the two of them.

Then, midway through her scan, in one of the back rows of the
orchestra floor, on the aisle stage left, she sees Dana. Or someone
she thinks is Dana, but Cate's desire that it be Dana fills in the rest.
She can't be sure, because she can't make out details at this distance,
and then the house lights are dimming and the curtain is going up
on Vita's living room. The old phone, heavy as a blacksmith's anvil,

goes off on the end table, its huge, jangly ring drawing Vita, hand-some in breeches, in through the garden door to pick up the receiver and shout, a little breathless, "Hullo? Yes? Well you see I was all the way down by the moat" to begin the play.

Looking down on her work as the play rolls out, sets thick enough to accommodate big characters, she is happier than she's been in a long time. She holds still a moment to feel her accomplishment. She designed these sets. She'll get to make others for plays as good as this one. She saved her friend. She has a fabulous dog. Dana is possibly sitting in a partially obstructed seat at the back of the theater.

When the lights come up for intermission, the bad seat occupied by the real or imagined Dana is empty. Cate goes out to the lobby, then onto the sidewalk in front of the theater, then into the crush in the ladies' room, but she's nowhere to be found. The mystery buzzes inside her in a low register through the rest of the play, and through the after-party until she is exhausted, on her way to the hotel in a cab, when it occurs to her that Dana—if it *was* her—has moved to the unsupervised area of the playground.

erasure

She comes home looking forward to spooling out her success for Graham. The reviews of the play have been mostly terrific. (One from a theater site was so critical, though, it set everyone off their pins until they agreed to gently set it aside as a peculiar outlier, a singed edge on their success.) Two print reviews singled out Cate's sets for praise. Molly and Lauren want to talk with her about something new. She's coming in on a high, but also agitated. She needs Graham's gravity and Sailor's happiness just for her being happy.

But Sailor isn't swishing back and forth on the other side of the apartment door, and doesn't come out from Graham's room. She goes in to look. The room has been cleared out. Cleared. The stupendous bed is gone, the folding tables and rolling office chair. The Ikea bureau. The garments that had been hanging in the closet. There's a surgical look to the scene. He probably wiped his DNA off the light switch.

A note is stuck to the door.

> Sailor's at Eleanor's.
> Can you pick him up soon?
> Thanks for everything.

Her cell announces a new message, this one on the latest encrypted app Graham installed on her phone. She opens it; it's a photo of him, an old picture she took during an early stretch of their marriage. A farm field in Michigan where they stopped once for him to pose in front of a creepy rural oddity. A brick right triangle poking out of the ground, a door on its high end. Clearly an enclosure covering the steps of a staircase going down into the ground, ground situated in the middle of nowhere.

And then the photo dissolves and the message never existed.

vue du lac

At the toll plaza, she takes Sailor out for a quick spin, puts him back in the car. "I will be three minutes, tops," she tells him. "Don't start barking like a maniac."

In the ladies' room, she's washing her hands when she feels a swift sliver, a whippy little breeze touching what she has come to think of as her new exposure. She checks to see what's reflected in the wall's length of mirrors. Regular women, one old but dressed like a teenager, one with two small kids she's trying to fit into a stall with her because they're too young to be left alone. So, all in all, a normal roadside population.

Before that afternoon in December, she was blissfully myopic, unaware that she might need to look over her shoulder; or sideways, into doorways as she came up on them. Or to scan the mirrors in a restroom. She used to walk leisurely through parking garages, even deserted ones, even at night. She stopped to help when approached by strangers on the street wanting directions. Now a heavy velvet curtain has risen, revealing all around her a lively pageant of possible danger. She not only sees it, but feels it whispering over her skin, as though, even when she's fully dressed, a fresh patch of nakedness has presented itself. The very peculiar thing is that this doesn't make her frightened; rather, it enlivens her.

Back in the car, she drives up through southern Wisconsin, also through March. The bleakness adherent to the month is that although the Midwestern winter is past its most brutal stretch, everyone is by now beaten down, and late assaults land on what's already bruised. A fresh cold snap holds no bracing novelty. Leftover snow is by now a pewter color that, on too many days, matches the sky. Eventually, though, at some point in March, winter gets broken. That happened yesterday. Today a watery sun hangs in a pale sky. Cate puts down all the windows so she and Sailor can smell the earth thawing on both sides of the highway.

After getting off I-90, Cate winds chaotically around Madison a little ("*Recalculating. At your next opportunity, make a U-turn,*" says the nonjudgmental WAZE voice) before finding Neale's address. The apartment is on the third story of a tan brick building in a complex of maybe twenty units with a developer-generated, meaning-free name—Wainscot Village—a featureless box fronted by a parking lot with covered spaces.

"Come on," she says to Sailor, opening the door on his side. "Time to get social."

Vestigial blue salt crunches under her feet on the metal stairs that run between the sections of the building. Sailor lags behind, peeing on several of the bushes that form a sort of hedge between the lot and the building.

"Hey you!" she calls down to him and he focuses and follows.

When they get to the door, Cate hears big life on the other side. Different sorts of clatter. Plates and silverware. Cabinets snapping shut with light thwaps. Voices without clear words. Orders given and taken, then laughter. Inside, Neale and Joe and Claude are getting ready for her. It's half past noon; lunch is assembling. And though the assembly is on her behalf, she pauses before pressing the doorbell. She fears that even with the door opened she will feel just as shut away from Neale, that this visit is a formality to firm up the lie that their friendship is still solid—a lie Neale has been heavily promoting ever since she decided to make this move. Cate hates these conversations.

She rings the bell and the door opens, revealing such a happy Neale—"Come in, come in, oh you look great"—pulling Cate by the hand.

Claude is working at the kitchen island, slicing hard-boiled eggs, then fanning the slices open, one to each plate of also-fanned lettuce leaves, next to small stacks of green beans. He looks up and smiles, flashing teeth blindingly white, endearingly crooked.

"Cate."

He's such a handsome guy, more so even than when he and Neale were together. Five years of meditation and organic gardening have left him sculpted in that yogi way and glistening with peace. He and Neale are wearing stretchy yoga outfits. They are, Neale explains, just back from teaching a Saturday afternoon couples class. Both of them are working at two local studios while they get their act together to open one of their own. Madison, they both think, is a town with deep, under-tapped yoga potential.

"He's arranging our salads," Neale explains. "Because he's French. No careless tossing for them. Take off your parka, give it to me, do you want something to drink?" Cate was just about to grab a can of pop from the refrigerator, the way she always does. But then she remembers this is a different household. She tacks around, stays put, and says, "By 'something to drink,' do you mean a juice that's bluish green?"

"I got diet ginger ale for you. I'm the perfect hostess. Do you want ice?"

"Why not?"

Neale grabs ice cubes out of the freezer, inadvertently putting herself in the way of Claude's reach for something on a high cabinet shelf. He kisses her at the temple, just a brush of lips. For some reason, Cate didn't factor romance into Claude's return. She thought that part was all over for them, that the new arrangement was just about calming things down for Neale, and helping out with Joe. This doesn't make Cate jealous exactly, but it does prompt a need to cheer herself up with a little schadenfreude, which means scanning all of the apartment's terrible design elements.

Everything is tricky here, pretending to be what it's not. Pressboard cabinets with a "walnut" veneer. Formica in a "granite" pattern. White metal folding closet doors with a "wood" grain. Windows with plastic inserts to make the glass look paned. Everything removed miles and miles from the walnut forest and the Italian granite quarry and the old-world mullion shop. Although the apartment does exist in the physical world, it is in a way, virtual. The air is thin—warm and dry as it comes out of the floor vents. She can see that Neale has tried to overlay this bleak rental unit with domestic touches that wouldn't have occurred to her back in her old house, where function was the only consideration, where form didn't even bother to follow.

Here, though, a fake fireplace has been filled with a grate and an arrangement of birch logs that will never be burned. On the far wall, though, a sliding glass door to a balcony reveals a real fire inside a small grill, which is currently aglow with coals. Claude goes out and slaps on two tuna steaks and sits on a bent lawn chair to oversee their progress from raw to raw-but-seared.

He knocks on the glass and waves Cate outside.

"We have, you see, a *très belle vue du lac.*" And he's technically correct. A narrow strip of lake is definitely visible between two other apartment buildings jammed in closer to the water. Which is very still, the ice just having melted. Neale complained on the phone about the saws of local ice fishermen, saying she'd probably be bitching about the engines of powerboats in the summer. But today all is very blue and still.

Rationally, Cate understands Neale's move. Everything she has done to put space and change between herself and the assault is understandable. Although Cate was there to save her, she was not reliably around once *Blanks* started sucking her away. Meanwhile, Neale couldn't be alone—how could she be? So she got free of the city and her neighborhood and her house and her hovering parents, grabbed a husband out of marital retirement, and bolted with him in tow, and this is where she landed—a manageable town surrounded by farms and prairie.

Nonetheless, Cate hates the move and takes it as a personal rejection. And is jealous of Claude. Her strongest emotions are particularly resistant to reason. And because of this, they stick out, obvious and pathetic.

Sailor has gone off on his own mission, to find Joe. The two come back through the hallway, wriggling around each other in a comic way. Sailor loves who he loves.

Joe fills a bowl with water and sets it on the floor. Cate tells him, "I got you something, some Basinski you may not already have." She pulls the album out of her backpack.

"Oh man, it's the white vinyl *Deluge*. Look, Papa." The accent is on the second syllable. Cate particularly hates when Joe gets all Frenchy with Claude. "Thanks, Cate." He comes over and gives her a sideways hug, banging his hip against her. Something has pulled him closer to her, she's not sure what.

"How's it going?" she asks him. He has grown a little just in the few weeks since she's seen him. He is sliding into his teens. He at first seems not to have heard her but then says, "It's okay. Really. Different, but okay." He's a little diplomat; he wants everything to be okay again for his mother. Also, he's thrilled to have his father back. He's not thinking this might once again be a temporary situation. Claude has, in the past, followed up hugely interested with not so interested after all.

Claude puts the salads on the table. Neale gets out of the oven a loaf of that bread that's almost baked and you just polish it off yourself. She tries to take it out barehanded, says *damn*, then drops it on the floor, then picks it up with a dishcloth as a potholder. Her hands are a tapestry of small suffering from pots of inadvertently spilled pasta water, thoughtlessly gripped oven racks and pot handles. It's like she has this one, very specific cognitive delay. It's too endearing. Cate feels a brimming at the back of her eyes.

Talk skitters around the table. Joe likes his new school here better than the one in Chicago except that it doesn't have Kiera. He
wouldn't say he has friends yet, but no one is beating him up in minor,
deviously non-bruising ways, which did happen in Chicago. The ca-
pricious and cruel tactics of the new administration, of course, drift
into the conversation. (The only conversations within Cate's earshot
that don't feature the president are those where a moratorium is im-
posed at the outset. "Let's not talk about him today. It's too depressing.") At the moment, he's trying to put in place a new travel ban,
which is almost exactly the previous travel ban.

"I'm waiting for France to go on the list of banned countries,"
Claude says. "We French are a danger to someone who likes his meat
well-done."

Neale wants to know about the new play Cate is working on, a
futuristic romance Molly and Lauren are trying out in the summer
on the Santa Barbara launchpad.

It's a struggle for Cate, getting through the meal. It's difficult eating lettuce, talking in an anodyne way about her work and not crying, all at the same time.

When they're finishing up, a tour of the town is suggested, also
a game of Clue, which is an old favorite.

"Just a minute," Cate says, looking hard at the bowl of fruit
Claude has set down in the middle of the table. "I think Sailor needs
to go out. He just passed a smoke signal. I got him a burger at the
rest stop." A lie, but who will call her on it? She should be able to sit
through this lunch and then have some fruit and a cup of Claude's
Marco Polo tea afterward, ask him about life in the ashram, listen
with Joe to some of the Basinski album she brought, but she can't.

"Back in a sec," she says, then heads for her car. Sailor follows without question. Not questioning sudden changes in plans is one of the best features of dogs.

Neale doesn't call Cate on her drive home. She won't be happy about Cate's escape, but she will get it.

They drive back on roads instead of highways, Sailor with his head out the window. When they are at a stop sign and Sailor sees three horses in a fenced-in field, he tries to climb out the window.

"If you want, we can go see them," Cate tells him. "See what's up."

She waits with him by the fence until one of the horses, heather gray, dappled with deep brown spots, comes over and dips his head so he and Sailor can make each other's acquaintance by twitching noses in the delicate air between their faces. Watching this, something pleated fans open inside her. The happiness of animals in a green field on a fine day, of course. But also a glimpse of the amount of information that can be given and received just by approaching without an already composed story, then holding still and paying absolute attention.

acknowledgments

Thanks to:

My excellent editor, Trish Todd.

My extremely able copy editor, Polly Watson.

Jane Hamilton, Mary Kay Kammer, Sara Levine, Steve McCauley, Julie Wlach, and Barbara Mulvanny for their sharp readings and excellent criticism

Michael Paulson, Daniel Ostling, Alex Fraser, Erin Gioia Albrecht, and Elvia Moreno for helping to fill in my many blanks about the art and business of theater and set design.

My partner, Jessie Ewing, for always showing me larger possibilities than I would have come up with on my own.